I0663670

Guardian Angel

The Main Character
Legendary Origin Stories!

BOOK -1

By Alexander J. McCarty

Editor/Cover Designer:

Gabriel McCarty

Cover Art: Cesar Escobar

GUARDIAN ANGEL Copyright © 2019 by Alexander J. McCarty

ISBN 978-1-943733-06-4

Published by Sphere of Compassion, Inc.

https://sphereofcompassion.com

authoralexandermccarty@gmail.com

https://facebook.com/authoralexandermccarty (Updates often with character art)

http://www.instagram.com/gabriel_of_the_exps

http://www.instagram.com/sphere_of_compassion

https://twitter.com/of_the_Exps

https://www.tumblr.com/blog/sphereofcompassion

Front and back Cover Art by Cesar Escobar

https://www.facebook.com/CesarEscobarArtworks/

Amorita Cover Art: by KurO's Artwork

https://www.facebook.com/kuro724/

Gobliy Cover Art by ToriFloopArt

https://www.instagram.com/torifloopart/

Front and Back Cover design by Gabriel McCarty

https://www.instagram.com/gabriel_of_the_exps

Books from *Sphere of Compassion*

THE MAIN CHARACTER!

Hero's Epic Journey Arc

The Main Character: Legendary Origin Stories!

OF THE EXPS

Rebellion Arc

Resurrection Arc

Table of Contents

Part -1: The Life of an Angel

Part -2: The Woes of an Angel

Part -3: The Life of an Angel

Part -4: The Power of an Angel

EXTRAS

Acknowledgments

This wouldn't have been possible without the continued support and help from my brother: Gabriel McCarty. We created this series and its characters together. He is always willing to help plan out scenes with me, brainstorm and brings these characters to life with his art. Oh, and did I mention that he edited this book too!

Special thanks to Cameron, who always gives me feedback as soon as I release a new chapter. Cameron also helped with design of Poppy and Yuki. But it was Hoshi Art, that took our design ideas and brought them to life!

Shout-out to ToriFloopArt for designing Gobliy and for all the help at conventions. The Gobliy design greatly shaped her character for the extra chapter!

Thanks to Drew and Michael for inspiring me with their stories, worldbuilding, advice, and dedication to writing.

Also want to thank everyone who has helped us at conventions! Random Ramblings Productions is a YouTube group that we are proud to sponsor and they're super helpful at spreading the works of Sphere of Compassion. Robby, Monica, Riley, Chris, Oscar, Rosemi, Gus, and Adrian have also helped us set up and manage our booths at conventions.

Extra shout-out to Cesar Escobar who created the front cover and for Hoshi Art who drew Yuki for the back cover of the print version of *Guardian Angel*. The Amorita on the print version is drawn by Kuro Neko!

I thank my id for keeping me vital and driven, my ego for keeping me positive and critical about my work and my super ego for directing my creative energies toward a better world for all living beings.

Lastly, I thank you, the reader, for purchasing this book. I hope you enjoy it and continue to support me and my future books.

Thank you! =(:3)* (That's a bunny, by the way.)

EXTRA SPECIAL THANKS to our Patreon Subscribers:

Drew Markowitz (writer of The Planetoids; a fun sci-fi fantasy animestyle novel series that blends Avtar style characters with Miyazaki style worldbuilding); see link.
https://amzn.to/2XeyHru

M. W. Arita (writer of Demi-Girl; an urban fantasy novel that explores the mythos of Japan!); see link.
https://www.amazon.com/Soulbound-Scar-Fantasy-Adventure-Demi-Girl-ebook/dp/B07N8DJ5H7/ref=sr_1_1?keywords=demi+girl+souldbound+scar&qid=1560791429&s=gateway&sr=8-1-spell

Andrea Martin (talented artist who not only created the first Sphere of Compassion fan art, but also helped design and create Boobslime for The Main Character!); see link.
https://instagram.com/andy112138

And another special thanks to Hoshi Art who has helped design many of the characters in this book and series!

Like the page!
https://www.facebook.com/hoshisweeteuart/

Introduction

Of the Exps is a universe of characters, lore and stories! This universe is explored in a linear matter, except for the flash back section of each book which gives us a deeper look into the spotlighted character and their past.

Inspired by M.W. Arita's grand vision for his franchise *Aeonian Covenant*, we decided to do our own thing. *The Main Character!: Legendary Origin Stories* will cover many important characters from the series and give them their own origins while introducing new characters, many of which will be add to the mainline series.

I really hope you enjoy Guardian Angel!

This book is dedicated to girl power, middle sisters and to every individual who lovingly supports their friends! There are tons of great female protagonists in anime and other that have inspired me! I hope Annie's story can help inspire you as well!

Part -1: The Life

of An Angel

Chapter 1: Angel's Sanctuary

The story you're about to read is about my life as a guardian angel. It has its happy moments, its scary parts and then are sections that make me cry just thinking about them. But it's an important story about the people who have made me into the young lady I am today. I'm proud to share it just as I remember it. An angel's memory is like an archive, so…welcome to my personal library!

My life began in silence. My mother was holding me, her messy baby, in her arms. She stared at me with glistening purple eyes and I stared back. I reached out with my stubby little hands and grabbed onto her webbed finger. I gave it a little kiss to thank her for bringing me into this world.

I grew up in our little sanctuary; a hut in the middle of the Forest of Lost Children. It was just Mommy and me for the first eight years. Angels age one fourth the speed that humans do, so I looked like a toddler at that time. I had a full set of hair, though it was still short, and I had strong legs that carried me all around our little village.

Mommy and I would knit clothing for each other and she would tell me stories about her incredible adventures and about grandma too. Grandma was a mermaid, an enchanting creature of the sea. That's why Mommy had such pretty scales on her body and flippers too. My grandpa was really cool too! He was a hero, a human warrior who fought against bad guys. Grandma and him met up on an adventure and after they snuggled all night long, grandma got preggy and then three years later, Mommy was born. I snuggle with Mommy all the time, but I never get preggy. Mommy said that's cuz we're both girls.

1

My papa was a great man too. Mommy was assigned to be his guardian angel and keep him safe. The two of them grew up together, they became the bestest of buddies and then they became even more closer! My papa was a legendary hero who took down a bad king alongside Mommy and his best friend! Hearing about Mommy's stories about her adventures with Papa always made we want to go beyond the forest and see the rest of the world.

I could talk about Mommy's stories forever, but you wanted to hear my story, so I'll get back on track!

One day Mommy brought over a visitor. It was an angel girl like me, but she was twice my age. I was so happy to have a big sister. Her mommy was a ShadowPup, big dogs that can shift into shadows. Whenever I ask her where her mommy is now, she goes quiet. So I stopped asking and we got along great! Things were even better than ever, at least for a time. Now that I had a sister, Mommy would leave us, sometimes for months. She was out searching for more sisters for me to play with. When I turned 16, she even brought me a little sister! That was the day I was promoted to middle sister. Tumble was what I called her and she was prickly but impossible not to hug. She was like a living tumble weed. Mommy thinks her mom was a WoodPrimordial, but those entities are apparently really special. Tumble is super special too! Even though she never talks, I never had trouble knowing what she wanted. The little prickly angel would always clung to my leg too so I never felt alone.

When Mommy wanted to go out again two weeks later, I got really scared.

"You can't weave us, Mommy. I miss you when you leave. It huwts, right here," I say, tapping my chest.

"Aww, my little one is worried about me." Mommy swept me up into her arms. "I have to go find you more sisters."

"I already have two sisters. I don't need any more. I don't wanna wose my one mommy." I sobbed in her bosom.

Mother's embrace would always calm me when I was needy or emotional, but I was too afraid at the time. I remember it so clearly. My body was shaking.

"Whad if you never come back?" I asked sniffling.

Mommy dried my nose off with her absorptive fingers and pet my head. "Then Luna will take care of you."

"Luna is a mega cool big sis, but she never cuddles me and she doesn't hold me when I cry. I need you, Mommy."

"I plan to return by the end of the month." Mommy crouches down. "These girls need me. They don't have a mommy. Don't you think everyone deserves a mommy?"

I grab Mommy's hand and nuzzle it while nodding. "Uh-huh," I say, stifling my tears.

"You have to be strong for you little sister, too. Don't count the days, my cherished one. Just spend time with your sisters and don't leave the forest."

I nod again. "I promise."

"Good girl." Mommy hoists me up, gives me a kiss on the lips and then sets me down.

I kept my emotions packed in for a bit but then started sobbing. "Mommy!"

Luna came into the hut.

I think she was listening the whole time.

"Dry your eyes. Do you have any idea how lucky you are?" she asks me with a scornful look.

"Lucky that I have a bossy big sister?" I asked, crossing my arms and puffing out my cheeks.

"You have a mother!" she yells, rushing into me and knocking me to the ground.

"So do you," I say, shielding my face. "Mommy loves you tons."

"You don't understand and you never will!" she gazed at me with eyes of hate.

I couldn't take it. Seeing my beloved big sis look at me like that made my tummy hurt. I leaped up and hugged her. "Then help me understand," I say, hugging her super duper tightly.

"Fine! You really want to know? I never met my mother because she was murdered! I know who did it too; but I just can't avenge her. I'm pathetic."

I kiss her lips and give her a big smile. "You're not pathetic. You're supah strong! Even stronger than Mommy. You're so cool, and athletic. I want to be just like you."

"Like me? Come on, short stuff, you don't really want that," she said, trying to wiggle out of my iron hug.

"I'm gonna help you get even stronger so you can get even with the bad guy who hurt your Mommy." I bite my thumb and place it against hers. "It's a bwood pwomise!"

Luna smiles, bites her thumb and presses it to mine. "Pwomise accepted," she said with a toothy grin. "But how are you going to make me stronger?"

"Duh, by cheering you on and showering you with wots and wots of motivational hugs!" I rolled around and hugged her, kissing her repeatedly.

"Okay. Okay. I'm motivated. Look, you know why your mom doesn't let us come with her, right?"

"Cuz it's dangewous and I'm still a baby nymph."

"That's right. I didn't want to have to train with you since your crying is so annoying, but an angel doesn't go back on her promises. If we want to get strong enough for your mom to let us join her dangerous quest, then we both have to get stronger. That means you're going to get bruised, cut and, well, you're gonna bleed a lot."

"Why would I get hurt?" I ask, letting go and cowering behind my hands.

"Because we're going to be sparring. The only way to increase our divine gifts is to use them. Our magic is like a muscle that we gotta exercise," she says, rubbing my chubby arms.

"Okay," I say with a salute. "But wait? What about Tumble? She wants to be with me the moment she wakes up."

Luna flicks my nose. "Well then you better get up early."

"Mmm," I nodded, eyes brimming with hope.

I was surprised when we first fought. I remember every detail.

"So, uh, whadda I do exactly?" I asked.

5

"Just try not to get knocked down. If you do, then I'm going to keep punching you, got it?"

"No way that sounds scary, sis. I don't wanna do this anymore!"

"Then your promise to me was empty!? What about your desire to leave the forest and go adventuring? Are you just going to give up on that too?"

"No I just."

"Shut up!"

"Huh?"

"If you have something to convey then do it with your fists. You feel that rage, right? Use it to knock me off my feet. Prove to me you aren't just a weak little cry baby."

I wiped my tears and rushed in. My fist hit her chest but she didn't budge. Her fists then hit me over and over. When I was about to fall down, she'd slam her fist into my chin to knock me back up.

I tried to shield with my hands but it hurt so much. "Stop!" I yelled.

"If I stop now, then you'll be the only one getting practice. You have to at least have pride as my punching bag, shorty."

"Can we please just stop for now?"

Luna swipes my feet and punches my gut as I'm falling. She then grabs me by my hair and pulls me up. "Do you think the threats outside will stop when you ask them to?" She tosses me back.

I stumble and fall into a mud puddle. "You ruined my dress," I said with teary eyes.

Mommy and I knitted it together. I miss Mommy so much.

6

"I warned you about getting knocked down!" Luna leaps on me and punches me repeatedly.

"Stop!" I yell, shielding my face.

"Your tears aren't going to help you!" she yelled, punching my arm till it snapped.

"You're killing me!" I wailed, trying to whack her off me with my broken arm.

"I'm saving your life!"

Luna kept hitting me for what felt like hours as I kept crying. My tears dripped down my cheeks and their inner prana was absorbed into me, filling me with energy.

Luna's eyes nearly popped and she grabbed her broken fingers. "Finally! I got a real wound! Nice one, shorty. You held out long enough for me to actually bust my hand punching you."

"Does that mean it's over?" I ask, trying to shake off my tears.

"Pretty much." Luna shoved her fingers in my mouth and down my throat.

I gagged and coughed, trying to pull away.

"Calm down, shorty." Luna pulls her hand out. It's sparkling with my saliva and it's being mended before my eyes.

"Woah! How did you do that?"

Luna giggled.

She had such a cute giggle, took away a bit of the pain.

"I didn't do this. You did, shorty! You healed me! The only way for us to improve our healing is to get hurt. Wow, I really messed you up. My bad. I

7

guess that means I get extra training though." She drooled all over her hands and rubbed them on my broken arms.

"Wow, that feels really good," I say with wide eyes.

"Yeah, but I think they're still broken. You're going to need constant healing all day. Guess we better snuggle up. Stay put," said Luna, rushing off.

I brought my hurt hands to my mouth and started licking them. "I can heal just like Mommy!"

"Yep. You're a natural healer. My hand feels just fine." Luna came from behind me and dropped a blanket over me. She then snuggled up next to me under the blanket. "Just remember, the more you get hurt, the more powerful I become. Hope that helps you deal with the pain a bit." She poked my belly and smiled.

"And then we get to snuggle more too, right?" I wrap my arms around her.

Ouch. They still hurt.

Luna turns her head to hide her cute purple blush. "Hey, uh. What do you see me as?"

"Huh? You're my sister of course." I lick her cheek and giggle.

"Yeah. Of course," she says, looking back at me with a smile weighed down by sadness.

It was impossible to not count the days Mommy was away. Every morning I'd get up when the Cuckatrice sang. Luna would always be just outside the hut, ready to fight me. I'd always lose. Every single time. I didn't even stand a chance. I'd get really excited whenever her fingers broke because that meant we got to gauge our power growth and snuggle! I remember asking her why she didn't just hurt herself with like a tree branch and then let me heal the wound. She explained that we're sisters so we should grow strong together. No cheating. By the end of the month I learned to not cry after my arms were broken. I became a real tough girl just like Luna. Sadly, our powers had reached a standstill. Two more weeks passed. No power growth and no word from Mommy.

"Tumble is starting to lose weight. She needs Mommy's milk. What do we do, Luna?" I asked one morning after our sparring match.

"I can't do anything without you. My healing still sucks! The only thing I'm good at is defense since I sweat so much."

"Should we go looking for her together?"

"No, Annie. Tumble is still too weak to go out there. I think she always will be."

"What do you mean?"

"She wasn't born right. That means she's always going to need you to take care of her, okay?"

"Yeah! That's my duty as mid sis!" I exclaim with a big grin.

"It's up to me. Ready or not, we're not making any progress by staying in this sanctuary. I'm going to go out and find her."

I grab onto Luna. "No. You're not allowed. I don't wan' you to weave and never come back like Mommy!" I whined.

"Geez, you're still such a crybaby." Luna licked my teary cheeks. "I'm going to come back. You can wait a week, can't you?"

I crossed my arms. "I don't wanna."

"Too bad. I'm the oldest sister so you have to do what I say," she said in brash voice.

I look up at Luna and my expression softens.

"What? What is it?" she asked with an annoyed look.

I hug her. "You're crying, Luna."

"Huh? No I'm not," she said, putting her hands to her face. "I…I am." Luna embraces me super tightly. "I love you, Annie. No matter what happens, I'll always love you." She kissed my forehead.

"Sisters through this life and the next!" I cheered, wrapping my fingers around her's and giving her lips a loving kiss.

Luna pulled away with embarrassment. "I'm gonna prepare some supplies. You have to promise me you'll stay put."

"But what if you don't come back this week?"

"I'm coming back for sure," said Luna with a smile.

A week passed. Luna didn't come home. Tumble must have noticed how I was feeling. She cried alongside me that night. I woke up next morning to see Luna. She looked scared and hurt.

I took off her clothes and lay her on the grass. "What happened Luna?" I asked, spitting on my hands and applying it to her scars.

"I'm leaving tonight again. I don't know if I'll return," said Luna, turning away from my gaze.

"Who hurt you?"

"Bandits. They thought I was a looker. Wanted to put me up for auction. Won't be scouting for products now after I tore out their eyes," said Luna with a dark glare.

"You can't leave me again! I need you," I said, rubbing her bruised cheeks.

"I have to. It's the right thing to do."

I hugged her tightly.

"Ow. Careful," said Luna, closing her eyes and cringing.

"I'm not letting you leave unless you tell me why you have to go!"

"Ugh! Fine! Just let go of me!"

I released her from my hug.

"Your Mommy has been captured by bandits. The ones I fought off were just some stragglers. They have a whole town of bandits and that's where your Mommy is. The slave auction is in three days so I have to go in and rescue her! I won't let you lose her."

I grab Luna's hand. "No! No! No! You're not going anywhere! I won't wose my big sister too." I broke down into tears.

"If I don't come back you can't come after me! I need you to promise me, Annie!"

"I'm going with you!"

"What?"

"We trained together and she's my Mommy, so I'm going to save her too!"

"You're a crybaby! You'll alert them of our position. What if you get captured and its all my fault? I can't go through that again. I won't lose you like I did...mother." Luna hugged me and cried in my arms.

"Mommy only got captured because she went out on her own. We're support angels so we gotta support each other! As long we got each other's backs, we can't lose!"

"The bandits we're going up against are merciless. There is nothing they won't do to you if you get caught."

"Then we won't get caught!"

"And if we do, what's going to happen to Tumble?"

"I said we won't and that's that!" I yelled, crossing my arms.

"I'm wasting my energy arguing with you. Alright, get prepared. It's a two day's walk from here."

"You got ya!" I rush off to pack my things.

"Wait! Before you go. I got something from a merchant. It's happy juice. Makes you giggle. Want some?"

"I love giggling!" I exclaimed.

Luna took out a vial and poured a little into my mouth.

"When does it start to take effect?" I rubbed my eyes.

I feel sweepy.

Everything went dark.

By the time I woke up, Luna was gone, the moon was out and I was in bed. I found a note attached to Luna's doll.

She would never leave behind her doll. It's her cherished gift from her mother left her. This isn't good.

I picked up the note. It was hard to read because I was tearing up. Bottom line is: she left without me, she knows she's likely going to get captured or killed and she loves me very much.

I have to find her.

My tears pumped energy into my body and put me into a hyper aware state. My hands started glowing and the energy materialized into a book. The book was fluffy and black. It reminded me of Luna.

I opened it up to the first page. It said what Luna was doing the day we met. Wait, it wasn't just what she did...it showed what she was thinking. I turned to the last page of the book and words appeared before my eyes. They were in my handwriting though. None of it made any sense to me at the time. The good news is, it didn't have to. It told me exactly where she was.

I closed the book, packed up my things, including Luna's doll, and headed for the exit of my hut.

Tumble stood just outside the door with her arms outstretched. "Uh-uh!" she mumbled with fierce eyes.

She's right. How can I get upset with Luna for leaving me if I do the same to Tumble?

I crouch down. "Come on, Lil Sis. Hop on my back. We have a perilous quest ahead of us."

"Mmmm!" Tumble put on a fearsome look and we charged off.

We arrived at the edge of the forest. The powerful barrier Mommy put up to protect us zapped me when I touched it.

"What do we do?" I asked, punching it over and over. "Luna and Mommy got out, so why can't I?"

Tumble shrugged. She rolled away.

"Hey, don't give up."

Tumble then rushed toward the barrier, rolling up into a fierce ball before colliding with it. She made it through but her skin had been torn from her bones.

I panicked. Hearing my little sister screaming was unbearable. I puffed up my cheeks with saliva and then ran through the barrier.

Pain surrounded me. Blood was everywhere.

I spit into the air and it landed on my face, healing it up. I gathered more spittle and applied it to my arms. I crawled up to Tumble and mended her wounds. Even after she was fully healed, she was still crying.

We didn't have time to stop though. Luna was already nearly a day ahead of us. We ventured on foot into the dangerous and exciting world beyond our home.

If we wanted any chance of catching up to Luna, we couldn't afford rest. Thankfully an angel's pee gives a strength boost and while neither of our lemon juices were particularly potent, they gave my legs the extra push we needed to continue our trek. We followed in Luna's footsteps, staying on course until we reached the next marker before moving on to the next. Reading the book made me feel like Luna was right alongside me. And reading her thoughts showed just how much she worried about me. Luna loves me wots and wots.

We had made up for lost time. Apparently by drinking blood, I went into a crazed state, which allowed me to ignore my aching legs and keep up a fast pace. We were just a few hours from both our destination and from Luna.

We had arrived at the Bandit's Village, which according to Luna's thoughts in my journal, was called Street Trash. It was more beautiful than anything I've ever seen though. The huts they had were mega tall! They shined in the sunlight and had dark windows, adding an air of mystery! The pathways were paved with rocks and they sparkled too!

"Isn't this place incwedible?" I ask Tumble.

Tumble holds herself and shakes her head. "Uhn."

I look back at the journal.

No. That can't be right.

It says. "I turn down the alley and am suddenly ambushed from behind. A parasitic blind fold is placed over my eyes and I feel a bunch of men grab onto me and inject me with something. My body becomes numb. 'I'm so sorry Annie. I couldn't save your mother,' I think to myself as I'm placed in the back of a cart.

"Luna's been captured! We have to go now!" I exclaim, picking up Tumble and rushing off.

We fall down the hill and land in front of an old MounTroll and his son.

The old man's skin is like stone, but the boy only has a few rocks growing out of him.

Real MounTrolls! Just like in my mother's story.

The old man's eyes creak open, shedding dust. "The God Sinka has blessed me. To think such valuable merchandise would just land at my feet. Two LustBorne! Get them, boy. You're old man is tired. We'll be able to move into the capital after this."

15

The boy took out a knife and rushed me.

Is everyone in the whole village a bandit?

Tumble rolls in front of me and catches the blade in her teeth.

Tumble just saved my life!

"Granpa, it won't budge," says the boy, being dragged toward Tumble.

"They are powerful creatures, but they are novices in terms of combat. Watch and learn boy." The old man's arm's released dust.

I saw the glint of a weapon and rushed in.

An arrow hit my chest but I managed to grab the weapon. I tried to wrestle it from his stone grip but I was no match.

The old man grabbed the back of my head. "You know, before the Fall, your kind were pets. Those were the good old days." He slammed my face against his rocky knee.

"Hey, hands off the girl!" yells the voice of a young man from behind us.

"You want the merchandise, then you'll have to pry it from my hands!" spat the old man, turning to the figure.

"Actually. You're going to release her yourself."

I looked out from behind the old man to see the figure toss a canister. It released a stream of smoke that relaxed my muscles.

I slipped out from the Old Man's grip and the rock boy fell over too.

The figure lifted me up and popped me into a basket on his back.

16

"Don't worry, little girl. I've got you." He picked up Tumble and tossed her in with me. "And your little friend."

"Thanks for saving us!" I exclaimed.

"Any hero would have done the same. Oh, I should introduce myself."

"I already know who you are," I said, poking my finger out from the basket and touching his back.

"You uh, you do?" he asked.

Mmm. I could smell his flushed cheeks.

"Yep! You're my hero!" I exclaimed, popping my arms out and hugging him.

Chapter 2: Yu-ki: The Pacifister

"Stay hidden. I'm going to get you out of here. Oh, and by the way, your hero's name is Yuki. That's Yu-ki."

"Yu-ki. We can't leave yet. My sister has been captured and my mom is at the slave auction," I say, tugging at his shirt from inside the basket.

"I just want to get you two to safety. After that, I'm going to free all the slaves," he said, heroism outlining his gentle voice.

I grab my chest.

He's incredible.

"Luna is right down this street. You're going to need help if you want to rescue her," I said, and was given an affirmative "Uhn" by Tumble.

"Fine but if things get crazy, then you leave me behind."

"You're not the boss of me. I bet I'm older than you. I'm sixteen."

"Seventeen," said Yu-ki.

"Wow, you're practically a man." I took in his scent. It was so youthful and strong. Made my head a bit dizzy.

"I think I found the cart. There are seven bandits guarding it. I'm going to set the basket down. Stay inside. I can handle them."

I pop out and leap off his shoulders. "Hey you boys like angels?" I ask, doing a cute pose Mommy taught me where I stick out my butt and put my fingers to my lips.

The human bandits approached and drew their weapons, long metal spears with a hooked tip.

"Wait!" Yu-ki picked up a barrel and set it down in front of them. He then climbed atop it. "These are little girls. By taking them, you're stealing them from their family. Take a moment to think of it from their perspective. I'm assuming some of you have families, maybe a daughter or a sister. What would you do if someone took them away?"

While he distracted them with a speech, Tumble snuck around to the cart and searched for Luna.

"If my daughter sold for as much as she's worth, then I'd sell her myself," said one particularly muscular bandit, stepping out from the crowd.

"Then perhaps we can make a trade. What do you want for the girl in that cart?" Yu-ki took out his satchel.

"Thanks. Saved me the trouble of searching your corpse!" The lead bandit pierced the bag with his spear.

Yu-ki pulled up his shirt as the sleeping gas burst from the satchel. He took me into his arms as my legs went numb.

He had such pretty brown eyes.

Tumble signaled us by hopping up and down.

She found Luna.

Yu-ki danced with one of the limp bandits all the way to the carriage. "See, isn't life more fun when you give instead of take?"

"I will track you down and slice off all your fingers before making you choke on them!" yelled the bandit leader before being dropped.

I hoisted Luna up and had her lean against me.

"Annie?" she asked in a daze.

"Yep. We're going to get you out of here just as soon as we save Mommy!"

"Who's he?" Luna rubbed her eyes.

I jumped up into his arms. "He's my boyfriend."

"Actually, I'm just a hero," he said, scratching his head with blush.

Mmmm. Those flushed cheeks are so tasty looking.

"Awww. He's shy. Yu-ki, admit you're my boyfriend or else I may have to prove it," I said, nuzzling against his chest.

"Annie, focus. The slave auction is being held at the center of the city," said Luna.

"Then why were those bandits taking you out of the city?" asked Yu-ki.

"It doesn't matter. I know where the auction is. You mother, she rescued me from this place. And now she's in danger. Works out fine for me. I get to clear my karma," said Luna, biting into her arm to wake herself up. "Annie, you and Tumble should get in the basket."

"Shouldn't you get a disguise too?" asked Yu-ki.

Luna tore off the cloak of one of the bandits. Her shadow then ripped the bottom part off. She draped it over herself. "I'll hide in plain sight."

I plopped Tumble in the basket before going inside myself.

"Hey, Yu-ki. You better treat my little sister right. If you break her heart, I'll find you and tear out your heart. Got it?"

"You are just adorable. Sorry but threats don't work on me. I'm ready to die anytime anywhere! It's not living life to the fullest that frightens me!"

"Then I'll make you afraid to wake up every morning to a life of constant torture."

"Hey, I'm a nice guy. I mean her no harm."

"Yeah. A bit too nice. Why put yourself at risk to help some strangers? Do you have sisters back home or do you expect some lewd reward? If you want one, then I'll take care of it. Leave the other two out of it."

"Hey, calm down. I'm a loner. And no, I don't have any sisters. I'm an only child. I ran away from home before I was taken to this place. This magical wonderland is where I truly belong," he said, waving to the PorcuPigeons.

"Stop right there," said a voice from in front of us.

I peeked out from beneath the basket and saw a soldier with cat ears.

"You're a hero, aren't you? What are you doing here?" he asks, ready to unsheathe his sword.

"Kitty!" Yu-ki hugs the cat boy soldier.

"I'm not a kitty! I'm a CatKin! Let go of me!"

Yu-ki released him. "Sorry, you just remind me of a cute wittle kitty I met on the street back home."

"Just go on. I've got an important job to do," said the cat boy soldier.

"Stay adorable," said Yu-ki with a salute before heading off.

Luna turned to my hero. "You do realize how dangerous those guys are, right?"

Yu-ki's face darkened and his voice along with it. "Yep. I'm honestly terrified of cats because of them. They wiped out my whole team." He slapped himself and gave a big smile. "Ever since then, I've been a lone wolf. I know how much cats don't like being touched so I thought flustering him would work and, well, it did." Yu-ki opens his palm.

"You stole from a soldier? That's a lot of Cat Coin."

"You shoulda seen what the bandit general was stashing."

"I'm not sure I approve of such a bad boy dating my little sister," said Luna, rubbing his crotch.

"I approve!" I shouted from the basket.

Yu-ki politely moved Luna's hand off him. "Hey, I'm not a thief. I only use money to save lives. I take it from those who would use it for violence and use it to create peace. Oh, looks like we're here."

I stuck my tail out from the basket and looked out with my fourth eye.

Wow. There are so many races gathered. Almost all of them bipedal. Are they all here for the auction?

Yu-ki navigated through the crowd. "Excuse me. Do you happen to know if the mermaid was already sold?"

The hooded man glared at my boyfriend. His entire body was cloaked except his eyes so it was hard to tell what he was. "You know what the real meal is here. The rest of these are just snacks. She'll be up right after this one, but don't expect me to lose to you, little boy."

"I'm seventeen! I'm practically a man."

"You're a boy, young enough for the brothel in town."

"Do you think I'm cute enough?" asks Yu-ki, batting his eyelashes.

The hooded man turned away with a bewildered look.

The speakers blared and my tail eye turned its attention to the podium. The host of the auction was a MounTroll that had priceless minerals in his body instead of regular rocks. "Well, everyone. It looks like we have a tie this round. You know what that means."

"Deal or death!" cheered the crowd.

"That's right. The second highest bidder can use their own bid against the highest bidder. The highest bidder must either fold or accept the challenge."

"Are they going to kill each other?" asked Yu-ki.

The hooded man looked at him, smiling through his mask. "Yeah. It's the entertainment part of the show. If you got the Cat Coin, you can fight me next round. I tend to forget people easily, but I'm sure if I kill ya, I'll remember you just fine."

"I'm flattered. Maybe even a bit excited," said Yu-ki, running his hand up the man's back.

The man took a step back. "If we do fight. Don't do that. Makes me think of my wife. And I come to places like these to forget about her. Oh, the battles about to begin."

"Today we have two legendary bandits pining after the same little Gobli. Who will take home this cute little morsel?" asks the announcer,

"Oh my god, I want to take her home!" squealed Yu-ki.

"Then you better go on up there! I'll watch your cargo," said the hooded man.

"Thankies!" cheered Yu-ki. He put his hand over his face. When he removed it he was harboring an intense glare.

"Excuse me Sir, but you haven't put up a bid yet," said the host.

"That's fine." Yu-ki sliced off the hosts' hand with a super sharp dagger. He then kicked the severed hand into the bidding box. "Consider that my payment."

The host was about to shoot Yu-ki, but the crowd cheered.

"You know, I bet your boss would be mighty impressed if things were a bit more interesting this time," said Yu-ki, shoving a Cat Coin in the host's sever.

"Ladies and gentlemen. It's a two-on-one! Two legendary bandits against this...uh, what are you?"

Yu-ki lifts up his shirt, showing off his sexy thin body. "I'm the Pacifister Yu-ki! Not the best name, but I can't argue with my wanted poster when I look this damn good!" He pulls out a poster from his pants. It's him with his hands posed like a cat and making a silly looking cat face.

"A bounty and a Gobli all in one. My blades sing for your blood," said the crouching two-sworded bandit.

The other bandit simply pointed a single needle at Yu-ki and hissed.

"Luna. What are we going to do? He's going to die," I said, poking her with my tail.

"We wait for the next round and then we get her. Doesn't matter what happens here," said Luna.

Yu-ki spun behind the thin needle wielding bandit and grabbed his arm. He jerked the arm around to deflect the dual sword attack, while backing away. He leaned back to speak to the Gobli in the cage. The Gobli was a little taller than me but I was still way cuter! Her skin was like chocolate and she had long ears that were drooping. The poor girl was draped in rags and bound in chains. "Don't worry. I'll get you home." He said, making her eyes shimmer.

"Looks like he found a new girlfriend," said Luna, sitting on my basket.

"No fair. I saw him first," I said, crossing my arms.

The needle wielding bandit tripped Yu-ki with his foot and flung him over his shoulder.

My hero landed flat on his back and pulled out a big sack when the two bandits approached. "You know what's the best thing about Cat Coin?" asked Yu-ki, tossing one up and down with his thumb.

"It can get you anything?" asks the dual-sword bandit.

"No matter the value, it's all the same size. So, unless you get a really good look, you don't know if three hundred coins are worth three Mews or thirty-thousand!" He swung the sack into the swordsman's weapon and the money tumbled out of it to the ground.

The two bandits dropped their weapons and immediately started shoving as much money into their clothes as possible.

Yu-ki stepped atop them. "Well, looks like I won." He tossed a handful of coins into the host's face and then sliced open the Gobli's cage.

Her eyes lit up with hope once more when he sliced her chains and lifted her onto his shoulders.

"See, isn't this little gift far more precious when she's happy? Look at those sparkling eyes!" Yu-ki leapt back when a dagger was tossed at him from the crowd. "Holy shit! That almost hit me!" he yelled before running off stage with the Gobli.

Luna was giggling. "Wow, you sure found a special hero."

"Yep. I'm gonna make tons of wittle sisters with him!" I exclaimed.

"Annie, you'd be making daughters, not sisters."

"Oh, not sure if I'm ready to be a mommy yet," I said thoughtfully.

The host reattached his hand. "Don't worry everyone. The thief who stole our product will pay with his blood. Anyone who catches him will get his bounty, along with a free annual subscription to our local brother Melting Pot. Now, without further ado, let us bring out the final item on our list!"

Four elves with chained colars brought out a glass encasing. Inside of it was Mommy.

"Luna. What's the plan?"

"The plan was for you to stay home so I could rescue her, but now we simply wait."

"Huh? We can't wait."

"Think Annie. Why storm the auction? We'd only get killed. We just have to follow whoever gets her and kill them. Easy squeezy," said Luna, squeezing my tail.

Is it really that simple? We're going to be a family again super soon!

"You may recognize this fiend from earlier this year. She stormed our auction and stole a ShadowPup from this very stage. This product is a genuine NymphBeast. That's extremely rare! But a full-grown adult like this is an anomoly! The powers of these divine creatures cannot be understated, which is why we have sedated it in a power sealing Goopy. Now, shall we begin the bidding?"

It suddenly started raining, but the rain wasn't coming from above. Instead, water droplets circled around the area.

"We're experiencing some odd weather; let's hurry up with the bidding so we can call it a day," said the host.

The water suddenly expanded, creating puddles across the ground.

"Luna, what's going on?" I asked, poking her leg with my tail.

"I'm not sure," she said.

The hooded man next to us started cackling. "Oh, this is going to be interesting."

Mommy sank inside her tank, seemingly vanishing.

"No magic allowed. If you're caught trying to steal her, you'll not only be killed but you'll be removed from the bandit records!" yelled the host.

Someone screamed in the back, then another. The crowd broke out into a panic.

Are we in danger?

I hugged Tumble close to me inside the basket.

"Your mom sure is amazing," said Luna with a smile.

My tail eye caught sight of her. Mommy would leap out from a pool of water, shoot a concentrated water beam, then ride it and slice through the crowd with her bladed fingers before vanishing into another puddle. She'd pop out, bite into the leg of a bandit and pull him into the puddle as he screamed. Body parts would then appear all around the portals.

Mommy looked so scary.

27

I covered Tumble's eyes while I gazed at the gruesomely majestic spectacle.

"Your mom's father wasn't a hero, Annie. He was an assassin," said Luna.

"Now what would an assassin be doing with a mermaid?" asked the hooded man.

Mommy popped out of a puddle. Her fangs were gone and she smiled at Luna. "You three didn't have to come all this way. I was captured so I felt I might as well clean out some of the trash before coming home. I'm sorry for worrying you." Her webbed fingers tossed little droplets that loving padded Luna's cheeks.

"Annie and I aren't weak. You have to trust us. We can help too. I want to liberate our people just like," said Luna.

Blades suddenly burst out from Mommy. Her blood sprayed over Luna and the basket.

Mommy. What's going on?

The cloaked man had long tentacles coming out from him, each one with their own weapon.

"Your mission has gotten in the way of progress," said the man.

Mommy turned around and slashed his head with her bladed fingers.

A black vortex was swirling where a face was supposed to be.

"Mommy will be with you all in just a moment," she said before sinking into the puddle.

"Luna! We have to help Mommy!" I yelled.

28

Luna picked up the basket. "If we want to help, then we'll leave before he decides to take us hostage so he can kill her. Sorry Annie, but that thing is beyond our abilities."

The sound of steam being release suddenly blanketed the area.

"Now what's going on?" I asked.

"No way," said Luna.

I could taste her fear. It made my body feel shaky.

A lance swooped by and sliced open the basket. Tumble and I fell out.

"Target sighted," said a weird creature made entirely from metal. It had an iron helmet and was clad in thick armor plates. An exhaust port came out from its back and released steam.

"What are Anima Collectors doing here?" asked Luna, biting her lip.

"Maybe they're here to help Mommy?" I asked, clinging onto Luna.

"Free merchandise!" yelled some bandits, rushing toward me and my sisters.

"I don't think so!" Luna's shadow picked up some fallen weapons and attacked the bandits.

The hooded man sent his blades at mother, but they missed and went into a puddle.

Mother popped out and shot him with a jet stream before pulling in the blood from the bandits' bodies. Her eyes went red and her whole body sharpened. Bone-like pipes came out from her sides and fired water bullets at the hooded man's tendrils. She then took the blade from a severed tendril and swung it around with her water whip, slicing a bunch of bandits.

Wow! My family is so cool!

29

"Let them fight. Collect the little ones," said another metal man.

Yu-ki dropped from I don't know where when the metal man approached. His super-heated blade slid down the metal man's swords before chopping off his hand. "Totally robotic which means you don't have a soul. Which also means, I don't have to hold back!" Yu-ki tossed a pouch on the ground that ignited the oil and caused a big boom.

My hero was sent flying back.

I leaped in the way and hit the ground with him. "What's with all those kissie marks on your face?"

"Oh, you didn't know? Gobli's like to mark their mates. She took a real liking to me. Didn't want to say farewell so she marked me for later."

"You're mine," I said, kissing his face repeatedly.

"I'm honestly not sure what's scarier. The horde of heartless machines, the veteran assassin over there, the deadly water goddess, who I'm assuming is your mom, or your persistency," he tapped my nose.

"Can you save Mommy?" I ask.

Yu-ki hopped to his feet and tossed a smoke bomb at the incoming machine men.

"Smoke has no effect on higher beings," said the machine man.

"It's actually a special spice. Smells nice, doesn't it?" asked Yu-ki, sniffing the air.

"I...can't smell."

"Oh, yeah, you're too superior for that. Good for you to since you won't smell that terrible rust."

The machine man's body was rapidly aging and becoming brittle.

"Heathen!" yelled another machine man, using his jets to fly toward my hero.

Yu-ki grabbed the rusting machine and used him to shield the blow. He kicked him and then jumped to the ground with me.

"Why are we ducking?" I asked.

"Oh yeah. I forgot." Yu-ki tossed another satchel that ignited the fire, blowing the two machine men to bits.

"You're amazing!" I leaped into a kiss with Yu-ki. I plunged my tongue deep in his mouth, wiggled it around every corner and even extended it a bit to go down his throat.

A special kiss for my special someone. So happy Mommy taught me how to kiss so good.

Yu-ki's eyes went really wide.

I pulled away and giggled.

"That was…something," he said, blinking repeatedly.

He suddenly dropped me.

That's odd. His arms are still holding me but he's up there.

Blood spurted out from Yu-ki.

A blade zoomed by and went through his legs.

"Shit. I messed up," said Yu-ki, before his torso fell on top of me.

My world went dark. Luna was fighting bandits and Mommy was going up against the man who just killed my hero. I was helpless but to watch.

Part -2: The Woes

of An Angel

Chapter 3: Sunny Village

Tumble stood on her tip toes and licked my cheek, bringing me back into the moment.

Her drool is so sparkly.

Oh yeah. Duh!

I gag myself and release a globule of spit. Tumble does the same and we both rub it all over his severed limbs. I keep my mind focused on healing so I don't absorb any of his blood. Once his severs were lubricated, Tumble and I reattached his arms and legs.

"I'm not going to die! I knew lolicons had to have some kinda super power!" he cheered, only able to move his face.

Hearing him say silly stuff brought tears to my eyes.

He was alive and I was going to keep him that way!

Something came crashing down from the sky. It was another metal man, only it was three times the size and wield a long sword. With a single slash, he cut through the bandits attacking Luna.

Maybe he's on our side.

It turned it's weapon on Luna and sliced through her shadow as she raised it like a wall. A powerful torrent of water washed the massive metal man away. Mommy rode the torrent, slashing at the extra big metal man.

The metal man's body became superheated, melting her wave before grabbing her in his arms.

"You need not worry. I will deal with that creature," said the assassin, sending chains out from his vortex and into Mommy.

Luna turned to face me. "You and Tumble have to survive. My story ends here. *Shade Pursuit*." Black energy came from her and entered my shadow.

"No! I can help too! I won't lose you!" My shadow moved on it's own and my legs along with it. I resisted with all my might, but only managed to slow the run into a walk.

"*Shade Beast*." Luna's aura enveloped her, giving her shadow claws and fangs. She leaped at the Machine Man.

I could see Mommy shooting water bullets at the chains bringing her into the vortex. For each one she cut, three more appeared.

Before turning the corner, with Yu-ki on my back, I saw the machine man grab hold of Luna. Its head opened up into a massive cannon that was building up energy.

I didn't see what happened, but I heard a wretched scream that shook me to my core.

Luna…

The shadow hex she put on my legs vanished. I couldn't walk. I could hardly breathe.

Tumble hugged me tightly and cried against my shoulder.

My body absorbed the energy, but it still wouldn't budge.

I was suddenly lifted off my feet.

Yu-ki held me to his chest as he ran away with me and Tumble in his arms.

Was Mommy killed too? Am I alone now?

Tumble grabbed my hand and forced a smile through her tears.

The three of us left Street Trash. I looked over my shoulder, seeing a cloud of smoke over the town. I coughed violently. It was as if the smoke cloud had cast itself over my happy life. My body had taken in its toxins and I had no idea how to expel them. We went deeper into the unnamed forest. Yu-ki set us down and turned away from us.

"My boyfriend and I were brought here together." Yu-ki wiped his eyes. "We are from another world, one without superpowers but with a wide variety of entertainment. Despite all the modern convivences, we were happy to get away from our world. Our parents never approved of us being together but that never stopped us. We would sneak out and go to the fair after dark. It was just me and Richie. We had the whole park to ourselves. When the assassin came, we both tried to defend the other. Ha-ha. We didn't last long. I remember dying in his arms. It was scary, but I could handle it because we were together. It was a cliché death. Hand in hand, just telling each other we love one another and that we'll see each other in the next life." He turns to us with a smile. "Well, that happened a lot sooner than expected. We woke up in this world, in a village not too far from where we are now. We're told to become heroes. Richie and I were big nerds so the idea sounded fun. We accepted and we rose up the ranks pretty fast. I was always into kendo and he was excellent at archery even before we came here. After a successful quest, we would always come to the stage and be rewarded. When I was getting a medal pinned to my shirt for successfully protecting the village from an enemy raid, Richie suddenly pulls me into a kiss. The crowd went wild. They were cheering and whistling. They loved it. They loved us. That night Richie and I decided we were never going back home. We finished quest after quest and well, it all felt like a dream. We were the famous hero couple: the PaciFister and the PeaceMaker. He would disarm them with his archery and I would go in for the knockout. We got overconfident. One day we were sent to take down a CatBoy general. His name was CatScratch. Richie's arrows were deflected and

I…I jumped down from a tree above the enemy. He couldn't react quick enough. I sliced off his arm, thinking he would be helpless. Next thing I see is the sword from that arm…in Richie's chest. I didn't even think about escape. I just went to Richie and held him close to me. I couldn't talk because I was so scared." Yu-ki turns away and sobs.

Tumble and I each grab onto one of his hands.

"You don't need to say anymore," I said, wiping my eyes with my free hand.

"I…I should have cut off that bastard's head. If I had, then Richie would still be here." Yu-ki gripped my hand tightly. "He smiled at me even as he left me. He said, it's a been a fun ride. CatScratch laughed at us, he mocked my tears and Richie's death. I was too damn sad to even get upset. Apparently, I was so pathetic that he decided not to kill me. Have you ever heard of something so pitiful?"

I held Yu-ki's hand to my face and nestled it, hoping my affection could whoosh away his pain.

"You think I'd learn my lesson, right? Well I didn't. I can't kill. Not even the worst guys. I saw a cat soldier soon after that and I sliced off his head. I kept stabbing the body over and over. I tried to bury sadness with rage but it didn't work. I didn't see that damn general's body. I only saw Richie. I can't kill without remembering his death. I thought of killing myself, but I couldn't do that either. Now I just live each day as a loner, rescuing as many people as I can with no regard for my own life. I don't know how long I've been alone. I'm sorry I'm rambling, but I don't…I'm not going to see you again. I don't want you making the same mistakes I did. Do what you have to do to protect those you cherish."

"You can't leave us. I'm scared," I said, holding onto him.

"I told you our story so that our memory lives on." Yu-ki takes out a fish scale. "It's still glowing. This means your mother is still alive. Now what kind of hero would I be if I didn't bring a girl back to her mother?"

"Wait!" I let go of Yu-ki and concentrate my energy.

I think of Luna and try to create a book.

If it appears, then that means she's alive and I can rescue her!

A book appears, but it's pink not black. I open it up.

It's not about Luna. It's about Yu-ki.

"The mermaid scale thing you said is a lie." I sob and punch his leg. "Why are you lying?"

Yu-ki picked me up and embraced me. "I just wanted to give you some hope. I'm sorry."

"Mommy and Luna are gone. You can't leave us."

"But I can't stay either. I'm terrified. If I let you down…if you two die because of me and my stupid code…then what the hell do I do?"

"If you leave us, then we'll die anyways. They're going to find us and kill us!" I whined.

"Not if we get you two to a village. Angels are worshiped by villagers and they're paired up with heroes. Richie and I were idiots, we didn't want an angel because we didn't want her to get hurt. She could have healed him; he could be here right now if I wasn't so stupid."

I poked his chest. "Nobody hurts my Yu-ki! Not even you. Do it again and I'll poke you harder," I said with a grumpy face.

"Fair enough. Okay, so I'll get you two to the closest village." He takes out a map from his pocket. "Aha! Sunny Village is just half a day's walk from here."

"So, you're going to take us there so we can get paired with a hero?" I asked, folding my arms.

"Yep. That's the plan," said Yu-ki, ruffling my hair.

I shake my head. "I already have a hero. Mommy always wants what's best for me. You're the best hero, so you are going to protect me."

"I failed you. I don't deserve..."

I poked Yu-ki's leg. "Stop it. I've already decided. You can't change my mind."

"Fine, then we'll go to the village and we'll get properly teamed up," said Yu-ki.

I look to my hero's book but Yu-ki closes it.

"Just trust me, okay?" asked Yu-ki.

"I'm an angel. I can read your emotions. Prove I can trust you."

"How can I prove it?"

I step on my tippy toes and make a kissy face.

Yu-ki sighs. "Okay. Fine." He crouches down and kisses my forehead sweetly.

I roll my eyes. "You're my boyfriend, not my mommy." I hop up and wrap my arms around his shoulders. Our lips are just inches apart. "Kiss me like you mean it."

Yu-ki blushes a super tasty pink color. I lick his cheeks as he rambles on.

38

"Oh. Okay see. I think there's some confusion here. I'm not a lolicon. I said that as a joke because I was overwhelmed. I had nearly died, after all. And well, it was after you gave me that rather, uh, passionate kiss."

"You're so sweet when you're being bashful," I said, rubbing my hands on his chest.

Tumble jumped up and down, cheering me on.

"My heart belongs to Richie. I can't be your boyfriend. Also, when you healed me, well, my arms got swapped. You don't want a opposite armed freak to be your partner, right?" he asked, putting his hand in my face.

Ouch. I really messed up. Poor guy. I gotta make it up to him!

My tail wrapped around his hand and made it caress my cheek. "Don't worry. I'm not asking," I said, sticking out my tongue.

Yu-ki needs someone to fill that hole in his heart. I'm gonna make it overflow with the super love energy he's gonna get from all my huggies and kissies!

I press my lips against his and drool into his mouth.

His eyes become more relaxed and he kisses back.

There we go. He's finally unwinding.

I tap his nose. "Why don't we lie down together? It's getting dark," I said, pointing to the sky.

"It's sunny out," he said with a curious look.

I poked his side. "Don't argue with me."

"Okay. Okay. Let's uh, find some where we can lie down together," he said with a nervous smile.

"Uhn!" exclaimed Tumble, gesturing to the leaf bed she had prepared.

"Thanks Tumble," I said, giving her a thumbs up.

Tumble responded with two prickly thumbs up.

Such a great sister.

Yu-ki eases onto the pile of leaves and I just stare into his eyes. He shuffles in place and turns away. "Since it's so late, we should really get some sleep," he says, putting a big leaf over his eyes to shield him from the sun.

I roll on top of him and kiss him again, drooling more into his mouth.

He no longer resists. He caressed my face as he kisses me.

I feel so happy! Yu-ki loves me! He really loves me!

Tumble pulls me up from him and removes his shirt. She then throws it up, having it land on the tree branch above.

Best sister ever.

Yu-ki shield's his face with his hands. "I feel funny," he said with a dazed frown.

I feel funny too. And my body feels really hot.

I realize my thighs are moving up and down Yu-ki's legs. "Whee!" I cheer, increasing the speed of my own volition while giggling.

I need to fully be in the moment. I don't want to miss a second of this.

I wiggle up to his ear and kiss it. "Yu-ki."

"Y-Yeah?" he asks, shaking a bit.

I grab his hands and caress them till they stop shaking. "My Mommy told me that when I find my special someone I shouldn't hold back my love. We're going to make a ton of little sisters!" I exclaim, barraging his cheek with kisses.

"Whoa. Slow down. You're only sixteen. I'm like a whole year above you. That's a huge gap that can never be overcome," he said, his cheeks flaring up.

"How old were you when you first made love to Richie?"

"I was fourteen and he was sixteen," said Yu-ki, scratching his cheek.

"Two whole years."

"Yeah…"

"You know what I think? I think that if you keep kissing me, then I'll grow up faster. A plant grows up super duper quick when it's showered with love, after all."

"Y-Yeah."

Once I make Yu-ki mine, he won't be able to leave me. It's what's best for both of us.

Suddenly I feel Yu-ki's hands on me. He's caressing my sides. He leans into kiss me.

The leaf falls off his eyes and I see them.

They're swirling and blissed out.

"Lots of little sisters," said Yu-ki in a daze, pulling up my shirt.

I yank my shirt down. "Sorry. Let's stop. I don't know what's going on," I said, pulling away.

My legs won't stop moving against him. It feels good. Way too good.

"I don't really want to stop," said Yu-ki, breathing heavily while tickling me.

"I...I don't either, but this isn't right. You're not you and I'm feeling light headed too. I wanted to forget the pain, but I...don't want to take advantage of you," I said, turning away from him.

Yu-ki embraced me. "As you wish. Let's just lie down together. I'll snuggle away those tears."

I nuzzled up to him and kissed his hand. "That sounds great."

Tumble dived into my arms, completing the cuddle puddle.

I woke up, kissing Tumble's cheeks.

She giggled, turned around and nuzzled me.

I looked up at the night sky. "Sorry about before, Yu-ki. I didn't mean to push you into...where's Yu-ki." I rolled over and he was gone.

Tumble pointed to a footprint the dirt.

A Gobli footprint. What if he was kidnapped? Wait, Yu-ki is way too strong. Oh no. Yu-ki left us for that not as cute as me Gobli girl!

Tumble started to cry.

It's all my fault. I scared him off because I was too pushy.

I hugged her and pet her lovingly. "We don't know for sure if Luna and Mommy are...gone. And if we talk to the locals maybe we can find the Goblin den Yu-ki ran off to. Well that is if he still wants to see me." I wipe my eyes.

Tumble pulled out a map from her pocket. She pulled me up to her and pointed to the nearest village. "Suunii."

"That's right. Sunny Village! Wait, how did you get this?"

Tumble hid her face behind her hands.

I pulled her hands away and smiled. "I'm not angry with you. Just be careful who you steal from, okay?"

Tumble saluted and the force of her hand hitting her head caused her to slip. She landed in the pile of leaves and giggled.

"Sunny Village is to the East…but which way is East?" I asked.

Tumble pointed behind me and nodded.

"I'd be lost without you," I said, hoisting her onto my shoulders.

We encountered a few dangers on the way to Sunny Village, but thankfully Tumble and I were able to charm any creature that tried to hurt us with our expertly practiced adorable duet dance routine. Together we were unstoppable and we were going to find out what happened to our family!

Sunny Village was a vibrant place. All the huts were wooden and colored bright fiery colors. There was even a sign that said "Welcome to Sunny Village. Toss Your Worries into the Furnace!" Tumble bowed to the sign.

It was still nighttime when we arrived, but the village was fully lit by Lamperns.

I stood up on my tippy toes and Tumble stood up on my shoulders, lifting the shade from the shortest Lampern.

"What wonderful reason have you decided to bother me for?" asked the Lampern in a jolly voice.

"My sister and I are looking for work."

"Sorry to tell you but there's no child labor in this village. It's all sunshine and smiles here!" The flames inside the Lampern took shape into a big smile.

"Mommy told me that Lampern's are Agni elementals that have been imprisoned."

"I'm sure your mommy had a really splendid reason for telling you something like that. But I'm free to leave whenever I want!"

"So, there's no place for angels to get work?" I asked.

A shadowy figure came out behind me. "Did you say angel?" The voice was a ghostly whisper.

I turned around. It was a hooded man like the one who hurt Mommy, but he was much shorter. Perhaps only a boy.

Tumble grabbed the Lampern and held it out defensively.

"No need for aggression. I'm surprised is all. We've never had an angel actually come here. Usually we have to purchase them."

"Wait, you mean you don't kill angels?" I ask, picking up Tumble and taking a step back.

"We don't do anything that isn't good here. And no. RiftRippers like myself are allies to angels. I know we're a bit scary looking, but we are your sworn friends."

"Then why did one of you attack my Mommy?" I asked with an interrogative glare.

"Must have been a freelancer. The less savory RiftRippers steal angels for villages in need. I wouldn't worry too much. Your mother is most certainly alive."

Mommy is alive! Yay!

Tumble set down the lantern. She climbed up the nearby bench and patted the RiftRippers head.

"Glad we got those bad vibes out of the way. My name is Sickle. My parents named me after Lord Death's weapon of choice…unknowingly that is." His shoulder's drooped. "See they were superstitious farmers who felt that having a sharp name would make me more adept with the equipment."

"Your kind, they have Mommies?" I asked.

"Yeah. I still live with my parents too. One of the perks of being a trainee. We're going on vacation when my initiation comes. I'm a bit apprehensive about it honestly."

"I'm sorry for judging you. We just had a really bad experience." I bowed to him.

"Cast those worries into the furnace! There's no bad or judgement in this place. Sunny village is a happy, prosperous town!"

"Can you help us find work? Tumble and I want to become brave adventurers."

Tumble rolled in front of me and struck a dramatic pose. I followed afterward, grabbing my tail like a sword and putting on an intense look.

"Sunny village hasn't had an angel since that shadow pup girl."

Luna!

"What happened to her!"

"She was…um…she left. Best not to talk about not so happy things. Why don't I take you to the guild hall. As a member of ISEKAI, I can get you a free drink," said Sickle, whipping out his badge.

I squinted and read the acronym. Imported Skilled Earthling Kid Adventurer's Initiative.

Sickle's smiled beneath his cloak. "The little portal emblem in the center shows that I'm part of the Import faction. Isekai has four main factions, the village chiefs, the importers, the heroes and the angels. On behalf of sunny village I heartily welcome you!" The RiftRipper hugged me and Tumble.

"How do you import heroes?"

Yu-ki said his lover and him were killed by an assassin. Did they force him here by killing him?

"I can't answer such an unpleasant question. Now come on, ISEKAI members get discounts on everything here!" he said, leading us down the orange tiled street to a building with a bubbly cat on the sign above it.

The person behind the bar was a Dwar. He stood atop a stool and was smiling from ear to ear.

"Two milks for our growing angels here," said Sickle.

"No. The only milk we drink is mommy's milk," I said with a firm nod. "We'll have some grape juice."

"Oh, that's even better. The grape juice here is incredible. Sorry, nobody is up at the moment. The village has a strict, err, I mean a healthy sleeping schedule. We go to bed when the Cuckatrices sing and wake up when they sing. As for me, I stand guard, I mean watch, in case visitors come around."

The bartender added some sprinkles to our drinks, set up a small slide and then slid them down into our hands.

I giggled. "This place is fun!"

"Yep! We try to make everything we do super fun!" cheered Sickle. "Oh, it's getting rather late. The inn will close soon. If we hurry, we can get you two a room!" He skipped out the bar and we followed.

The inn was the prettiest building of them all, a blend of all the brightest colors came together to make a beautiful rainbow along it's wooden walls.

"Sickle is here with some guests!" cheered the RiftRipper, picking up the BellBloom flower and jingling it.

Such a pleasant sound. Like a river's current and a Cuckatrice's song melded together.

Sickle hopped behind the desk and took off his hood. He was a human like Yu-ki. He had bags over his eyes, pale skin and a quaky smile.

"How can I help you young ladies?" asked Sickle.

"Um, we'd like a room to stay in, Mr. Sickle."

"I run the inn for the night shift. Don't worry, I'm not dissociative, though it's not uncommon for RiftRippers to become dissociative after initiation. Let me check our record book." He lifted up the notebook and cycled through the pages. "Room 297 is our best room and the only place worthy of our special guests!" He lifted up a VocalVenus, a yellow funnel-shaped plant that had dozens of roots that went up the wall and through the ceiling. "Hello, room inhabitant, we need you to vacate the room immediately. You will be relocated to another of our high maintenance rooms."

"Oh, we aren't picky. We can take any room and we only need one bed," I said, holding Tumble close to me.

"I would vacate this entire building for you angels. If you had any idea how important you were, then you'd understand. This entire village is at your disposal," said Sickle with a bow.

Wow. I never expected to be so beloved. Yu-ki was right, they really do worship us here. Maybe this place could be our new home.

An old man apparated before us. "Why was I told to leave my room? You do realize I'm the village chief, don't you?"

The Old Man had wrinkles that looked like the mystical runes on GlyphTurtles, a permanent smile, and a beard of vibrant purple leaves.

Sickle gestured to me and my sister.

"Go on, speak," said the Old Man, who had vines coming out from his white pupils.

He must be blind.

"Two guardian angels have come to our village and are looking for work," said Sickle.

The Old Man bowed in every direction, chanting a hymn I couldn't quite understand. "This village is at your service, my goddesses."

Goddess! Wow, are Tumble and I really that special?

The Old Man's vines branched out till they touched Sickle. "There you are. What are you waiting for? Go and bring them to their room. We can figure out a sleeping arrangement for me later. I'd sleep on this cold wood if the little goddesses willed it!"

Sickle hopped over the desk and led us up the stairs.

"That old guy, um, what's his name?" I asked.

"Old Guy is fine. You can call him whatever you like," said Sickle.

"We think Tumble's father was a WoodPrimordial. Is that what he is?" I ask.

"Yep. His flesh was sliced to make every building you see. Without Old Guy, this village wouldn't even exist." Sickle took us to the room.

The door was made of redwood and was super shiny.

"Uhhh," said Tumble, waving at her reflection on the door.

Sickle opened the door. "I'm not even allowed to look inside, but I hope you all enjoy your stay. If you need anything at all, we'll be forced to comply," he said with a big smile.

Tumble and I entered the room. It was a calm green color, nothing like the rest of the village. The bed had a small lake inside it, but Tumble and I made sure there were no fishies trapped in it.

Tumble lifted up the pillow and rested her head against it. She then collapsed to the floor.

I felt the material and then grabbed my ears. They were the same.

The pillows are made from Sleepy Sheepies. Does that mean that they were killed?

Tumble popped up and pressed the pillow to my head.

It was so soft. I drifted into a deep sleep.

The Cuckatrice's song woke me up. Tumble was nestled close to me.

There was a knock at the door.

"Who is it?" I asked, fixing up my hair.

"It's Old Guy, the village chief. We've prepared you a hearty breakfast and want to bring you to the temple as soon as possible. We've rounded up our finest heroes and will have them compete to see who are the two most worthy!" he exclaimed.

I hopped out of bed and opened the door. "We only need one hero! Tumble and I are sticking together."

"What about if the four of you came together as a group?" asked Old Guy.

Yu-ki had a partner but he didn't have an angel. I suppose the more heroes the better.

"Do you have fresh fruits? We'd like to meet our hero soon, so we'll just snack on the way," I said, walking out the room, hand in hand with my little sister.

"As you command." Old Guy vanished and then reappeared with a fruit bowl.

It was a rainbow of different juicy delicacies.

"Only the finest and purest food for our little goddesses," said Old Guy.

Wait, he keeps calling us Goddesses. I hope we don't disappoint these people. Our powers aren't exactly the strongest.

Old Guy took us to the temple. It was tall and colored like the sun, with the brightest wood used at the top of the structure. The doors opened and we were blessed by a ray of light.

Wow.

Fifteen shirtless young men were on the temple podium, flexing their stuff.

Temples are awesome.

"We're a small village but what we lack in size we make up for with spirit," said Old Guy, the wrinkles on his face bending into smiles.

"So, what kind of test are you gonna give them?" I ask.

"Well first we have to test compatibility. The bond between an angel and their hero is of absolute importance," said Old Guy.

"Great, so, uh, how do I do that?" I ask with a friendly smile.

"You have to kiss them, of course," said Old Guy.

He expects me to just kiss a bunch of hot guys and cute boys I just met? Awesome!

"So, do I just uh, get up there and smooch it up?" I look over the crowd gathering in the pews.

Wow, they all look super happy.

"Am I going to do that in front of everyone?" I ask, twiddling my finger in my hair.

Not sure how I feel about that.

Old Guy led us up to the stage. "An angel's kiss is a spiritual sacrament. The entire village is gathered here to witness the miracle."

"Umm, Tumble is a bit young for kissing. Maybe she can just go for hugs instead," I said, giving her a hug which she gladly returned.

"That's absolutely fine. You're the only one who needs to test the bond, after all." Old Guy stepped up to the podium and started chanting.

The boys walked behind the vibrant red curtain in the back.

"The Great Goddess, queen of all angelic beings, has blessed our constant positive energy! Two angels have come to grace us, and they are here to stay! Give praise to the angels!" he cheered.

The Great Goddess, exalted is she,

Created angels and all we see,

Her tears becomes life

Her blood gives us hope

Her love, infinite as the sky,

It moves forth the gears of time.

Blessed are her angels,

Purer than faith.

Blessed be the heroes.

Our valiant saints.

May their bond

Live on and on

And may we live to see

A world that angels ushered in

Where everyone is free!

Blessed be the Goddess

Both merciful and wise.

Blessed be her children

Blessed be their lives!

Tumble was dancing to the music all along, and invited me to join in too. When the song was over. The temple fell silent. Everyone was concentrating together. Tumble opened up her arms and took in the positive vibes. The boys were then brought in, led by a cloaked figure, likely a RiftRipper.

The first one in line was the strongest. He had a rough edge behind that big smile on his face. The RiftRipper chanted as he led the boy to the very back of the temple, behind the curtain. After a few moments, the curtain opened. The boy was completely naked and bound in place by a red chain around his arm.

Mommy always told me to listen to my intuition. But I didn't know what to think. This was surely an odd ritual, but these people were super nice. There's no way anything bad would happen.

A mobile staircase was placed by the window.

The way his naked body shimmered in the sunlight was enchanting.

Before I knew it, I was on the top step.

I leaned forward and gave the hot boy a gentle kiss.

I save real kisses for guys I know.

He sucked my tongue into his mouth.

Wow. He's a really good kisser.

My tongue was trapped between his teeth.

What's going on?

Blood mixed with saliva.

I looked into his eyes and saw only malice.

Chapter 4: The Angel's Curse

Just as I was about to pull away, I heard the head priest.

"And thus, the mixing of blood and saliva come together to awaken the dormant power resting in our brave heroes."

Wait. So, they're supposed to bite my tongue.

I look into his eyes once more and see joy.

Did I imagine that dark look in his eyes?

The hero breaks the kiss, sucking up the trail of drool before it could land on the hallowed temple ground. Two cloaked men lead me down the steps and then close the curtain behind me.

The head priest continued his chanting. After finishing, he turns to face the two priests standing by the curtain. "When the next hero is in place, open up the curtain," he said in a hushed voice.

The curtains suddenly opened on their own. The hero I kissed marched to the front of the stage. "The angel's gift has awakened me!" He created mist from his feet and then twisted it with his hands, to create a sword of fog. "I will be her hero. I swear an oath upon this village that I will protect her with all my heart. There is no need to continue with the others. I, Braven, am the strongest of all of Sunny Village's heroes!"

Mmmm, confident guys are soooo hot!

"Very well. Create the bond! It shall last until the day you leave us, hero!" exclaimed the head priest.

Braven sliced his hand and placed it atop my head.

The blood trickled into my mouth.

54

It was so tasty and made my head feel dizzy.

"The sacred bond has been formed!" cheered the head priest. He signaled the two other priests to bring us behind the curtains.

I grab Braven's hand. "So, you promise not to abandon me?" I ask with watery eyes.

"To do so would be to dishonor all that have come before me. I will not let that happen," he said with sexy conviction.

The priests led us to the small changing room behind the curtain. They then put on blindfolds.

So many strange customs.

The clothes my mother and I made together were taken off me by the blind priests. When they tried to remove my bloomers, I covered myself and told them to stop. They bowed and then brought me my new outfit. The white angel leotard, complete with stockings and arm sleeves, seemed to fit me perfectly. Metal greaves with their upside-down golden cross emblem were fastened to my feet and hands.

They felt a bit heavy.

The priests put on a wide white church hat on my head. It went right over my cute little black and purple horns. After that they fastened a headband over my third eye. Thin clear contacts were placed over my eyes.

Aw, I hope they don't think my eyes are ugly.

I looked in the mirror and did a little twirl.

I loved the outfit. The white color accentuated the caramel color of my skin and the pretty pink color of my hair and eyes, which now were white and pink instead of black and pink.

"Is everything to your liking?" they asked.

"Almost." I removed the hand gauntlets. "Sorry, they're too heavy and I can't feel with them." I grabbed the scissors and a needle with some thread. With them I cut heart-shaped windows just below my knees and one at my belly.

Tumble loves poking my belly so I gotta keep it accessible or she'll be sad.

I walked around a bit. "These greaves hurt my feet." I said, taking them off.

The priests removed the metal plates on the greaves and attached them just above my feet. "Is that better?"

I stretched my toes. "Yeah! That's great." My tail eye spotted something super cute and snatched it off the priest's robe. "Sorry. It does that sometimes," I said, wrestling my tail to get the pin it stole.

"Everything we own is yours to take, my angel. I'm honored that you like it," said the priest with a bow.

"Thanks a BunBun bundle!" I hugged them and then placed the adorable sheep hairclip in my hair.

The priest bowed to me graciously, moved to tears.

I looked back at the large mirror.

Oh yeah, now I'm gonna get those hearts thumping!

I was led out of the changing room and past the curtains. The people in the pews chanted with new fervor.

I waved at them with a big smile on my face.

Wait, where's Tumble?

My little sister came out along with Braven. She was staring at him with intense discernment. She too was clad in an angel leotard and her hair had been tied into twin pigtails. She had two baby blue pom poms in her hands.

I hugged her and she smiled at me. Her glistening hazel eyes smiling with her tiny mouth.

Awww, little sis looks adorable!

Tumble looks me over and her eyes widen. She takes off one of the large bows in her hair and wraps it around my tail. "Mmhhm." She gives me a thumbs up.

"You really look like an angel now," said Braven in that strong but weathered voice I had already fallen for.

"And you look…wow." I said with sparkling eyes and a bit of drool.

Braven was looking hot! He had thin metal plates covering his legs and two larger folding plates on his knees. His pants were tight so I could see all his juicy curves. He also had on a red belt with little yellow totems on them. His short-sleeve shirt was a crop top, so those abs were displayed for my viewing pleasure. He had shoulder and elbow guards as well, along with metal finger gloves. His blond hair looked even sexier with the single bell earring he put on his right ear.

Braven grabbed our hands and bowed.

"May the Great Goddess grant protection to our angels and their chosen hero!" exclaimed the priest.

After the ceremony the head priest, Old Guy, brought us to his room, my room, to enjoy the feast he prepared. There was a single massive plate of fruits in the center of the round table.

"Ooooh," said Tumble, rubbing her face against the fruit before eating it.

"Enjoy the meal," said Old Guy before disappearing.

Braven pierced a bunch of grapes with a single thrust of a needle and then popped it into my mouth. I sucked up all the grapes, making my cheeks all puffy. I chewed them up and then drooled half into Tumble's mouth.

"You two are uh, very close," said Braven, turning away from the sight.

Poor guy, seeing me and little sis must remind him of someone he lost.

"Yeah, were as thick as the Bramboo trees!" I exclaimed, tightening my muscles and standing on my chair.

Tumble climbed up my body and put her hands over my head, completing our pose.

"I've never seen a Bramboo tree," said Braven, grabbing a Snapple and bringing it to my face.

I sat back down and bit into the Snapple, giggling as it made little pops on my tongue. "Neither have I but my Mommy…she, uh, she saw them and she told me all about them." I shook my head and forced a smile.

Come to think of it, Yu-ki was always smiling. What if he came from this place?

Braven slowly skinned a Pinch, a delicious gummy fruit. "How many heroes have you had?"

"Oh, uh, just one. He kinda left me…for a bunch of Goblis," I said with a frown.

"I've worked with many heroes," said Braven softly.

Tumble poked his cheek with a banana.

"Sorry, she doesn't like seeing sadness," I said, lowering her arm.

"Then she'll fit right in," said Braven with a forced smile.

"Hey, do you know someone called Yu-ki? His hero name was the Pacifister."

"Yeah, he was an old friend of mine." Braven took the banana from Tumble's hand and ate it.

If Yu-ki trusts these people, then so do I!

After eating we were led by two very chipper guards to the quest board. It was a large wooden board with different papers stuck to it, each one offering a different quest.

I picked up the first one I saw. "There's one for cleaning someone's house. Isn't that kinda a waste of a hero's talents?"

"Killing isn't all we're good for," said Braven, scanning the board.

Tumble found a poster for clearing the forest of bandits and jumped up to show me.

"Not sure we should start with something so dangerous," I said with a nervous look.

"You see this belt? Each of these totems is given to me for a completed quest. I can handle anything." Braven looked away as he talked to me.

Is he hiding something? I could check his journal, but Yu-ki didn't like it when I did that. I'll have to check when I get some alone time.

"Hey, how come none of the missions are outside the village?" I asked, shifting through many pages.

"Sunny Village must be maintained. We're different than most places. See this mark?" He showed me the cane symbol on one of the quest sheets. "That means only a hero is allowed to undertake this mission, but the rest can be taken up by anyone. The entire village is responsible for the happiness of every member."

"Wow! So, it's like you're one big family! That's so cool!"

Braven smiled. "Let's head to the village hospital. After we've healed the people there, we can do something a bit more dangerous." He held up a quest sheet with a gold cane emblem.

That must mean it's only for really brave and powerful heroes!

I stood on my tippy toes and read it aloud so Tumble could hear too. "Cleanse the village of ghosts." My eyes shimmered.

"Don't be afraid. I've dealt with ghosts before." Braven looked down at me. "Are you smiling?"

"Ghosts are real! That means that maybe we can see Mommy," I hugged Tumble and cried.

"I doubt such a pure creature would be bound to this world. Angels live without remorse," said Braven, walking off.

I rushed up to him and grabbed his hand. "Let's clear all the missions. Then we can go on a big adventure outside the village!"

"Focus on the matter at hand." He led me and Tumble to the hospital. It was a bright pink building with smiley faces painted on the outside and inside.

Patients were resting on futons along the floor, resting peacefully.

"Why are they all sleeping?" I ask.

"If they were awake, then they would be suffering." He leans over to me with an intense look in his blue eyes. "Outward displays of suffering are not allowed here. We must be courteous to others." He puts a jar up to my mouth. "I want you to fill this up."

"Okay, but uh, my saliva is best at healing when it's fresh. I learned that the hard way," I said with a smile. I spit into my hands and rubbed them on the patient with scars on his legs.

The wound healed in just a couple seconds.

"You're more powerful than I expected." Braven walked past me and smiled at Tumble.

She had already healed four men with separate injuries.

"Hey, so uh, where are the girls? I only see boys and men here. Not that I mind," I said, my tail rubbing up and down Braven's leg.

"They aren't here. Don't ask too many questions. Stay focused."

Braven sure likes to put up a tough exterior. That just means that when he finally opens up to me, the Kindness inside will be all the sweeter.

We finished our hospital duties early and we even cooked together. The not so rich families were overjoyed when we delivered them piping hot vegetable soup. We went back to the Quest Board multiple times. Doing all manner of odd jobs till the sun went down. New jobs would pop up all the time so the missions went on for nearly a year. After every completed quest Braven would reward me with head pats. And while we were doing all manner of quests, from labor, to teaching, matchmaking and exploring, I started my own creature encyclopedia. One day I wanna publish it to the world. Eventually Braven, Tumble and I completed every quest on the board.

"You're a hard-working girl," said Braven with a smile.

"Yep and all that sweat has made my skin like iron!" I grabbed a twig and smashed it against my leg.

"The graveyard is outside the village. You should wash up before you go."

"Won't I need the extra defense in case they attack?" I ask.

"The ghosts won't attack you. And if they did, then I'd use my wraith dagger to get them to back off." Braven smiled.

Aww. He had such a sweet smile.

"Hey, so uh, after the mission. Do you want to spend the night in our room?" I ask, giving him an adorable look.

I won't mess up like I did with Yu-ki.

"Perhaps," he said before walking off.

Tumble lifted my arm up and then leaped into a high-five.

"Thanks!" I embraced her and snuggled her. "Let's get all cleaned up for our big mission."

Tumble saluted. "Mmhm!"

As soon as we got to our room we stripped down and went into the bath.

It was warm.

Tumble scooted up to me and started scrubbing me with prickly hands.

"Stop. That tickles." I giggled, grabbed the soap bar and counterattacked.

62

Tumble and I wrestled in the tub and our worries went away amidst the fun of our mock battle. I allowed her to win and then I scrubbed her scalp.

"How do you get so many twigs in your hair? Not all of these are ingrown," I said, pulling out some dirty sticks.

Tumble shrugged.

"So, what do you think of Braven?"

"Uki," said Tumble.

"Yeah. I miss Yu-ki too. But Braven is really hot. And he's strong too, so we'll definitely be safe."

Tumble turned around to face me. She poked my belly and then tried to leap out of the tub. My tail grabbed her and pulled her back in. "You shouldn't underestimate me." I poked her belly over and over, making her giggle. I held her close to my chest. "Let's bathe together here every night."

Tumble looked up at me and beamed.

We got dressed up and met Braven at the entrance to the village.

"The graveyard isn't too far from the village, but stay vigilant. This is a real quest," said Braven, leading the way into the unnamed forest.

I signaled Tumble to watch the middle and I stayed in the back.

Braven closed his eyes and focused his energy. Rain came out from his hand and sprayed the trees in front of us. "I only sense trees and some bugs. Nothing dangerous."

"Wow. That's a really cool power. How come you can do that, but I can't?" I asked.

Mommy had water powers so why not me?

63

"You awakened this power in me. It's my potential. Shame this is all it can do," said Braven.

We made it to the graveyard without any monster encounters.

There were graves everywhere.

I grabbed Braven's hand. He was shivering. "At nighttime I come here...they speak to me."

"Well, what do they say? How can I help?"

Braven stared at me intensely. "Is this really what you are? An innocent, hard-working angel?"

"Don't forget loving middle sister," I said, snuggling Tumble.

Braven turned away but I could feel his hand shake more. "You had an elder sister?"

Sickle didn't want me to mention her, but Braven is really nice. Oh! Maybe he can help me find her.

"Yeah! Her name is Luna. She was attacked. I'm not even sure if she's alive," I said with a sniffle.

Braven turned and smiled at me. "That's good."

"Huh?"

"As long as there's even a bit of doubt you can hold onto hope." Braven covers his face with his hands. "Nearly my entire school was slaughtered by the same RiftRipper. So...these graves...they're my classmates. I didn't know all of them, of course, but...I feel responsible."

"What killed them the second time?" I asked softly.

"Tell me more about your sister. I think I may have known her by a different name," said Braven.

Why is his smile unsettling me?

"Was she part YomiHound?" he asked, his eyes sharpening.

I took a step back. "Umm, maybe we should head back," I said, grabbing onto Tumble.

Braven tossed Luna's doll at my feet. "I found this in your bag when you were taking a bath. She had the exact same toy." His fists were shaking.

"I don't know what you think she did, but...I know she didn't do it," I said, making sure Tumble was safe behind me.

Is he going to attack us?

Braven grabs my arm. "You don't need to trust my words. You can read it for yourself. You have my blood so summon my book!"

"Okay, but first. Promise you won't hurt Tumble."

"I'm not going to hurt her. Now summon it!"

I called forth the book with shaky hands, but it didn't come out.

Braven cut his finger and shoved it into my mouth. "Try again."

I nodded, shivering in fear and summoned up the book.

He snatched it as soon as it was summoned.

Braven's book was red and had a sheep emblem on it just like my little hair pin.

"Where is it?" He searched through the pages. "Aha! It's here!" He took out a dagger and grabbed my hand.

Tumble leaped up and bit onto his arm.

"Let go!" Braven yelled. "It can only be activated with angel blood and I'm not allowed to hurt you even a little."

"Tumble. It's okay. I want to know. Maybe it can help us find Luna." I held out my hand and closed my eyes.

Braven poked a hole in each of my fingertips and then placed my hand on the page.

My awareness left me.

I was now seeing the world through Braven's eyes.

He was standing alongside a group of heroes, all male. I recognized one of them. It was Yu-ki! And the guy Yu-ki was holding hands with must have been Richie.

Awww. They are so cute together!

"Come out, demon!" yelled Braven, standing just outside the cave with a mace in his hand.

"Why should I listen to the demands of a petty human?" asked Luna from the cave.

Just hearing her voice warms my heart.

I felt an odd mix of my own warmth and Braven's malice.

"Why should you fear a bunch of petty humans?" asked Braven, readying his mace.

"I don't." Luna came out.

Yu-ki stepped up. "Why don't we solve this through a dance battle. Come on, Shade, show me what you got!"

"I don't think your friends want peace," said Luna.

One of the hero's fired an arrow at her.

A figure jumped out from behind Luna and took the arrow head on. The figure was a hero and made no sound as he writhed around.

"See! I told you all! She's brainwashed them!" yelled Braven.

"We don't know if that's really what happened," said Yuki, rushing with his lover to help the injured hero.

"They just couldn't resist my charms. Come and kill me if you want, but you'll have to cut down a dozen of your fellow heroes to do so," said Luna, petting one of her hero pets.

Why is Luna acting like this?

I try to shout out in my own words to stop the conflict, but it's no use. Instead Braven's voice comes out. "How many have you killed?"

"None of them." Luna smiled. "They just love me so much that they blindly throw themselves in front of me. It would be cute if they didn't scream so loudly. Thankfully I've removed the tongues of these ones."

Braven rushed in with his mace but a brainwashed hero deflected it with his shield.

"You never accepted my kiss. Afraid of what it would do to you?" asked Luna, tearing the mace from Braven's grip with her shadow.

The mace slammed into him, knocking him down.

"Let's head back," said Yu-ki, stepping in between the two with Richie at his side.

"The villagers won't believe us! We have to do something or she'll kill more of us! She's the one behind the YomiHound attacks!" Braven stood up. "Those heroes were dead the moment their lips touched that demon!"

Braven pushed Yuki and Richie aside.

The heroes rushed in and fought against Luna's horde.

Richie held Yuki back from jumping in to stop the fight.

Braven closed his eyes each time before his mace smashed the head of Luna's minions.

The battle was over in less than a minute, with the heroes either dead or too injured to fight.

Yuki and Richie immediately tended to the injured heroes.

Luna's shadow gripped his legs with her shadow. "If killing didn't weaken my powers, I would end you right now."

Braven spit on her face.

Luna licked it off her cheek. "You act like you're the victims, but I'm supposed to be responsible for tending to a whole village of cowards. Why should I have to waste my power on weaklings?"

"Those weaklings were my friends!" yelled Braven, slamming his head into her.

Luna clenched her teeth and growled. "I'm leaving this worthless village tonight. Your friends died for nothing and it's all your fault."

The page must have ended. I came back into awareness. My eyes were drenched in tears.

"I'm so sorry."

"I couldn't leave the village to go after her. If I did, then my classmates would have to fight alone. I lied about the emblems on my belt. They're the totems for the heroes that your sister killed."

"You feel guilt still. And you're burying it with hatred."

"You don't know anything about me. You thought I was some brave hero when we met. The truth is that when I saw you, I was terrified. So were the other heroes. I don't know what happened when she kissed them, but they changed. They followed her like a shadow and gave up their lives for the girl who had ruined them. I was half-expecting to suffer the same when I kissed you. But I got lucky. I was ready to die to protect them, but I was still scared." He pulled a mace out from behind a tombstone. "I'm not afraid anymore." He swung the mace and everything went black.

I woke up inside the temple. My head was throbbing.

"You have such a sweet smile, but it's a lie. It's all a lie," said Braven, turning away. "You know at first I thought these powers were useless." He looked up at the rainstorm inside the temple. "They mask sound. You can scream all you like. Absolutely no one will hear you. I've got all night to avenge my comrades."

"I'm not Luna. We can find her together! I'll get her to tell me everything!" I yelled.

"Stop looking so innocent!" Braven jumped on me and pinned me down. His knife pierced my clothes and cut my skin. "I don't care if you're responsible or not! You're a demon just like your sister!"

"I'm your angel. I'm not going to run. We can figure things out together." I forced a smile through my terror.

This isn't the real Braven. I can save him. I have to!

69

"Stop being so damn sweet!" Braven shoved me to the ground. "It only makes this harder for me."

"I want to help," I said, standing back up and facing him.

Braven took out the quest sheet. "We're going to solve this final quest together. Once you've suffered enough, the ghosts of my friends will be appeased. They'll finally let me rest!"

"There are no ghosts. You need to forgive yourself!" I yelled.

"Of course you wouldn't hear them! You're a demon! They hate your kind!"

I licked my finger and applied it to my wounds.

"Don't you dare heal yourself. Do it again and I'll hurt you more!" Braven slapped me.

There's no use in talking to him. He's lost it, but if I run. He'll go after Tumble. I have to lure him out.

I ran for the window.

Intense pain exploded into my back. I tumbled to the floor, screaming in pain.

After all we've been through...how can he do this?

"You tried to run so you asked for it." Braven pulled out the knife. "Well, well, look at this." He grabbed onto my black wings. "Proof you're a demon. What else are you hiding from me?"

Braven slammed my head against the ground and then pulled me back up. He tore my headband off. "A demonic eye! Is this what turned my friends into slaves!"

My wings whacked the knife out from his hand.

"Good. We want you to put up a fight." He slammed me to the back wall.

"This is where the spirits gather. Not the graveyard. This is the place where their lives were ruined! And this is where they will find peace." Braven fastened the chain onto my wing.

I stared him down. "Hurting me will only cause you more regrets. We're friends, Braven. It hurts you to hurt me."

Braven stared down at me. "You still look at me with hope in your eyes. My mission is to wipe your kind off the map. I didn't kill your little sister." He takes out a pouch of money. "I sold her to someone who would finish the job for me."

I couldn't see. My eyes were so drenched in tears that everything was wet.

"You're lying. You said you wouldn't hurt her. You're not capable of that."

He has to be lying.

"I was capable of killing my fellow classmates to get to your sister. You think I wouldn't send a little demon to her grave?" He tossed me her pom poms.

I held them to my face and took in the scent.

They were hers, but that doesn't mean he really sold her. I need to know the truth.

I stared at him defiantly. "Prove it to me! Show me the book!"

"I don't have to prove anything to you demons." He picked up his journal and set it on the side of the back window. "Did you know that heroes are branded? They give us numbers so they can keep track of us."

I reached for the book but he burned my hand with a heated blade. "Yu-ki and I were friends. When he left the village, he left me his weapon. How fitting that this weapon will be what ends you!"

"No. Not Yu-ki's weapon. He would never hurt me." I sob into my hands.

"I hope your sister is alive and that she's reading this right now!" yelled Braven. "Oh, and once I'm done with you, I'm going to track down your mother!" He takes out Mommy's scale from his pocket and cuts me with it.

I miss Mommy.

"See that shine! That means she's alive!"

Yu-ki said that but he was lying. Wait, but that doesn't mean it isn't true. Mommy needs me and so does Tumble. I have to survive this. I have to kill Braven!

Chapter 5: Sunny Village's Secret

I starred daggers at Braven. I threw a punch at his arm. My tail slid up my arm and wrestled the scale out from his hand. He slashed at me as we struggled, cutting my clothes but not my skin. My wings grabbed onto his wrist and squeezed them. My tail moved his arm when he jabbed at me, redirecting it to slice the chain around my wing.

"Only your blood will appease them!" Braven kicked me off the window and into the wet grass outside.

The rain he created had formed mist.

I crouched down to hide from his sight.

"I don't want to kill you! If you suffer enough, then they'll be at peace. Shade must pay for what she did!" Braven tore off the little totems from his belt and tossed them at the ground, trying to locate me.

If I move too much, he might hear me.

I closed my eyes and prayed for protection.

"I lied before! These totems aren't for missions I've completed. They're for the heroes that died! Their souls are trapped in the totems. They are screaming to me. Begging for me to make you suffer!"

Luna and mother aren't safe as long as he's alive. I have to find a way to end him. Why am I shaking. I have to be strong like my sisters.

A totem hit my back.

"I can hear you sobbing! Sadness isn't allowed in this village! You can't break the rules just because you're suffering! I suffer all the time! Every night I go out to the graveyard to cry!" Braven rushed at me.

It's over. I'm going to die.

"Protect me!" I held out Luna's cherished doll.

A shadow rose up in front of me.

A RiftRipper? No.

"Ha! Maybe your sister was witnessing your agony, after all!" yelled Braven, swiping Mommy's scale at the ShadowPup.

Luna has to be safe! She sent this puppy to rescue me! I just know it!

The pup's head sharpened and then jutted out.

Braven dodged it and rushed to me. He lifted me from the ground, making me drop the doll in the process. "Luna. You don't want your sister to die, do you? Call off your familiar and I'll let her go!"

I bit into Braven's hand with my sharp teeth and fell to the ground.

The shadow pup's head jutted out once more. This time it penetrated Braven's armor.

The shadow spike came out the back of the large rock behind the crazed hero, meaning he had been pierced straight through. When it pulled out, the blood splattered on my bottom lip.

Braven backed up against the rock and then collapsed. He looked up at me weakly. "When a demon kisses someone who isn't strong enough...she takes their loyalty and their lifespan. My friends only had a few years left in them. There are so many heroes just like them. So many heroes that I've failed." His head drooped. His hand fell to the side, still gripping my headband.

I instinctively licked the blood off my cheek.

Incredible!

My mind was going hazy.

I went to him and grabbed onto his belt.

74

Remember the good times we had. Stay focused.

I wrapped his belt around my waist.

I will find out the truth. I will find Luna.

I saw the bloody wound and my eyes widened.

More.

I licked the blood and gasped.

Why does it taste so good? No. I need to find Tumble. Get the book. Where's the book? The temple window. Yeah. Just go to the temple window.

My legs wobbled as I walked away from Braven's body. My body was burning up. I clenched my chest but the heat continued to assault me.

I climbed up to the temple window.

The book was right there.

I have to wake up.

I grabbed Tumble's pompoms and held them to my face.

It did nothing to clear my mind.

I set them down at my side and gripped my face.

The book was right there but my hands weren't listening to me.

Wait. It's dissolving. My one chance at finding Tumble is slipping away!

My whole body lit up from the inside. Blue light came out from my skin, appearing as tattoos. The energy exploded out my book, forming two white and pink wings. My hair tingled and expanded with golden energy. Lastly, a veil of pink energy formed around me and framed my dizzy face.

I wobbled back and forth, squirming in place.

Angel's have perfect memory, yet I can't recall what happened next.

I woke up. My head was still a bit dizzy but I was back in control. My tummy felt knotted. I turned to where Braven's book was, but it was gone. I fastened Tumble's pompoms to my side and hopped off.

Braven's body was gone too.

I picked up Luna's doll and ran off toward the graveyard.

That has to be where he made the exchange.

I arrived at the front gate of Sunny Village. Sickle was standing guard.

"My sister was taken away! We have to find her!" I gripped his cloak and cried.

"Braven already spoke to me." Sickle lowered his head.

I stepped back.

He allowed this to happen?

"He tried to fight off the angel thief, but he wasn't strong enough," said Sickle.

I don't know what to believe anymore.

"Then why aren't you going after them?" I asked.

"A veteran RiftRipper took her. I'm only a trainee so I had to stay behind. Our strongest heroes and RiftRippers went out already to retrieve her."

"I want to help too!" I stomped my foot.

"My apologies but you can't go out without proper protection. There's a chance the thief will return to take you. You should find Old Guy. He is the most powerful being in the village. He will keep you safe." Sickle pat my head.

"Why isn't he going out to find her?"

"He is a Wood Primordial. His kind bind themselves to villages. They are immortal as long as their zone isn't destroyed, but they cannot leave it." Sickle looked down at me. "What happened to you? Your clothes are cut. Whoever it was that dared to harm you shall face my wrath," said Sickle, the constant joy in his voice quivering.

"Why can't people cry here. It's good to cry," I said, sobbing into my hands.

"I'm not permitted to say. Come with me. I'll bring you to your room." Sickle grabbed my hand.

I pulled away.

"Please don't make this difficult."

"You said I need a hero to go out there with. Round up whoever is left. I'm going to make a bond."

"I'm not really authorized to..." Sickle looked away and scratched his head.

"You can't deny the whims of an angel." I said, crossing my arms.

That energy and those wings...did I imagine all that? No. I can see it clearly in my mind's eye...along with Braven's body.

I gripped onto my belt.

I'll carry on his mission for their sake and my own.

"Fine. I'll bring them to the temple. Alright?"

"Yep!" I smiled.

I waited at the temple, jumping at the slightest noise.

Has Braven's ghost come for revenge?

I gripped the flaming dagger.

Yu-ki, please, keep my spirit strong.

The door opened.

I turned to face it, my legs shaking.

Sickle entered, alongside a single hero. "You're not going to be happy. All the other hero's were sent off to save your sister. This kid is the only one left." The trainee gestured to the hero.

The boy was around fourteen and had black and red round glasses. The meek cutie was wearing a stylish pinstripe suit and absolutely no armor. Something must have hurt him because this hero was in a wheel chair.

I put the knife in my bag and approached the adorable boy. "My name is Annie."

"Uh, hi Angel. I'm uh. I'm nobody." His shoulders slumped.

"You're not nobody. Did you get hurt trying to protect my sister?"

He shook his head. "I had Parkinson's before I even arrived at this place. The journey didn't fix it, but it did stop the progression so no way am I going back to Earth."

"Now, now, hero. Stay positive," said Sickle.

"The progression of what?" I tilted my head.

"It's a disease. I lost movement in my toes first. It kept growing until I couldn't walk. I'm not able to fight with the other heroes. But I help them make plans and I get really happy when my strategies work!"

His sweet brown eyes were glowing.

I went around the back of his chair and hugged him. "You just need someone to support you." I poked his nose. "And you gotta eat lots of fresh fruits."

"Thanks. I'm Ruiz. So, what is the plan?" he asked with a smile.

I swallowed hard and fidgeted as I paced around him. "So, uh. I don't really know what will happen. I've heard some bad things and I honestly don't know what's true and what isn't. I may shorten your life it doesn't work or accidentally make you my slave. Or...who knows really."

"These people have taken great care of me. This village is my home. If you're saying there are risks, then that's fine. I'll deal with what happens and forge my path forward. Plus, you'll back me up, right Angel?"

"It's Annie," I said, sticking out my tongue.

"I don't feel right giving you a mortal name. I hear you Angels can even resurrect the dead." His constant smile expanded.

"I...don't know if I can."

Maybe there's someway to tilt the odds!

I clap my hands and put them out.

Ruiz smiles and joins in.

Oh yeah. I got this. Braven taught me this game. I almost feel like I'm playing patty cake with him again.

Ruiz stops playing and wipes a tear from my eye. "You okay?

"Yeah!" I hop in place and then pursed my lips. "Are ya weady?"

"Yeah. Let's do this!" exclaimed Ruiz.

I leaned in, bit my lips, and kissed him.

My blood and saliva mixed. My tongue guided it down his throat alongside a silent prayer of protection.

I pulled away and covered my cheeks with my tail.

Why do I like kissing so much? I don't want to mess things up like I did with Yu-ki.

Raul clenched his teeth.

Sickle picked me up. "Best you don't see the rest."

I struggled out of his grip. "I'm not leaving him. He's scared. If he doesn't make it, I'm going to be by his side!" I grabbed Ruiz's hand.

It was shaking.

Is he going to be okay? Did I kill him!?

Ruiz cries\d and gripped my hand tighter.

I hold his hand to my face. "You're strong. You can do this! I need your help to save my sister!"

Ruiz stopped shaking. He looked at me and his eyes were glowing. "I feel incredible." He leaned forward and placed his feet on the ground. He started to stand but then sat back down. "Okay. I still can't walk. But I definitely feel something."

"Usually the heroes awaken their ability in battle. If you want to join the search for your sister. You best go now," said Sickle, guiding us out of the temple.

We went out and searched all night. I called Tumble's name till my mouth was sore. Ruiz was kind enough to give me his water. I was still wary of hero's after what happened with Braven, but I grew fond of Ruiz. I wasn't ready for another romance and was afraid I'd mess it up again. We were friends and we were happy just being friends. Sickle told us to turn back once the trees went black.

"You see this goop? This forest has been taken over by a Queen Goopy. It's not safe to travel any further."

"But what if my sister is there?" I asked.

"Chances are the RiftRippers already found her and have brought her back. We should return to Sunny Village," said Sickle.

"Don't worry, Angel. We can look again tomorrow," said Ruiz, smiling at me.

His smiles are amazing! They feel so real and they make me feel warm without making me dizzy.

I nod. Muttering a silent prayer for my little sister's safety.

"She's fortunate to have you," said Ruiz.

"Were you part of Braven's class?" I asked.

"Yeah. I still have nightmares about that day. Seeing all my classmates slaughtered like that. Then I wake up and the killer is making me hot soup and checking my temperature. It was surreal. Braven helped me back then. My family got separated at the border, so my big brother had to stay behind with my dad. I made it Florida with my mom. Braven told me that he would be my new brother. I was bawling so hard he had to rush me out of the village. Haha!"

"Why are you trusting me. You barely know me," I said.

"Angel's are supposed to take in our troubles. That's what I was told. I was supposed to tell you all this earlier but I was shaken up at the time. I saw a YomiHound. And get this." He leans up to my ear. "She had a mermaid scale in her mouth. Now, you may not know this but Braven said a Mermaid's blood, if taken forcefully, can heal anything. It could give me the ability to run again! Wouldn't that be awesome!?"

Oh no. Is he going to try to hurt Mommy too? What should I do? Things went crazy because of misinformation. I have to tell him everything.

"That scale is mine. It's from my mother."

"Really? That's incredible."

"She is incredible and I won't let you hurt her."

"Are you kidding me? Of course I'm not going to hurt her. In fact, I'm going to help you find her."

"You are!" I grabbed his hand and bounced up and down.

Not going to lie. I may be ogling my buddy right now? I can't help it though. Kindness really flips my switch.

"Yeah. I research them thoroughly. I know all about their powers too. They are living legends. Oh, but enough fan boy-ing. I haven't tested it myself but apparently when the moon is full, the scale releases a light that leads to the one it came from."

That's almost too good to be true!

"When is the next moon?" I ask, leaning over his chair.

"A couple weeks away."

"Then let's build up our strength these weeks so we can find her!" I exclaim, giving Ruiz a fist bump.

We made it back to Sunny Village. We stayed at the main hall, waiting for some news about my sister till morning. I woke up and my new best friend had laid out a bed for me. I was all snuggled up and in pajamas.

Awww! The pajamas had a pattern of little sheep.

My tail rubbed up against his leg as I awoke. "Did you strip me?" I asked, sticking out my tongue.

"Nope. I just laid out the bed. Sickle changed your clothes. Don't worry, I came from a big family. I've seen my cousins naked all the time."

"Did you like what you saw?" I asked, grabbing my tail to keep it still.

His eyes got big. "You have wings! And they're cool! Like bat wings! Can I touch them?"

I shook myself back to my senses.

Geez. I gotta get those morning vibes under control. Don't want to scare off my new bestie. Wait. Tumble!

"Did she show up?"

Ruiz shook his head. "Not yet. Sorry, Angel."

"I'm the one who should apologize. I don't mean to make you uncomfortable," I said, holding my tail close to me.

"Who cares about that? We have an important mission. After the morning session, let's start training! I want to find out about my new power." Ruiz put out his hand and made zappy sounds.

He's too cute.

83

I went to the temple. Old Guy was there, so I rushed up to him.

"Take your time, little goddess."

"My sister is missing. Is there anything you can do to help?" I ask.

He smiled extra wide. "No. My dear, but you can."

"Huh? How?"

"Angel's are fueled by emotions. They sponge up energy." He leans down to me. "Do you know what the most powerful energy is?"

"Love?" I ask.

Old Guy dramatically raises his hands. "Devotion! An angel must sponge up the devotion of her followers in order for her power to grow."

"You mean my healing?"

"Not just your healing. Angel's keep all the bonds they make. That means you can find both your sisters."

"But I never drank Tumble's blood. I never made the book."

"You are connected to all your people. How do you think your mother found your sisters?"

How does he know so much about us?

"I'll do whatever it takes," I said with fiery eyes.

"Such a brave spirit. Shall we get the ceremony started?"

"Wait. Um, there's something you have to know. Braven…"

Old Guy covered my mouth and leaned in closer. His eyes were glaring at me through his smile. "He left the village. I've already informed them. Don't rock the boat, my dear."

That power. It's like he could crush me without lifting a finger. What is with this place? I'll leave as soon as the next full moon comes.

"Now, let the healing ceremony commence!" he exclaimed.

Even though he had turned away I could still feel those eyes gazing into me. Eyes devoid of love.

The ceremony was very unpleasant. A line of sick people, all male, lined up to give their illness to me. Supposedly angel's can't get sick because of how pure we are, but my stomach was in knots.

My nose was dripping too.

Why do I have to kiss all these strangers and why are they all guys? No point in asking Old Guy though.

Old Guy continued chanting but I swear I heard his voice in my head. "Angel's can't get sick. You are an angel, aren't you?"

It was that same terrible emotionless tone that chilled me to the bone.

I held my nose to keep it from dripping and put on a fake smile as I waved all the sick people goodbye.

I turned away from Old Guy, clenching myself. "Am I done?"

He crouched down and put his robe to my nose. "Go on. Blow."

I cleaned out my sinuses into his sleeve.

"You best get some rest now. I've moved Ruiz to your room. Don't worry, I'll make sure he doesn't flee the village like that other boy did." Kindness beamed from the old man.

"His name was Braven," I said softly.

Old Guy's soulless eyes peered into me again. "Was?"

His ghostly voice made me jump.

I ran to my room. Ruiz was already there, drawing something.

"I think I may have figured out what my power is," he said with a smile.

"Riuz...I need to talk to you." I sneezed and covered my nose.

He scooted way back against the corner. "Whoa there. When did you get sick?"

"I'm not sick. Some Puffles just got in my nose," I said with a smile.

"Puffles are about the size of my fist. You're sick. But that doesn't make any sense." He opened his book and searched through it. "Angel's aren't supposed to get sick. It's impossible actually."

"That doesn't matter!" I yelled.

"It does to me. I get sick very easily. I hate it."

"Ruiz. Let me speak! Sorry." I fixed up my angel leotard and put on my serious face. "I don't think Tumble was taken by an outsider."

"Honestly I don't get how she was taken to begin with! Braven was like our top hero! Sure he didn't have power like Yuki, but..."

I grabbed his hands. "Yu-ki had powers!"

Ruiz pulled his hands away and wiped them on my blanket. "Yeah. He could imbue objects with different attributes."

"Like sleep?" I ask.

"Yeah and fire! Do you know Yuki?"

"Uhuh. I met him before I came here. He's doing just fine, don't worry," I said, rolling my eyes.

Ruiz looked at me quizzically.

"Is there still snot on my face?" I ask, wiping my nose.

"Why would Yu-ki date you? He was a one man kinda guy."

I scratched my head. "I might have been a bit forward…actually forceful is the better term."

Ruiz grinned. "Wow. You must have some gumption. Anyways, Braven is way too strong to lose."

"Maybe for any of the hero's. But not a veteran RiftRipper."

Please Braven, tell me you didn't really sell her off.

"Yeah. I don't like talking about those guys. They freak me right the hell out."

"Hey. So I think Old Guy has my sister. He's definitely hiding something."

"No way. Old Guy is the nicest person here. Do you know why he sent the RiftRippers out to find heroes?" Ruiz looks at me for a second and then continues. "He wanted to help out the villagers. Everything he does is for them. We're like a hive and he's the queen bee. Hmmm, odd analogy."

"Well, he's definitely hiding something and I want to find out."

"Relax. The most suspicious thing I've seen him do is leave the village at midnight."

I tossed a pillow at Ruiz.

"Hey, what was that for?"

"Wood Primordial's can't leave the village. Isn't that what you said?"

"Ooooh. You're right. Hey, but he's not faking being a Primordial. Just like you aren't faking being an angel, right?"

What if I'm not an angel? Braven said my people are demons. What if he's right?

Ruiz woke me up with a gentle whack of the pillow. "You okay. You were looking way too serious."

"Yeah. Oh. You mentioned your powers! I almost forgot. What are they are?" I asked, following Ruiz to his work desk.

There was a map with Sunny village at the center.

"Cartography." He smiled at me.

"Maps?"

"Here let me show you." He pulled out a paper. It was a stick figure with a tail and…

"That's me!" I exclaim.

"Yeah, I love to draw but I suck at it. Has nothing to do with my disease. I just can't put my thoughts to the paper. Now, look at this." He lifts up the map to show another picture of me.

It captures my fun-loving determined attitude, my super sleek curves, adorable eyes, and my heart.

I suddenly find myself locking lips with him.

Ruiz pushes me away. "Are you crazy!?"

"I'm sorry! I didn't mean to. Please don't hate me!" I exclaim in tears.

"You're sick! You can't go kissing people or you'll spread it."

He's right. Old Guy was making me spread sickness, but why?

Ruiz poked his chest reverently while muttering.

"Whattya doin'?" I ask.

"Praying to Jesus Christo that I don't get sick."

"So, you don't hate me…for stealing a kiss."

"I'm fortunate to have you as my friend, quirks and all," he said, giving me a thumbs up.

"Awww. Thankies!" I give him a thumbs up too.

I miss Tumble.

"So…your power is artistry?" I ask.

"It's more than that. I mapped out the entire village while you were at the procession. I think I can channel spirits."

I slipped on a pillow and fell on my bum. "You mean like, ghosts?"

"More like deities. I don't know."

"Well that deity better not try to steal my friend or I'll knock it's lights out," I said with a big smile.

"You want to follow Old Guy tonight?" asked Ruiz, drawing with his left hand while looking at me.

Okay. That is a really awesome power.

"Yeah. And you're not stopping me. This may be a lead on finding out what happened to my sister," I said with a firm stance.

"Okay. Want some lunch?" he asked, offering me a sandwich.

I held my nose. "What's that smell?"

"It's a Cuckatrice sandwich."

I whacked his hand. "No! No hero of mine is going to hurt my animal friends."

"I didn't hurt him. He was already dead."

"I'm taking charge of your health from now on. Fruits and vegetables only. Mostly vegetables."

I want all the fruit.

"No bread?"

"Bread is ok."

"Thanks, Angel. I'm sure to get better in your care," he said, smiling at me.

I won't let anything bad happen to my new friend.

We snuck out just before midnight. We didn't know exactly where Old Guy slept but it didn't matter because Ruiz knew where he exited the village. Old Guy merged with the wooden gate and then appeared on the other side. We lay in wait behind a rock. I silenced my breathing before we followed along. We went followed him all the way to the river.

Old Guy opened his vest and poured some sort of powder in the water.

I looked to Ruiz and he shrugged.

Neither of us knew what it was.

A voice came from behind us. "Don't you tire of poisoning your people?" The voice was seductive and sophisticated, somewhat femine too despite clearly belonging to a male.

The figure walked right past Ruiz and I. He was a very elegant man, with gorgeous pink hair and wearing all sorts of colorful...

Animals! He was wearing animals and they were still alive. They were molded into clothing but somehow still drew breath. What kind of person would do something like that?

Ruiz started shaking. "Flam." His voice was a cold, dead whisper.

Old Guy turned to face the intruder. "If I don't give them the sparkling water, then the village will collapse. You know this, so why even ask."

"Your village is kept safe by secrets and by contracts," said Flam with a wicked smile.

"When your reign is over, my people will be free of your toxic haze."

"I'm offering you a single chance. Hand over the angel." He turns to the bushes we're hiding behind. "She's immune to your sparkling water's effects anyway. The only thing she'll bring to the village is trouble and misfortune."

"She's a naïve one. Thinks she can hide her angelic aroma. But she is a sacred guest. I will not turn her over."

Flam's eyes twisted with cruelty. "Then your entire village will make for a glorious tapestry of death and misery!"

I stepped out from behind the bushes. "I'll go with you."

"No, blessed child. Stand down. I'll take him on." Old Guy's feet released roots that bore deep into the ground.

"Your powers weaken the further you are from the village. And once every inch of it is ashes, you too will die, Old Man!" yelled Flam, his scarf poised for battle.

"No! Nobody else is going to die because of me! Just take me away!" I yelled.

Ruiz rolled out from behind cover. "If we attack together, we can take this dictator down!"

"Little boy." Flam's aura erupted out into a rainbow of malice. "You haven't the faintest idea of the forces you are facing!"

Chapter 6: The Hero's Bond

Massive wooden pillars sprouted from the ground, lifting Ruiz and I out of the way of Flam's scarf.

Did that thing just smile at me? If I can just determine what creature it is, maybe I can find a way to defeat it.

"You should run. I'll hold him off." Old Guy brought his aura-laden hands together. "***Wrinkle Condense***."

The trees in the surrounding area were brought into close proximity.

"Once I have my eyes on something, it is already my possession," said Flam as his scarf coiled up the large wood to reach me.

"***Wrinkle Distortion***." Old Guy turned his hands, bending the trees around Flam. The deadly enemy was trapped and his scarf stopped before it could reach us.

The scarf sharpened as it recoiled, slicing an exit out from the wooden prison.

Flam then sliced the slab to wood flakes and emerged, gripping his chest. "Your devotion to your people tickles my very heart."

The scarf shot toward Old Guy, who slammed his fists together to create a special barrier. The scarf disappeared upon hitting the front of the distortion and came out the back of it.

This is insane. Mother told me about the power of WoodPrimordials but this is beyond that. Was one of these gods really the father of Tumble?

Ruiz grabbed my hand. "Okay so honestly I'm terrified and I have no idea how I can use my powers to stop him."

I gripped his hands tightly.

We're both shaking.

"How tough are you?" I asked, keeping my eye on the battle below while running in place.

"I can take a hit. What's your plan? And why are you doing that?" he asked with a nervous smile.

I coated my hands in sweat. "I'm going to need you to get hurt."

"What the hell kinda plan is that?" Ruiz released my hand.

"If you're in danger, I can transform and protect you...hopefully," I said, staring intensely at the battle below.

"Yeah. Maybe we should just try to stick the landing and then run away instead," said Ruiz, gauging the distance to the ground with fear-stricken eyes.

"If you get hurt, then maybe I can fly us out of here. My normal wings are for grabbing but maybe, just maybe, my angel wings can get us down from here."

Old Guy bent the space between his palms to redirect Flam's two-pronged scarf attack. "Forget the boy. Run to safety. He's deadweight."

The scarf coiled around a tree and sliced it, causing it to topple toward Old Guy.

The Wood Primordial made a motion with his hands that sliced the tree in two.

"We have to do something!" I hopped into Ruiz's lap and gripped the wheels on his chair.

"Don't do anything stupid!" he yelled, grabbing my arms.

"Sorry," I said with a nervous grin. I kissed him as I rubbed my sweaty hands on his legs and shirt.

Ruiz freaked out, releasing his grip on me.

I closed my eyes and drove us off the pillar and to the ground twenty feet below.

Something's on my leg.

Flam's scarf pulled me out of Ruiz's lap and flung me into a tree.

Oh no. Please be okay.

I reoriented myself after pushing the leaves away from my face.

His wheel chair was toppled over on the ground, but where was he?

I slid down the tree and saw my hero in the villain's clutches.

Flam had his scarf tie my hero up like a present, with a bow tightly fixed around his throat. Wooden vines crawled up Flam's legs but were turned to stone at a glance. "You are quite the catch. You know, I could give you the power to walk again," he said, caressing my friend's face with his sharp rainbow fingernails.

"Please do, so I can run the hell away from you!" yelled Ruiz, struggling to break free.

"Oh, you tease me with that little show of desperation. Show me more!" He clawed at my hero's chest, shredding fabric and flesh like rice paper despite the defensive buffs I gave him.

Ruiz screamed in agony.

I wanted to look away, but I had to focus on him and his suffering.

Please, give me the power to help my friend.

I silently prayed to myself as my friend whined for his life.

Wooden vines suddenly came out from below and wrapped around my legs. They pulled me away from the battle, from Ruiz.

I grabbed onto anything I could.

I won't abandon him.

I felt light come out from my body. "I won't lose anyone else!"

Wings sprouted from my back.

This Guardian Angel won't fail ever again.

My wings aided me, giving me the strength to break free of the vines. I zoomed into Flam.

He expanded his handkerchief into a curtain that covered me.

Tiny mouths bit at my skin, tearing off bits and pieces of me.

This pain will only make me stronger.

A wrinkly hand tore through the blanket of mouths and pulled me out.

"I know I've caused you great pain but I need your help. Go to Sunny Village and save as many of my people as you can." His hands moved alongside his wrinkles, distorting space.

"But what about Ruiz?" I asked, reaching out toward my hero.

"Even the most gifted heroes are expendable. You are a sacred treasure that must not fall into his clutches." Old Guy completed his incantation and tossed me in the portal.

No. My friends aren't expendable!

I flew out of the portal before it closed and slammed into Flam from behind.

His tie die shirt grew hands that grabbed onto me. They then expanded, pining me to the ground below him.

"Alright boy. Moment of truth. Who dies?" Flam's scarf pulled Ruiz in toward his menacing gaze. "You or the girl?"

"She has her whole life ahead of her. As for me, my body becomes more and more like stone." He stared at the rock-like vines.

Old Guy turned away from the sorry sight. He created a portal to Sunny Village and left us.

Is all this my fault?

Flam's scarf tightened around my hero's throat.

I mustered up all my strength to push off the ground only to be slammed down by more hands.

"I...I don't want to die," cried Ruiz.

Why am I so weak?

Flam licked my friend's tears, shivering with ecstasy. "Say it." His voice was a ghostly whisper.

The scarf coiled around my hero's and snapped them.

"Say it!" yelled Flam.

Ruiz clenched his teeth. His trembling eyes released a burst of tears.

I have to save him.

Ruiz closed his eyes. "Kill her." He opened them. "Kill her and let me live!" he pleaded.

His words hit my core.

My wings faded, and my energy dispersed.

Flam pressed his lips against Ruiz's. He passionately kissed the shivering boy. "Do you love me, hero?"

The scarf brought Ruiz's broken arms behind Flam's back in a tender way, making it all the more disturbing.

Ruiz sobbed. "I…I do. I love you like life itself," he said, with terror clouding his eyes.

"Then I shall keep you safe, my little snowflake." Flam's arms moved up Ruiz's legs all the way to his face. He kissed his neck. "Mmmm. I'm satisfied for now." The cruel villain turned to me. "I'll return for you after you have your big family reunion. Take my advice. Flee from the village." His fabric hands tossed me against a tree. "Going in there is a death sentence."

Fabric littered the area, consciously swaying in the wind to block Flam's leave from my sight.

I buried my face in my hands and sobbed.

Ruiz is lost. It's my fault. Braven too. And Tumble. And Luna. And Mom! Even Yu-ki. It's all my fault.

"Angel. Are you still there?"

My head popped up. I wiped my tears away, revealing the form of my dear friend.

"I'm sorry. I…I was so scared. I can't move. Please save me," he said, reaching out to me.

"I'm the one who's sorry." I walked up to him with shaky legs. I put his arms on my back and started to drag him.

Ruiz clenched his teeth to muffle his screams.

I gently released his arms. "I have to go. I'll be back, okay? I'll be back and I'll heal you then." I looked off at the smoke cloud coming from Sunny Village.

I gotta to rescue 'em.

The smoke assaulted my throat and brought tears to my eyes. The buildings were burning. Humans were running in a panic, most of which I didn't recognize.

What am I even here for? I'm going to die.

I found a young boy under some rubble. I pulled him out.

His legs are missing. I gotta stay focused.

I spit on my hands and rubbed them on his wounds.

No way I can give him new legs, but I can at least stop the bleeding.

"Where's my dad? He was with me," cried the boy, holding onto me.

Something moved behind me.

I turned around.

Black teeth and red eyes gazed past me and at the boy.

A ShadowPup.

"Luna! It's me! If you're listening, then please leave him alone."

The pup's face sharpened and jutted out.

I jumped into the attack, slicing my hands to stop it. The blade pierced through my hands and bore straight through the boy's heart.

I...failed.

Tears came out from my eyes in globs.

The ShadowPup turned its attention to me.

Luna wasn't coming to save me. My sadness was going to end me.

An arrow shot into the pup and caused it to disperse. It came back and then left to find new prey.

"Well, well, what do we have here?" asked a figure, approaching from the smog.

It was a cat boy soldier.

I stood my ground and grabbed onto a metal pipe nearby me.

Ow! It was still hot.

It seared my hands but I kept hold of it.

"Stay back," I said, searching for an escape route.

He drew a sword and knocked my weapon out from my grip. "A real angel. Bringing you in would earn me a gold star." The soldier cut my arm with a swipe of his blade. "Then again, so will killing you."

I rushed toward him and tried to wrestle the sword out from his grip.

The soldier let go.

I fell on my butt.

The CatBoy approached a man who was fleeing. "Dad. It's me," he said softly.

"Son…"

Huh? These murderers have family…in the villages they attack. Ugh. Nothing makes sense anymore.

"Sister was taken. I couldn't save her. But I'm going to avenge her. And you too." The cat soldier took out a dagger and repeatedly stabbing his father. "You have to suffer father…so I can be strong."

What do I do? Should I try to save him? No. Too risky. I gotta look for someone else to save. From now on, I'll be my own hero! Like Yu-ki!

I ran off, shielding my eyes from the smoke while still looking for villagers to save.

There was a man with his face to the ground. I rolled him over.

Ugh. I recognize him. He was one of the ones who gave me their sickness. Actually, it was worse than that. He put his tongue in my mouth. He…exploited me. Why should I save him?

I took the dagger out from his trembling hands. When I looked into his eyes all I saw was a terrified creature about to die. I felt pity for him, which upset me even more. "No more bad stuff." I glared into his eyes.

He nodded with a face full of desperate tears.

I snorted my rage out. Spit on his wound and then rubbed it in with my foot. "Consider this your second chance. Now go out there and save as many people as you can!"

The man nodded and rushed off.

What am I doing? I have limited time and saliva. I shouldn't waste it on someone like him. Ugh, I'm a terrible hero.

I wiped my tears and ran inside a building where I heard screams. "Don't panic. Your resident guardian angel is here to save the day!" I exclaimed, sliding into the room.

What I saw made my body shiver.

Four bodies, two of them children and in the center was a cat boy soldier with two swords and swirling sadistic eyes. He was dressed in a pink and blue maid uniform and was keeping rubble from coming down on him by forming some kind of barrier.

"A LustBorne," he said with a wicked grin.

"I'm an angel!" I yelled, trying to boost my courage to keep my legs from shaking.

"And I am the CatBoy General assigned to conduct tonight's tragedy. My name is CatScratch."

He's the one who killed Yu-ki's lover. I gotta be careful.

"Why did you kill them?" I scanned for a weapon.

"Oh, they're still alive. I just caused enough damage for them to go into a tearful panic. The YomiHounds can deal with the rest. It's more poetic this way. But don't you dare think me soft!" He yelled and pointed both blades at me.

My body suddenly became heavy. I fell to the ground, unable to push myself back to my feet.

What did he do to me?

CatScratch smiled. "After killing my family, every kill afterwards just feels empty. I yearn for that feeling again. That moment of madness transformed me from a lost and weak child into a purpose driven and powerful warrior. You're feeling the effects of that power right now!"

I was lifted off my feet and pulled toward him.

It's now or never.

I whipped out my dagger and sliced his arm.

He reeled in pain, causing the building to topple on top of him and the family.

They died because of me.

I didn't have time for remorse. I ran away in terror.

I tried to save them and I failed at it. New plan. Get out of here, pick up Ruiz and get as far away as possible.

I ducked when I heard a loud sound.

The burning wood from the house shot out in multiple directions, one of them slicing my leg.

I spit on my hand and hobbled as I waited for the wound to heal.

What gives? It should heal immediately.

I head toward a house for cover but it's suddenly gone.

Or not?

The house smashed into another house that was parallel to it a moment ago.

I was brought to the ground. My body then twisted to the shape of a chair.

General CatScratch took a seat on me. "Break time. I'm not going to miss my chance to see our beloved leader in action. You should enjoy the show too."

I didn't have much of a choice.

The wooden rubble of the two crashed houses moved. It twisted and fortified itself.

A figure was seated atop it.

Flam!

"You missed, Old Bat."

"That isn't my name," said Old Guy, seated on a swirling vortex of wood above the village.

"Old men should die and let the young take over. I'm doing your people a favor by freeing them of your stagnation!" yelled Flam, sending pieces of flaming rubble at the WoodPrimorial.

Old Guy deflected most of the attacks, but a few hit their target. It didn't matter though once he increased the speed of the rotating wood storm. The fire was put out almost immediately.

Old Guy sent the entire storm of rubble at Flam, riding the last one and chanting. The wood took the shape of a dragon and zoomed toward the cruel villain.

"You're too late!" Flam opened his palm to reveal a shattered orb.

The wood dragon fell apart and Old Guy collapsed along with it.

"Every Primordial hides its core in its village. You're probably wondering how I know such an ancient well-kept secret." Flam hopped off and rode his scarf to the weakened Old Guy. "Let's just say that one of your kind told me in return for his villages safety. Your kind aren't entirely beholden to the archaic code, after all."

Come on! Angel powers! Hurry up and activate! I gotta save Old Guy. I don't care if he's a creep and a liar. He's not all bad and I want to save the good parts!

Energy burst out of me, sending the cat boy general tumbling off my back.

My wings came out and I soared to Old Guy's side.

"I'm not going to let you die!" I exclaimed, gripping his hand while glaring at Flam.

Flam waved at his general. "Stand down, CatScratch. I'll take it from here. Go out and make sure there's at least one survivor from each family." He looked out at the screaming villagers and the pack of hounds slaughtering them. "As best you can." He said with a blush.

"Those survivors will seek your death," said CatScratch.

"Oh, I'm counting on it. Hee-hee," said Flam with a girly giggle.

Why can't I find the wound?

I searched Old Guy's body, but he was uninjured. Despite this, life was draining from his face.

Old Guy looked up at me in furious tears. "You were supposed to save us!" He pulled his hand away from my grip, shredding it in the process.

He had become so frail.

"You aren't an angel! You were ill! You're a demon! A demon who has cursed my village!" He shaped the nearby wood into sharp spears and willed them to end me.

Blood gushed out from his throat.

Flam cleaned his bloody scarf and smiled at me. "You tried your best and you failed. Go on, cry. It's okay." He pulled me into his arms and cradled me like a child.

I didn't feel like crying.

I bit into his neck with my sharpest teeth and then pulled back, tearing off bits off his skin.

If he can bleed...he can die!

105

I was suddenly above the ground. The scarf was around my throat, strangling the life out of me.

"Oh, that defiant look is so moving! Even now you seek my death! I want to see it fade out. I want to see those tears before your eyes go completely hollow!"

A shadow rose out beneath us and took the form of a hooded man. A blade emerged from the man's back and sliced the scarf.

The RiftRipper pulled me in with a tendril and then the world around me was distorted and darkened.

Part -3: The Love
of An Angel

Chapter 7: Pink String of Fate

I came out in an unknown forest. By the time I got back to my feet, the RiftRipper was already leaving me.

I rushed after him. "Wait up!"

He turned to face me. His face was a void.

He's not the same one who took Mommy away. That's good.

I took a step back and shuffled my feet. "Thanks for saving me."

He approached as if his body was gliding across the ground. His head tilted in an unnatural way. A bladed tendril came out from his cloak.

Wait...what if he saved me to capture me?

The blade patted my head gently.

"It's my pleasure, dear."

Oh, so he's nice like Mr. Sickle.

He turned away.

I reached out and grabbed onto his cloak. "There's a big cloak guy like you! He has my little sister. Do you know where he is?"

"No. I am searching for him too."

"If you find him, can you bring her back."

He crouched down over me. "I would not dare make a promise I cannot keep. What I can promise you is I will lay down my life to retrieve her," he said, shaking a bit.

I went on my tip toes and patted his head. "You're a good guy. What's your name?"

"I discarded my name when I took up this duty. My enemies call me the Broad Spectrum Assassin."

"Oooh, fancy, hee-hee," I said with a big smile.

"Staying near me puts you at risk. I must go," he said as he sank into his own shadow.

Welp. I'm alone now.

I hold my hand to my chest.

But I don't feel alone. I should see how Ruiz is doing!

I focused my thoughts on my friend, but images of him telling Flam to kill me kept popping up. The journal half-materialized before vanishing.

Okay, let's try Luna.

I focused on her but nothing came up. I turned my attention to the sky. The moon was only a crescent.

If I'm going to find Tumble, then I'm going to need to wait for a full moon. Till then, I'm staying put.

The wind whooshed by and made me shiver.

I'll find a nice place to rest for the night.

I went through the forest. It was unlike anything I had ever seen before. The trees were covered in some sort of sticky sap. I kept turning around because I felt like I was being watched. There were no creatures in the area, minus a few buggies. I found a kinda comfy log and rested my head against it.

"Don't worry sisters. I'm going to find you both." I closed my eyes, bathed in the moonlight.

The next couple days I stayed nearby and gathered Rain Berries. I found a spot with tons of berries and…

What happened here!?

Empty armor with rust or blood was stuffed behind one of the bushes. I looked behind another bush and there was more empty armor.

Someone must have killed these heroes.

I stuffed the berries into my shirt and surveyed the area.

The trees were no longer slimy. When did that happen?

I went into a panic and rushed out of the area. I tripped over something and fell.

The berries scattered all across the grass.

My foot was stuck in a puddle of goop. My foot was being dissolved. It stung like crazy.

Okay. Take a deep breath and figure a way out of this, Annie. Your sisters are counting on you! Okay, this creature must be a Goopy. I never wanted to meet one in person. Think about what Mommy's journal said. What was their weakness?

A young man suddenly rushed up, holding a torch. "You finally showed up!" he yelled, holding the flame to the Goopy.

Fire! That was it!

The Goopy released my leg and rushed along the ground to a hiding spot.

The young man chased after it while I healed my foot with my saliva.

Goop fell from the trees around the young man.

"Yeah! Bring it on! I'll kill you all!" he yelled, waving his torch.

The Goopies rose up and took human shape.

"Oh, I know what my comrades looked like and don't think I won't hurt you when you're wearing their faces!" he rushed at one of the Goopies and burned it.

I'm a Guardian Angel so I have to give this hero support!

The jewel on the goopies' heads turned a violent red color as their body became jagged.

"No! You're not taking me too!"

Two lunged at him and bit onto his arms.

I pulled out Yu-ki's fiery dagger and ran to help him.

"Don't be an idiot! Get out of here! Warn the others about this place!" he yelled, swinging his dagger at the enraged goopies.

"I will!" I yelled back. "I will make sure these bad creatures never hurt another hero!"

I ran off with tears in my eyes.

I have to get stronger to keep my word.

Night came and the moon was full.

This was my chance!

I closed my eyes and focused on Luna, holding out my pinky. I thought of the pinky promise we had made and when I opened my eyes, there was a long pink string of energy.

The string went past the trees in the distance.

It would lead me to Luna.

I held out my other pinky and thought of Tumble.

Sure enough, another pink string appeared.

Yay! I'm going to rescue them!

I ran off toward that direction all night long, leaving the forest entirely.

When morning came and my strings vanished, I collapsed.

I woke up to the sound of a Cuckatrice. I could tell from the pitch that it was a girl and based on the volume of the song, she was close by.

I'm going to find her!

Mommy was a brave adventurer who chronicled every creature she met. So, I had definitely seen her drawings of the magical bird, but I still really want to pet one!

Using my mega good hearing, I followed the sound all the way through the prickly forest to the bird.

She had beautiful green and purple tail feathers, with swirls that looked like fearsome eyes. Her wings were short and stubby which was super adorable!

I rushed to the bird as she sang and grabbed her in my arms. "Heya, I'm Annie. Nice to meet'cha," I said, petting her affectionately.

She responded with a "Buckaw" and snuggled my chest.

Cuckatrice's are the prey of so many predators. They have little wings and chubby bodies which makes it hard for them to escape. But they also posses powerful magic that weakens the predators. It's said that their songs can turn an Ebony Panthera as docile as a newborn KitCat. Not only was this Cuckatrice ultra cute, she was a powerful ally.

After spending a couple days with my new bestest bird buddy, our bond went to the next level. I could understand her completely now. What once sounded like "Bock Bock Buckaw!" now was easily understood as "I love you too." Her name was Phoenix and she was looking for her family too. Apparently, some bad heroes took them away from her when she was out foraging. I told her that I would ask anyone I found if they had seen her kids and husband.

My charm power without Tumble at my side, couldn't pacify most of the creatures. But I wasn't alone anymore. The two of us had each other's back. Phoenix would weaken any predators and I would then scare them off. We were an awesome team.

It was almost a whole month before the next full moon.

Once it came, we traveled together. I carried her in my arms and ran to my destination with newfound energy.

The forest got darker and more prickly as we ventured in deeper but we stayed focused.

The next morning I awoke to someone grabbing my butt.

I grabbed their hand. "What are you doing!?" I yelled.

I recognize her! It's the Gobli girl. The one who stole Yu-ki!

I backed up and looked over my shoulder.

Phoenix was still asleep in the leaf bed I had made her. And there were at least ten Gobli.

They were wearing human clothes, I think. They had pretty pink dresses that kinda clashed with their scary looking thorny maces. I was taller than even the tallest one of them.

"Where's Yu-ki?" I reached for my dagger, but it was missing.

The Gobli girl pointed and laughed at me, showing off the weapon she stole.

Nasty girl! Took Yu-ki and my keepsake. Not on my watch!

I rammed into her and grabbed the blade. I pointed the burning tip at her. "Go away or I will hurt you," I said, puffing out my cheeks and standing on my tippy toes to look bigger than I was.

A Gobli rushed up and slammed her mace into me.

I coughed up blood and my vision went hazy.

Phoenix rose to attention and rushed in front of me. She spread out her wings and warned them to back off.

Aww. She's the best.

The Goblis left, along with Yu-ki's sword.

Phoenix is great, but I'm going to need a powerful hero if I'm going to rescue my family.

We were extra cautious the next couple of days but the danger died down once we were out of the prickly forest. When the next full moon came, it brought us all the way to the top of a small mountain.

No way. What am I supposed to do now?

The string went out past the massive body of water.

When I was teleported, I got sent to a completely different island!

I fell to my knees and sobbed.

Phoenix nuzzled me. She told me that I needed to move on. That both our families were already dead.

We cried together that night, staring out beyond the endless ocean.

In the morning we were both thinking clearly. We decided that finding a village was our best bet. It's likely that's where her family was taken and maybe I could find a RiftRipper that could teleport me back to Sunny Village so I could find my family. Problem is, we couldn't see any villages from the mountaintop.

If I only I had saved that hero.

With no clue where a village was, we decided to just hug the shoreline and make our way across it. We were so happy when we met with a merchant.

"Hello, Sir?" I waved at him.

He turned, his eyes golden nuggets and his hands coated in silver. "Yes, little missy."

Oh no. He was a MounTroll.

I took a step back.

"No need ta be alarmed. I'm a merchant not a bounty hunter," he said with a golden grin.

"Sorry. I uh, had some bad experiences at Street Trash," I said.

"I'm impressed ya made it out of there, little angel," he said, eying my clothes.

"We were wondering where the closest village is. And also, is there a way to cross the big lake?" I asked.

"You'd need a ship, a crew and a captain, none of which comes cheap." He grinded his fingers together, creating dust.

"Well, how can I make money?" I put on a pouty face.

"You could waste years of your life doing quests for the villages and get your CatCoin from raiding corpses. Or…" He leaned in and his eyes got big. "We could work out a deal."

"What is the deal?" I asked with a scrutinizing look.

"Angels sell for a lot of coin. I'll give ya twenty percent."

"I'm not letting you sell me off to some random person!" I yelled.

"No random person can afford angels. It takes an entire village to come up with enough coin. You wanted to go to a village. Why not makes some money while yer at it? It would be more than enough to get yerself across the sea to the next island."

I looked at Phoenix. She shrugged.

The idea makes sense, but can it really be that easy.

"Actually we'll just, uh, walk to the village. Which way is it?"

"Information is not free. Look, ya got nothin' ta lose. You could even leave the village after I sell you."

Ugh. He's right.

"Okay, but I want my money up front!" I stood tall. "Um, how much was it?" I ask, still keeping my proud posture.

116

"Gheheh! No worries, little angel. We MouTrolls, the real ones, believe in the force of Karma! Cheatin' ya out of yer money would only cause me harm. I didn't get rich by swindling people. I got rich from word of mouth and corpse raiding. Thank the ethers that we don't take all that shiny baggage with us when we move on," he said, wiping away a tear.

"The coin?" I asked, opening my palm.

"We don't know how much we can go for until we get the buyer. Hop on my cart and I'll bring ya to the village."

"Thanks, mister MounTroll."

"Merchant will do just fine for a name," he said, flashing his shiny teeth.

I allowed merchant to cuff me, all the while Phoenix glared at him.

He rang the bells on his cart, creating a terrible sound that was meant to keep monster's away. I covered Phoenix's ears every time right before he hit the gong.

"So, this island...does it have a name?" I asked.

Merchant slowly turned to us and smiled. "Abandoned. Pleasant name, isn't it?"

I will make it out of this place.

Merchant was suddenly blasted off the cart.

My ears bled and my head got dizzy. When my eyes came into focus, there was a beautiful young lady with short red hair, freckles and a black hood. The numbers fifty eight and a heart was on her left cheek. She was holding my shoulders.

"Are you okay, kid?" she asked.

I noticed an emblem on her belt.

She must be a hero.

"Yeah. I'm fine. Just a bit dizzy," I said, wobbling a bit.

"Sorry about that. I use too much power when I get emotional." She clenched her gloved fist. The tension left when she looked back at me and she offered her hand. "I'm Racheal by the way."

I shook her hand. "I'm Annie. Oh, and that guy you blasted is merchant. He was just taking me to the village."

"In chains?" Racheal rolled her eyes. "You can't be that oblivious." She crouched down. I looked at her chest and noticed a bunch of numbers had been tattooed across it.

Just like Braven said. The hero's are branded.

"Are you staring at my boobs? Geez, you angels really are always horny, aren't you?" she asked with a grin.

"No. That's not it at all," I said, waving my hands with a blush.

"No worries, I'm not upset." She turned around. "Get on my back. Dark and Broody isn't far. I can take you there."

"Okay, but I need money for a boat and a captain and a crew," I said, counting on my fingers.

"Oh, a little adventurer, are you? When you leave, I'm coming along." Racheal picked me up and plopped me onto her shoulders.

Phoenix hopped onto my head.

"Sure, you can come too," said Racheal, looking up.

Merchant got up. "Are you really stealing from me?" Crystals came out from his hands and aimed at Racheal.

"She's just a kid, you creep!" Racheal put her hands together and sent out a sound wave.

The projectile mineral and Merchant were both sent flying. Merchant smashed into his carriage.

"He really wasn't trying to hurt me," I said, shaking Racheal.

"You can't trust anyone. Especially not merchants," she said, running off with me.

The atmosphere changed when we stepped into the new village. It became heavy. The air was harder to breath. The dark blue and black buildings all drooped, adding to the negative atmosphere.

"Isn't this place cool?" asked Racheal, skipping down the snow-covered streets.

"Can I speak with the guy in charge?" I asked.

"Ooh, you're focused. That's good. Yeah, I'll take you to her." Racheal lowered her head solemnly and groaned to greet the other somber villagers.

This place is the opposite of Sunny Village. Why can't I just go to a normal village?

"Phoenix wants to know if you eat Cuckatrice's here."

"Yeah. Sometimes they send us out to bring back food for the village. I personally haven't been able to eat meat since I got here," said Racheal with a shrug.

"We gotta go rescue the animals!" I exclaimed.

"Hold up, there are rules here. If you have a grievance, you have to bring it up to the elder."

Don't worry Phoenix, we're going to rescue your family!

We were brought to the graveyard.

"Hey everyone! You won't believe what I found!" Racheal picked me up and introduced me to each tombstone.

"Did you know all these people?" I ask softly.

"Eh, only a few. But I love graveyards. So creepy, right?" she gave me a big smile. "I have a special power to talk to ghosts. Problem is they never talk back. Maybe I'm too pastel for them." Racheal put her hand on the tombstone. "Look Annie, a Crimson Spider!"

"Those are incredibly deadly!" I exclaimed, pulling back.

"Yeah! I know, right?" she placed the spider on her nose. "And they tickle too." Racheal giggled.

Suddenly this place doesn't seem so sad.

"So, this is where the village leader is?"

"Nope." Racheal points to a sleeping bag lying on the ground near some particularly creepy trees. "It's where I sleep. Just wanted to show you around the place." She opens a bag and tosses me some Banana Berries. "Sometimes I hear groans in the middle of the night and get so excited that I lose sleep! Haha! This place is amazing!" she exclaimed with wide eyes.

"Where you born here?" I asked.

"Nope. I was born in Ontario Canada, nineteen ninety so I'm twenty-two now. Single mom, never knew my dad. No siblings either. No boyfriends.

I actually came across this place at an anime convention. I was selling my critically ignored independently created horror comic 'the Missing Piece.' I'm wearing the cosplay for my main character, Amanda." Racheal points to the metal puzzle piece shoulder guards on her and the emblem on her belt. "The plan was for me to reinvigorate the horror genre like Saw did! But, at the last convention I was boothing at, things got a bit hectic." She scratched her head.

"You were killed?" I asked softly.

"Yeah! Blood everywhere! But these things need buildup!" Racheal took out a flash light and crouched down to me. "It was just another day of below average sales and above average enthusiasm. I had recently seen Saw five in theatres and oh man did it inspire me! I was on my fourth comic, it was where I would introduce these creatures that feed off misery called the Barren. See, to me, true horror isn't the threat of dying, but losing who you are! Feeling trapped or broken! So as I'm sketching out a creepy forest, I hear a scream. Some guy's in a Batman outfit got his head sliced off. It was surreal. I was freaking out, and I didn't run. Funny cause I always hate when the victims don't run. But I was frozen in terror completely. The dude in the cloak, with bloody knives coming out from his cloak and just floating in the air- crazy shit, I know- he kills a whole group of people as they run by. Literally their bodies just fall to the ground in bloodied segments."

How terrifying. Yu-ki, Braven and all the heroes had to go through the same thing. It's too awful.

Racheal wiggled in excitement. "I was freaking out! I always wanted to witness something crazy and man was this crazy. The creepy shadow man approached my booth. I couldn't look into his eyes because he had no face. It was the most unsettling thing. I made a mental note before I pissed myself in terror. Mmm, it was such a rush! I kinda just stared at him with an open mouth. Racheal leans in close to me and deepens her voice. "'Racheal Summers, you have been selected.' I feel the metal blades brush up against my leg." Racheal bites her lip and glides a single finger up my leg. "Mmm, I was so turned on. Anyways, so I mustered up all my strength and spat out a response. 'I get to live?'" Racheal suddenly brings her fingers to my face. "His blades brush up against my cheek. 'You must die.' I blacked out immediately. But when his knife pierced my chest I came to again. At that point I was no longer excited. I was sobbing. Some guards came in and opened fire on the creature but the shots passed straight through him. The creature's head tilted and saw my open comic. He made some sort of otherworldly sound. He followed my panel plan and sliced my skin off bit by bit. I was crying and screaming. I didn't know what was going on. It felt so fake but the pain was so real." Racheal bounces up and down in excitement. "He legit skinned me alive. I mean, I died somewhere in the middle of it, but holy shit my death was epic! The scariest thing I've ever witnessed for sure! But yeah, after that, I awoke in this village and got trained to be a hero."

I hug her tightly. "I'm so sorry you went through that."

Racheal points to my wet legs. "Ha! You pissed yourself. Looks like I still got my knack for storytelling."

I crossed my legs and lowered my head in embarrassment.

Racheal gripped me. "Don't you feel that adrenaline! I wish I could live ever moment like this! Hyper aware, fully conscious and pumped with energy. Now, lets go to the creepy swamp out back, and get you cleaned up for your big important talk with the village head." She lifted me up.

Racheal is a funny girl. But she's nice.

She took me to the creepy swamp. The trees in the area creaked and there were bizarre animal noises.

"No shame in being afraid. And no worries. I will protect you," she said, taking off her clothes.

Wow. She has freckles on her chest too. That's super cute!

"Staring at my boobs again, huh?" asked Racheal, covering her chest.

"How many years have you been in Dark and Broody Village?" I asked.

"Four years and not once have I failed a mission. See, I was a scared little girl so I took self-defense, Tae-Kwan Do, even Kendo. I wanted to meet a crazed killer but I also wanted to be prepared to beat his ass down if he broke in the house. Nobody is hurting my mom," said Racheal, punching the air.

Wow! She's super cool.

"Who, branded you?" I asked, looking away.

"The cheek tattoo is what my character wears. Amanda Panda was supposed to be the fifty-eighth victim of the killer, but she ended up kicking his ass. It was her girlfriend's idea to add the heart."

"Do you channel her courage by dressing up as her?" I asked, stripping down.

"Yeah, you could say that. Fear is such a rush, and a true hero uses that rush as fuel to kick ass." Racheal suddenly hops out of the bath grabs onto my wings. "You have butt wings! You're like a little Dante. That is the cutest thing ever! Why did you hide these from me?" she asked, beaming when my little wing hands grabbed her finger.

"I didn't want anyone to know I'm an angel. We're kinda a target apparently."

Racheal takes off my hat. "You have horns too! Demon horns!"

"Angel horns!" I yelled.

Racheal bows down. "Oh, dark emissary, I humbly pledge my allegiance to you. Grant me the power to destroy those bratty popular girls at my high school."

I poke her nose and slip into the swamp.

Oooh. The water is cold and mucky.

Racheal slid in and then pulled me close to her chest.

Her skin is so soft and pretty.

"Do you see it?" She points at the branch. "A Blood Bat is right above us!" She squealed and squirmed in delight. "I gotta try this." She took her fingernail and cut her palm.

I don't think I'll ever meet anyone like her again.

The bat came down from his perch- you can tell it's a boy since his ears are less pointy- and cautiously landed on her hand.

"Sooo cute," said Racheal wiggling with joy.

The Blood Bat bloated up like a toad and then flew off.

Racheal came up and tickled me.

"What are you doing?" I asked, trying to fend off her assault.

"You are magnetic! I had heard angels attracted creatures but I have never seen a Blood Bat in all my years here. Poppy gets the guys for sure, but not too great at attracting monsters."

"Wait, there's another angel here? Can I meet her?"

"Yeah, sure. But she likes being the center of attention. Didn't like it when I tried pig tails because I was too cute. You're waaaay cuter than me so don't let her bully you, okay?" said Racheal, stretching her arms out.

"No worries! My big sister taught me to stand up for myself." I punched the water, splashing Racheal's face.

"She is so lucky to have you. With a cute, brave little sister like you cheering me on, I bet I could double my page count."

"You still write?"

"Yeah. This place is awesome, but I have to get back home and continue my series. My mom is waiting on me…and I did write my own ending to the Saw franchise, but that doesn't mean I don't want to see it for myself. Some new kid that showed up nearly spoiled it for me!" yelled Racheal "I broke his nose" She said with a grin.

"As your Guardian Angel, it's my job to protect you so your dreams can come true, big sister!" I exclaimed, hugging her.

Racheal embraced me and cried. "You're so cute and sweet. It hurts!" she exclaimed, thrashing me around in the swamp.

"And you're so pretty," I smiled. I looked at her bare chest again.

"Fine you can touch them," said Racheal, rolling her eyes.

"How did you get those numbers?" I asked softly.

"We're expandable, little sister. Oh my Cthulhu, can I call you little sis?" she asked with shimmering eyes.

"Well, that is what big sisters are supposed to call their little sisters," I said with a sunny smile.

Racheal hugged me tightly. "You're sooo much better than Poppy."

"And you're the prettiest hero." I leaned in and kissed her lips.

Huh? Why did I do that? I like boys!

My face flared up like a tomato.

"I'm so sorry! I'm sure you have a boyfriend and I'm your little sister not your lover and I don't want to scare you off. Can't we just stay friends forever?" I asked, grabbing her hand and sobbing into it.

"Whoa. Calm down. Sister's kiss each other all the time, right? And no…" Racheal's shoulder's slumped. "I don't have a boyfriend."

"But you're so pretty," I said, rubbing the freckles on her cheeks.

"I'm also…you know, weird," said Racheal with a nervous chuckle.

I kissed her cheek. "I enjoyed that kiss. So…I guess I'm a little weird too," I said, hiding my flushed cheeks.

Racheal pulled me out of the swamp. "Let's get dressed and meet with the village chief, little sister."

After we got dressed, I wiggled in place. "Can we uh, kiss again?" I asked, shifting my hips.

"Aww, you want practice? That is so cute. Wow, I'm like a real big sister now. With our powers combined, we can surely get boyfriends!" she exclaimed, lifting me up in her arms. She kissed my lips.

It was such a sweet and soft kiss. Like the one's Mommy gave me.

"I still can't believe you never had a boyfriend," I said.

"Well, I did date once, tried to do a blood pact so we'd be together forever. I went just a biiiit too fast," said Racheal with a nervous chuckle. "Hey, don't feel sorry for me. You haven't had a boyfriend either," she said, poking my belly.

"Actually, I had three." I stuck out my tongue.

Ruiz kinda counts and Braven was clearly into me, so yeah, three.

Racheal's head slumped. "Ugh. Losing to my own little sister."

Phoenix nuzzled her foot. "Aww, thanks, birdie. You're right, it's not too late for me!"

"Wow! You understood Pheonix?" I asked.

"Not a word, but Amanda does. Can speak to ghosts and animals. She's the best!"

"Nope." I scrunched her cheeks with my hands. "You're the best."

Racheal smiled. "The elder is right down this path."

A wretched scream came from behind us.

"Stay here. I'm going to see what happened," said Racheal, setting me down.

I grabbed her hand. "No way, Big Sis! I'm going with you!"

We arrived at the house and heard all sorts of banging.

"Okay, I'm going in!" Racheal kicked the front door open.

A hero was on the ground, his neck was black and his arms were sliced off. Looming above him was a RiftRipper.

Oh no. It's him. The one who took Mommy from me!

"It's unfortunate you witnessed this," said the murderer, his blades turning to face us.

Chapter 8: Racheal: The Silent Symphony

The door behind us slammed shut.

The man who took away my Mommy glided across the ground to end Racheal.

"You aren't getting me again! *Sound Shot!*" Racheal slammed her hands together, creating a sonic wave that pushed the assassin's blade's aside.

My feet moved on their own. A furious fire was heating my insides.

I grew aura wings and slammed into the attacker. "Where's my Mommy!?"

He's going to tell me even if I have to hurt him lots and lots!

"You know Betrayer too?" asked Racheal, firing sound shots at the incoming bladed tendrils.

Phoenix spread out her wings. Her eyes glowed and grey energy coated her body. She screeched at the RiftRipper.

"Such things only work on mortals." Tendrils came out from under his cloak and sped toward me.

"*Sound Shotgun!*"

My ears bled as a powerful sound wave zoomed past me and exploded into the ceiling.

Rubble buried Betrayer and stopped his attack.

"Get out of here! I'll hold him off!" yelled Racheal.

No. I'm never going to lose anyone else. I will protect Racheal.

My tattoos glowed and I summoned up a black book wrapped with chains and with red swirls on the cover.

This must be Racheal's book. I'm going to make sure her story continues.

I slammed my hands together. "***Sound Shotgun!***" The sound wave blasted Betrayer at point blank range.

Did I just use Racheal's power!?

"Awesome hit, Annie!" Racheal lifted me into her arms and made a run for the door. "We have to get as far away from him as possible."

"We're an awesome team!" I exclaimed, firing sound bullets at his incoming tendrils.

Two tentacles came out from the ground and wrapped around Racheal's legs.

I fell out of her grip and landed on my booty.

Racheal was slammed against the wall before being thrown aside into the kitchen of the house.

My shadow rose up behind me and grabbed onto me. "Your mother is dead. Try to leave this place and you will be forcibly reunited."

Mommy...

A sound shot hit my shadow's face and Racheal stood by the door way, bloodied up.

I can heal her as soon as we beat this guy.

A single blade went into a rift and came out of multiple rifts around Racheal.

If I hurt him, then she'll get hurt too. What do I do?!

"You shouldn't throw your life away," said Betrayer, gently caressing her body with his blades.

"Why did you kill Richard?" asked Racheal in tears.

"A job. One you will not speak of to anyone," said Betrayer.

An old woman with black bark as skin and dark circles over her eyes appeared between Racheal and Betrayer. Her corrugated forehead and permanent frown gave her a heavy gravity of negativity. "Get out, boy." She clawed a spatial distortion into existence and swung it around, slicing all the tendrils around Racheal.

The RiftRipper sunk into the ground as a shadow and left.

I rushed to Racheal's side and spit on my hands. "I'll get you healed up in no time!" I exclaimed, rubbing her wounds.

"Holy shit that was a rush!" exclaimed Racheal, hugging me.

"Thanks for saving us, Village Chief," I said with a bow.

"Oh, I'm just an Old Bat," said the woman, slicing off bits of her skin and expanding it to fix up the house.

Racheal looked up. "Ancient One, do you have any idea why Richard was killed?"

"Betrayer is a RiftRipper who seeks to bring ruin to ISEKAI."

"Then why go after Richard? He didn't even have powers."

Old Bat crouched down to the boy's bloodied body. "Such a shame," she said, shaking her head.

Racheal crouched over. "Oh my god! His guts are spilling out. This is disgusting!" she exclaimed with a giddy smile, putting his intestines back inside him. "I can feel his insides. I never got this close to him befoe." Her bottom lip quivered. "Wow! My hand is in an actual corpse!"

Old Bat chopped the air, instantly distancing Racheal from the body. "We must respect the dead," she said sternly.

"I am respecting him! I'm in complete adoration!" exclaimed Racheal with big eyes.

I went to the body. "Maybe it's not too late." My aura wings coiled around my hands. Energy radiated from my palms.

My powers are getting stronger and stronger. I didn't even know I could do this.

"You're wasting your time," said Old Bat with a solemn look.

"Do it, Annie! Oh, I hope he comes back as a zombie!" exclaimed Racheal, bouncing in place.

Phoenix hopped into the old woman's arms.

"Why did you bring these dangerous creatures into my village?" asked Old Bat, glaring at Racheal.

I raised my voice while staying focused on healing. "She's with me! Phoenix is looking for her family. I heard you kill Cuckatrices in this village. As a Guardian Angel I demand you put an end to this violence."

The air distorted around me as Old Bat laughed. "Haven't even introduced yourself and you're already making demands. You will learn respect, girl."

Racheal rushed up to Old Bat as she turned away. "She wasn't trying to be rude. She's just a bit overwhelmed is all. I mean…we did just witness a murder," she said, biting her lip.

"Yeah. I'm mega sorry for being rude. Every second counts. Her husband and six children were all taken from her. We just want to reunite her with her family," I said, bowing down. "Oh, and my name is Annie."

"Annolette?" Old Bat's eyes widened. "Was your mother an Aquis?"

"Nope. She was part MerMaiden though," I said.

Old Bat put her hand on my head. "The Aquis can take whatever form they wish, my dear. Your mother is indeed a legendary being."

But she's dead now.

Old Bat collected my tears as they fell and contorted space to grab a bottle from the kitchen. She collected the tears in the bottle. "You shouldn't be wasteful." She reached into her pocket and took out a glowing scale. "You're going to need all your energy if you're going to bring back your mother."

The glowing scale. Then she is alive!

The tattoos on my body glowed and water came from my hands.

Old Bat sliced my arm with her fingernail.

The blood mixed with the water and sealed up the wound.

"You are indeed a gifted child," said Old Bat with glowing eyes.

Blood spurted out from the corpse. It coughed.

Wait. I did it. He's alive!

Racheal hoisted me up and snuggled me. "You didn't tell me you were a necromancer!" she exclaimed, rubbing cheeks with me.

"I had no idea I could do that! I just gave it a shot and it actually worked!" I exclaimed, kissing Racheal's cheeks repeatedly.

"I'll consider your request after you prove your loyalty to the village," said Old Bat.

"But what if her family is killed tomorrow morning for breakfast?" asked Racheal.

"This village is maintained by rules. Defiance of the smallest degree can create cracks. Those cracks can spread and then it all comes crashing down. This girl's arrival spelled doom for Sunny Village. I won't allow the same to happen here."

How does she know about that? Ugh. That doesn't matter right now.

"Please. I beg you!" I exclaimed, pressing my face to the ground. "I already saved one hero's life. I will fight for your village, just please save her family and all the animals trapped here!"

"There is no hope for this village. It's kept together by loyalty and consistency. This conversation is over."

"Wait, don't go!" I grabbed onto her cloak.

"Insolent child," said Old Bat, glaring at me.

"There's a forest covered in slime. Lots of heroes died there. One of the heroes, he died protecting me. You have contact with the other village chiefs, so please warn them."

"A hero that dies so easily isn't worth concern."

"Please tell them." I looked up at her in tears.

"Where is this forest?"

"It's uh…somewhere on this island. I'm not exactly sure where. What is this island called again?"

"Abandoned. We live miserable lives but better to live in misery than to die in glee like those poor fools at Sunny Village." Old Bat swirled out of existence.

"Annie! Come here!" yelled Racheal from the other room.

"Richard isn't just back to life. He's more muscular. You turned the little twerp into a hunk," she said, rubbing the resting hero's muscles.

"How did I do that?"

"No clue, but it's awesome! You're so magical!" exclaimed Racheal, making a little jingle with her fingertips.

"Racheal, you gotta tell me what she meant when she said this village is hopeless," I said with a super serious look.

Racheal scratched her head. "You're safer the less you know, honestly."

I grabbed her hands. "Please, tell me."

"Old Bat and the heroes, we lost the fight. This village is owned by the Love Dictator. The meat, the animals captured, are for his soldiers. Messing with that could put everyone in the village at risk." She raised her hood and turned away. "I've said too much."

I lifted up Phoenix. "You have a mom back home. I bet she loves you a lot."

"Yeah, she did. Raised me all on her own," said Racheal, wiping away her teary eyes.

"Well Phoenix loves her kids just like every other mother. They're probably sad and scared without their Mommy." I gaze up at her with teary eyes "Please, tell us what you know."

Racheal closed her eyes. "Breaking the rules here and getting caught…is a very bad idea." She grabbed a vase and tossed it to the ground.

The vase shattered without a sound.

"But I've never been caught," she mouthed to me, followed by that adorable grin.

134

I grabbed my chest.

My heart is racing. She looks so radiant.

Racheal crouched down and picked up her book from the floor. "I'm going to rescue her family. You can monitor my progress from here. Just uh, promise me you won't look at any of the past pages. I'm sure there is some stuff in there that would freak you out." She handed me the book.

I set the book down. "I'm going with you."

"I'm the only one who can move without a sound. Either you stay behind or I'm not going. This is a big gamble for me, but not doing anything, well…then I wouldn't be a hero." She forced the book into my hands and held herself with shivering arms. "It always bothered me. Those poor animals don't have a chance in hell at survival. It's not a horror film; it's a fucking snuff film." She looked up and smiled at me. "Thanks for inspiring me to do the right thing." Her shimmering eyes gazed into me.

She's beautiful.

I patted my cheeks. "Alright, you can go. Buuuut, you gotta do something first."

"Make you a promise I can't keep? Not gonna happen. The place has CatBoy soldiers surrounding it. I'm quite likely to die."

I shuffled my feet and wiggled around. "Umm, ya gotta kiss me first. For um, luck?"

"Sure thing, little sis." Racheal crouched down and gave me a little peck on the lips.

I lowered my shoulders and rolled my eyes. "I meant a real kiss." I stuck out my tongue a bit.

"Sure thing. After I come back," she pushed my tongue back into my mouth with her gloved fingers.

"Hold up." I exclaimed.

"Every second counts Annie."

"You need Pheonix or you won't know the right ones to save."

Racheal stopped in place and clenched her fist. "A great and wise man believed that everyone deserves a chance to live a cherished life. I'm going to free every Cuckatrice in that wretched building. I want to carry on the legacy he started." Racheal reached into her cloak and pulled out a red mask that looked like a face with missing puzzle pieces where her eyes were. "Time for Amanda Panda to kick some ass!" Racheal rushed out of the building without a sound.

I sit by the sleeping hero and followed Racheal's quest in my book. She snuck past the guards and made her way inside the building.

Let's see if this works.

I bit my fingertips and placed them on the book.

If I could see Braven's past, then maybe I can see her present.

I place my fingers on the book and close my eyes.

I open the door after making sure to silence it.

Just another day for Amanda Panda!

Inside are some guards, hiding their adorable cat ears under police hats.

Ugh. I'm the reason this place has so many guards. No worries, Racheal. You got this.

I silenced my footsteps and pointed in the distance.

I created a loud explosion sound at the very back of the building.

The guards rushed to the back area.

Wow. So far so good. These powers really are super rad.

I ran down the hallway in total silence.

How am I going to free all these animals? Oh, what am I thinking!? If I do, then Old Bat will know its me! Annie really shouldn't have had that conversation with Old Bat. Oh well. Time to be a hero.

I placed my hand on the first Cuckatrice door. My sound wave blasted it open.

I vomited upon entering the room. It smelled like feces and dead bodies.

Ugh. Can't believe I used to eat these guys.

I grabbed my stomach. The room was totally dark.

These poor birds have probably never seen the sun.

I take out a flash jelly from my cloak and put it on my hand. The area lights up.

The birds are all scrunched up together, with barely enough room to move around.

The birds looked up at me and rushed toward the door, singing a melody of joy.

I put an imaginary silencer on my finger and fired at the birds as they fled.

There are too many of them.

I fired silencing shots from all my fingers at the fleeing birds, hoping that I didn't miss any.

"Hey, what was that!" yelled a guard.

Shit! Looks like I did miss one!

I mimed a grenade and threw it outside, through the wall.

"It's coming from outside!" yelled a guard.

With Annie by my side, I'm finally no longer alone. I can feel her reading everything I'm doing right now. Oh, I hope I don't think anything embarrassing, like about how cute her butt is. Damn it. I'm no good at this!

I peeked out from the prison cell and saw that I had at least forty more doors to bust down.

How am I going to get all of them to safety? There's no way. But I gave them a chance to escape. The rest is up to them.

I ran by and blasted the doors open one by one. There was a guard who noticed me, but only one.

He turned to holler to his allies, but not before I tossed a silencing air dagger into his throat.

I rushed up and pile-drived him to the ground, making a disorienting low pitched demon laugh.

He got scared and reached for his knife.

I put on my invisible sound gloves and punched him repeatedly, making little squeaks at each impact.

This is too much fun.

He sliced my thigh with a hidden dagger.

138

I winced in pain before placing my fingers in his ears. *"**Sound Burst!**"*

A symphony of fireworks went off in his head, busting his eardrums and knocking him out.

Oh, yeah. All in a day's work.

"You again!" yelled a voice.

I turned around to see four armed guards, including our resident CatBoy general: NeedleStack.

NeedleStack was wearing spiked bondage gear around his ligaments. His chest was covered by a pink frilly apron. And he had that cute sailor cap on, dignifying him as a general. His body was covered in fuzz and his head looked like a tabby cat, complete with a cute little pink nose. His jade eyes glared at me.

I'm going to die! Better make it flashy!

I grabbed the sword from the downed CatBoy and ran my hands up it. *"**Sound Imbue**, **Cacophony**."*

I quickly put a sound barrier around my ears before clashing swords with the first CatBoy.

The sound of a jet engine burst out from the impact. It still rattled my eardrums and disoriented me but the other CatBoys, even the general, were on the ground with blood gushing from their heads.

I turned to run and felt a prickle in my foot.

Not good.

The splinter in my foot expanded into a thorn. It kept expanding till it was coming out both sides of my feet. I collapsed and my mask fell off on impact.

No! No! Amanda needs her cursed mask. I need it or I'm going to piss myself in terror!

"Don't move or I'll expand the next one," said NeedleStack with a grating rough voice.

I could feel a slight prickle on my chest. And then I felt my undies get soaked.

"I surrender," I said, wiggling my legs in excitement.

I'm about to die again. Mmm, what a crazy rush!

He turned me over with his stiletto army boots. "If it isn't the jewel of the village?"

"You say that like it's a compliment. I'm only the jewel because I'm the only hero here without an angel."

Yeah. Don't let him learn about Annie.

"If you were any other hero, I would have killed you. But you're a legend! Racheal: the Silent Symphony!" exclaimed NeedleStack, twirling a long metal thorn.

"Glad to see someone appreciates me around here."

NeedleStack pierced my leg with the metal thorn. "Why are you stealing from us?"

"Girls do crazy things when they're in love," I said, forcing a smile.

He turned the thorn, making me gasp in pain. "Test my patience and I will kill you."

"I've wanted to free the animals here for a while, just didn't have the courage."

"Then there must be a new development." His smile widened. "A new angel perhaps?"

"More than that…the Betrayer was here."

NeedleStack's eyes got wide. "Then you best be careful."

I am abruptly brought back into my body.

Racheal is in danger. I have to go rescue her!

I get up from the bed to see a large shadow looming over me.

Betrayer!

"Don't get in my way!" I yelled, starring daggers at the massive RiftRipper.

"You were shaking so I brought you back to awareness."

His tendrils spread out, blocking the exit to the room.

"I will give you a choice. Heal the girl or reunite with your little sister." A portal opened up in his chest.

What should I do?

I broke down into tears. "Why are you testing me? Why did you hurt my mother!"

"Calm yourself. Nothing I do is personal or maybe…" His body contorts into an unnatural shape "all of it is?" His tendrils turn to face him. "What do you all think?"

"I don't know where that portal leads! How can I even trust that my sister is there?" I asked, stepping up to him.

"Silence!" His shadow spread out like wings. "And listen."

There was no mistaking it. I could hear her sleeping on the other side. My sister was in there. She was alive.

"Serving your kind is in my genetics. But how I do so." He twisted his body into a thin spear and then reformed behind me. "That's entirely up to me." He opened up the portal in his chest again. His head fell off his body and looked up at me from the floor. "Have you decided?"

I held my shivering body.

Tumble was alive. I have to see her. But if I don't save Racheal...she's going to die. Racheal and I are going to make the journey together! Yeah! I've decided.

My lip quivered. "I...I want to see my little sister again!"

Wait. Why did I say that? I can't just leave Racheal to die? Can I?

My hand was already in the portal. I reached out for Tumble.

I'm not going to abandon either of them.

I reached into the darkness and gripped her arm. I then pulled with all my might and fell back on my butt.

"Not playing by the rules." His body loomed over and became jagged. "That calls for a penalty."

My arm was gone. It got separated from me when he closed the portal. But I wasn't wounded. There was just a fleshy stump, with functioning veins.

My arm was over there but not separated from me.

"New decision: stay here or fight me to get to your hero."

I wiped my tears and stood up. "I'll fight you if I have to."

Betrayer's body contorted into hands that clapped robotically. The shadowy tendrils blocking the door then snapped back to his body. "That courageous spirit shall lead you to ruin if left unchecked. Just as it did for your mother. Sacrifice is the lifeforce of this world. Do not forget that." He spun into a single dot and then out of existence.

I ran to the scary building. I slammed into the door three times before it opened.

I ran toward Racheal but massive spikes suddenly grew around her, making a wall that blocked her off.

"Ah, this must be the little angel," said an oddly dressed CatBoy. "I am NeedleStack. Known for being the most powerful of the CatBoy generals."

"I don't care who you are! Stay away from my Rachie!" I yelled, creating a sound blast with my hand.

NeedleStack at me and grinned. "You are all that stands between me and my final gold star."

"He's not lying. He's the one who took over this village...the village he once was raised in!" yelled Racheal.

"Then let me heal her and I'll go with you."

His eyes popped. "Really?"

"I swear!"

What he doesn't know is I have my tail crossed. Hee-hee.

NeedleStack shrank the spikes around Racheal.

I went to her side and immediately got to healing her wounds.

"Hey, Big Sis. I think we can take him down together," I said softly.

"Too dangerous. And he lives here. We can't just beat him up and escape. There's no escaping them."

I grabbed her hand. "Then we won't beat him up. We'll kill him."

Racheal's eyes got wide. Her mouth quivered. "Really?"

"Yeah. It'll be our secret…our unbreakable bond."

Racheal seized me in a hug. "Let's do it."

"I'm not deaf, you know," said NeedleStack, his hands coated in thistles.

"Then you were already warned," I said.

"I'm no longer keen on taking you in alive," said NeedleStack, tossing the thistles my way.

I clapped my hands, pushing the bad pointies aside.

Racheal kicked off the ground, and sliced NeedleStack's chest.

A thorn grew out from the wound and pierced Racheal's shoulder.

I slammed my hands together and created a soundwave.

"Die! *Prickly Poison*."

My legs burned with pain.

Racheal's shadow suddenly stood up and sliced off my legs.

Oh no! Not the Betrayer too!

"This battle has been delayed." Betrayer dived into NeedleStack and opened up his cloak. The two of them then vanished from sight.

"That bastard will be back! You have to heal!" yelled Racheal, tearing the spikes out from my severed legs.

144

He saved me. But why? My head is dizzy.

"I'm honestly feeling pretty tired," I said.

Everything went black.

Chapter 9: Poppy the Hapi

I awoke in an unfamiliar room. Everything was pink and purple. There were rainbow banners above and adorable animal paintings below. Hearts, stars, and cute birds decorated the walls.

Is this where Yu-ki lives?

"She's awake! Thank you, Poppy!" exclaimed Racheal.

"Yep. She owes me her life." I feel something fluffy press against my chest.

My vision cleared up.

There was a super colorful Hapi girl in front of me. She was older than me, about sixty, or fifteen in angel years. Instead of hands or claws, she had beautiful brown wings with pink and blue glitter. Two tuffs of feathers covered up her chest and joined to make a heart shape. She was wearing a open neon green bra that framed the feathers which was clearly designed for her. The adorable girl had short ocean blue pigtails with a pink flowery bonnet, with heart ribbons connected to it.

Another angel? She looks so cute. Must be a really powerful angel.

Her dazzling orange eyes turned mischievous.

"You owe me too, virgin girl," said the Hapi with a sly grin.

"Yeah, sure, whatever. I'm just so happy she's okay." Racheal grabbed my hand. "I can't lose another friend." She started crying.

"Ugh, stop trying to be so pathetic that guys will bone you out of sympathy. It hasn't worked before. It won't now," said the Hapi angel, patting Racheal's back.

Racheal broke down in tears and sobbed.

"Hey, don't be so mean to her. She's my friend," I said, puffing out my cheeks with a glare.

"Hey, relax. I saved your life. I'm allowed to tease her a bit. By the way your adorable savior's name is Poppy."

"That is such a cute name!" I exclaim, hugging her.

Poppy nods self-assuredly. "Yep. Yep. It sure is."

Racheal pulled me off from Poppy and lifted me into a warm embrace. "Oh no. You aren't taking her too, Trappy."

"It's Poppy! And I have no interest in her." Poppy hopped onto the bed.

She has talons for feet. Aww and cute brown tuffs just above them.

"Hey look, you're almost as tall as me now," said Racheal.

"Shut up!" yelled Poppy. "Racheal, the innocent virgin lamb and a lamb angel. You two are just perfect for each other. I'm not going to get in the way of that. In fact, I fully support it." She patted my head with her wing.

Ah. So soft. Like a pillow.

"I'm not into little kids!" yelled Racheal, her face getting flustered.

Poppy leaned back on the bed, wiggling her feet. "Of course not. But hey, nobody else will love you, so why not take what you can get. A hero taking advantage of a little girl's innocence. How pathetic," she said, looking up with a mean grin.

"That's what you think. But I blew one of the guys the other day."

Poppy sat up with wide eyes. "What!? Which one of those mortals dared to cheat on me!"

147

Racheal stuck out her tongue. "It's a secret."

Poppy snorted. "You mean it's a lie."

"Honestly it was so dark. I couldn't make out his face. Oh, but he was so tasty!" exclaimed Racheal, wiggling.

I had no idea Racheal had so much experience.

"Get out!" yelled Poppy, pushing us out of the room.

Racheal and I left the building and walked outside.

"Why is it so dark if it's the morning?" I asked, looking up at the black clouds above.

"Poppy wants to be the only source of joy so she got one of her many boyfriends to create a dark coating over the sky. I don't mind it. Actually makes me chipper." She grabbed my hand. "Really happy you're okay. Last night sure was crazy."

Wait! Phoenix!

"Where is Phoenix?" I asked with urgency.

"I'm taking you to her right now."

"Thanks!"

"Yeah. I told her to wait for us. We don't know if her family were among the Cuckatrices I freed last night. She wants to meet with them alongside us."

"Wait. You can understand her?"

"It's one way only! My powers let translate my words into other sounds but I can't understand what she says. Which really sucks. I used to talk to ghosts as a little girl, wish they could talk back to me," she said with that adorable dorky grin.

"Carry me," I said, standing on my tippy toes.

"Sure thing, Annie."

We met with Phoenix just outside the village's entrance and then journeyed up hill. We eventually arrived at a forest clearing with tons of animals.

"Look at all of them!" I exclaimed, almost falling off Racheal's shoulders.

"Yeah. You inspired me, Annie. I saved every last one of them. There's no doubt going to be repercussions when the village finds out, but you know what." She looked out at all the free people. "It's so freaking worth it!"

Phoenix hopped out of my arms and rushed to the other Cuckatrices with teary eyes.

She didn't have to look for them.

Five other birds came out from the flock and nuzzled her.

Her family. She found them all.

Racheal went up to the birds and crouched down.

Phoenix snuggled against her hand. She chirped a thank you, but it was weighed down by her heavy emotion.

Racheal pet her. "It's fine. No need to thank me." My hero chirped a response to Phoenix.

My heart started racing. Racheal is just the sweetest girl ever!

149

I chirped to Phoenix too, congratulating her on reuniting with her loved ones.

She nuzzled me, bringing me to tears.

She didn't have to say it. I could feel that this was the last time we'd meet.

I grabbed Racheal's hand for stability and the two of us waved the happy bird family farewell.

I'm gonna miss her. But she's free now. They all are.

Racheal picked me up and rested my head against her shoulder. "Shall we head to the guild hall?" she asked in a gentle tone.

I wrapped my arms around her. "Yeah. I'm gonna get you a boyfriend."

Tomato! Her cheeks look like a juicy tomato!

Racheal pulled up her hood, hiding her blush.

We walked down the gloomy rocky path to a building that looked like it was melting into the ground.

"Why does it look like that?" I asked.

"Because. We're in Dark and Broody Village! Old Bat is depressed, so naturally the buildings are too. This whole village is made of her flesh. I know, crazy, but it's true."

Just like Sunny Village.

"So, uh, how many heroes are in this village?"

"A bunch. But don't worry. You got the best one right here!" Racheal grabbed my hand and pushed open the door, which had the words "you're going to die anyways" painted on it.

That's not very pleasant.

I immediately felt heavy upon entering the building. The negative energy surrounding the thirty plus heroes was making it hard to even stand. Most of them were wearing black cloaks like Racheal, hiding their faces under their hoods.

Racheal hopped on top of one of the skeletal tables. "Hey, everyone! Our village finally has a new guardian angel!" She hoisted me up in both arms.

The negative energy vanished.

"So cute!" "Oh wow, a real life girl." "If I die now, I can be happy!" "Finally, this place has been given a blessing!" cheered different heroes.

"Hold up!" yelled a voice from the back.

It was Poppy.

"Anyone who gets near that girl is excommunicated from my harem. If you don't want to be left unsatisfied and unprotected, then don't even think of cheating on me! You don't even know if she's a real angel! She's probably just some little girl that Virgin Lamb dressed up."

"I am a real angel!" I yelled.

"Admit the truth, Racheal," said Poppy. "Admit she's not an angel and I'll allow you a night with one of my very well-trained men." The Hapi girl pressed her talon against the hero's face.

"Screw you! Annie is better than any boy. She's my friend and my little sister!" yelled Racheal.

151

"I remember when you wanted me to call you big sister." Poppy took a banana from the fruit bowl and approached my hero. "We can still make that happen," she said, poking Racheal's face with it.

Racheal took the banana and bit it, making the guys cringe. "I don't need you. I have…where did she go?"

I was on the guild hall's stage. "Watch the angel take flight!" I exclaimed.

Come on powers. I need you. For Racheal!

My aura wings spread and I took flight. I soared around the room as the guys cheered for me. I spun hearts in the air and made bell sounds with each twist. My performance ended by gripping onto the top of the long pole at the center of the stage. My tail grabbed it and I spun around it, blowing kisses and posing adorably before something slammed into me.

"What are you doing!" yelled Poppy, pinning me down with her talons.

"Proving I'm an angel just like you!" I exclaimed with a fierce glare and puffy cheeks.

The men cheered us on to fight and strip each other.

Racheal stepped in and grabbed Poppy. "Let her go."

"No! I worked so hard to get control of this village. All of those guys wanted to kill themselves. Every single one of them. But I danced, snuggled and literally blew away their worries! Their lives belong to me!" yelled Poppy, loud enough for the guys to hear.

The room was suddenly filled with crying men and boys.

"We love you Poppy!" "You were my first." "You're beyond the boundaries of sex." "You're a goddess!" "We'd never leave you!"

I know how to get out of this situation. Sometimes it takes true bravery to stand up. Other times, you gotta suck in your pride and bow down.

"Everyone! I'm not a real angel," I said softly.

"What?" "My dick lied to me!" "Are you going to say you're a boy too?" "Fantasy is the only reprieve from a hostile world." The men were all freaked out.

"I'm just a trainee. It's the truth. Poppy here, she's my teacher."

"Huh?" Poppy looked at me with a blank stare.

"An angel that dominates other angels!" "So hot!" "Strip her down!" "Stroke her ears!" "Double fellatio!" yelled the men.

Why is everyone in this village so crazy?

Poppy released me and turned to the crowd. "That's right! This little angel trainee is my student. And only good boys will be allowed to train her," she said, grabbing the air and making a jerking motion.

The men cheered. Some fainted. Other's praised their dark gods for the blessing.

I seized Poppy in a hug. "Thanks sensei!"

"Huh? I mean oh uh…hi?" she asked, fumbling around.

Aww. The real Poppy is so cute.

"So, when are my lessons?" I asked.

Poppy shuffled in place. "Oh I uh…I dunno."

The men were muttering amongst themselves. Doubt was brewing.

"Let me just get a quick bite to eat and then I'll meet you just outside the guildhall. Hey boys." She winked at them. "On to Glory!"

"I must be alive because my heart bleeds." "Life is meaningless without MOE." "You can drain me all of all my essence."

"Oh and by the way I know one of you cheated on me with Virgin Lamb," said Poppy, glaring at the guys.

Racheal grabbed me by my hand and walked me out of the guildhall, being sure to snag a bunch of grapes in the process.

"Did I do good?" I asked, once we were outside.

Racheal affectionately slugged my shoulder. "Yeah you did. Never seen Poppy so flustered."

"Aww, thanks, Rachie."

Racheal ruffled my hair. "You are too cute. Never thought I'd ever be so lucky as to get a demon for a little sister."

"I'm an angel," I declared, waving my bat wings.

Whoops. Wrong wings.

Racheal crouched down and nuzzled my wings, poking my little hands. "Can you feel that?"

"Yeah. It feels funny."

"Oh, sorry. So, you really think you can learn from that Hapi?"

"Yeah! I really do. She's like me so we gotta be friends. I've decided."

"Aww. I love your enthusiasm!" cheered Rachael.

"Hey, did that guy who you umm, blowed on? Was he nice to you?" I asked, fiddling with my fingers.

Racheal's shoulder's slumped. "I just said that to tease Poppy. She's made sure no guy will touch me no matter how bad I want it. If they do, they get a death sentence."

"She kills them!?" I asked with wide eyes.

"No, but she won't heal them. Or make them feel good."

"Oh." I grab Racheal's hand. "That's not a problem anymore, then. Is it?" I grinned.

"How so?"

"Well, I can heal them!" I exclaimed.

"That reminds me. I'm going to go see how Richard is healing up."

"And I have training!" I punched the air.

Racheal crouched down and kissed my cheek. "Just be careful."

"I'm not going to get hurt."

"No. I mean be careful not to become like Poppy. When she first arrived she was a scared lost child. This village changes people. I let it change me but you undid that damage. You gave me my courage back. Don't let it change you."

I saluted. "Roger, Sir!"

"See ya!"

"Wait!" I exclaimed, grabbing onto her.

"I'm going to need kissing practice if I'm going to be a great angel! And you promised that when you returned from freeing Phoenix's family that you would give me a real kiss!"

"Did I say that?" asked Racheal, scratching her cheek.

"You did."

My hero turned away. "Well I may have sorta, already given it to you…when you were sleeping."

"Huh?"

"I was hoping that whole true love's kiss thing was more than just a fairy tail. I mean if romantic love can work, why not sisterly love, right?"

"Well I was asleep so it doesn't count." My tail grabbed her hand.

"I'm not good at kissing! Okay?" Racheal wiped her eyes. "No experience."

"Then we'll get good together." I hopped up into a kiss.

Racheal grabbed me and tilted my body before placing her lips against mine.

My cheeks flared up.

My lips feel electrified! I didn't know she had lighting powers too!

"Hey there," said a voice.

"Eeep!" Rachel jumped and dropped me on the ground.

I looked up at her.

Wow her boobs are big.

Racheal turned away, blushing like it was her first kiss. "Poppy. What do you want?"

Poppy stretched out her leg, which was decorated with multiple bracelets of different colors. She picked out the two black bracelets and handed them to my hero. "One for you and one for your girlfriend."

"We were rehearsing for a play!" yelled Racheal.

"Really? About what?"

"About two sisters in…just go away, Trappy!" yelled Racheal, running off.

"Too easy. O-hee-hee-hee." Poppy held her sides as she laughed.

"Hey, why are you being mean to her?" I ask, running off to Racheal.

"You wanted lessons. Then stay here. I can teach you how to get a boyfriend or a girlfriend." Poppy's wings climbed up my sides.

My body's all tingly.

"H-How did you do that?" I asked, fiddling with my hair and wobbling.

"Oh, come on. You're an angel. We die without male essence. Quit acting so innocent."

"Male essence? You mean kissies?" I ask, kissing her cheek.

She jumped back and wiped her cheek. "Don't try and make me gay, you little tease!"

I bowed to my teacher. "Please. Teach me how to be a better angel. I need to be strong so that Racheal and I can journey beyond this place."

"Wait. So if I teach you how to be a proper guardian angel, then you'll scurry off."

"Well I need a ship first and a crew."

"O-hee-hee! I can sell some of my boys if you have the coin."

"Wow! You're really nice!" I exclaimed, shaking her wing.

Poppy pulled away. "Benevolent is the word. I have one rule if I'm going to teach you. You're not allowed to pass me up at anything. Got it?"

I looked at her with a sad face.

"What is it?" she asked, looking to the ground.

"Whoever said mean things about you, they were wrong!" I exclaimed, patting her head.

Poppy's cute cheeks lit up with embarrassment. "I'm not ugly! I'm beautiful! Everyone here loves me! They always will!" she exclaimed, holding her sides. "I'm not a miscarriage."

Poor girl has been through so much. I've gotta help her too!

I squeezed in under her wings and hugged her. "You're super beautiful!"

"Stop it," she whined. "Stop being so cute." Poppy pushed me off. "Get up! We've got training to do! I'm going to teach you everything I know!"

"Yes, Sir."

Poppy spanked my butt with her wing.

It was so soft.

"Am I being rewarded or punished?" I asked, my finger against my bottom lip.

"I'm telling you to get a move on! Our powers are an ancient secret. Follow me to the training grounds."

I nodded.

Poppy led me to a large shack made out different colored slabs of wood. "This place is brimming with negativity."

"Why is that? Are there ShadowPups that eat you if you're happy."

"No, idiot. It's because of the shitty situation they're in. This village has a cost. If they don't get enough money per month, they lose the right to eat the food, drink the water, etc. And if they're caught stealing, they're executed."

What? That's crazy!

Her eyes became hollow. "Let's just go inside."

Poppy opened the door to reveal the training room.

There were pinky glittery punching bags, hoops dangling from above for flight practice and lots of banana shaped objects. Tons of paintings of her decorated the walls.

She really is an idol.

"Okay, let's see how strong you are. Give that prissy little flirt a good punch!" she exclaimed, pointing to the punching bag.

I slammed my fist into it, making it squeak.

"Ha! That all you got. I'll show you how to make this bitch really squeal!" Poppy backed up, got a running start, jumped up, spread her wings to increase speed and then dropkicked the punching bag.

Owwie!

The bag squeaked so loud I had to cover my ears.

Poppy turned and smiled at me. "Sorry you had to see me so ugly like that. I have some anger in me." She grabbed my hand with her wing. "Don't tell anyone, okay?"

I smiled. "I won't. And I think you're really cute when you get mad. Sorry."

Poppy's expression softened. "It's not easy. Pretending to always be happy. But it's my job." She spread her wings. "It's our job now!"

"If you're sad or angry. It's okay to show it."

Poppy shook her head. She jumped off the trampoline in the room and took to flight. "The heroes of this village need us to be perfect beacons of hope. Doesn't matter if we're tired, irritable, or our throat is sore from too much service. We just gotta bury it and keep smiling. It's our job." She flew through all the hoops and then landed. "I won't accept you as an angel if you don't give it your all."

I hopped on the trampoline and pictured myself flying.

My wings didn't come out and I fell on my butt.

Poppy grabbed my booty wings. "That was pathetic! What are these things even for?"

"Watch and be amazed!" I jumped up and landed on my wings. They walked along the ground for a bit. Then I lost balance and fell over. "Whoops."

Poppy facepalmed. "They don't do anything. Do they?"

"They can grab things."

Poppy seethed. "Oh! So you think you're better than me because I have no hands and you have four!"

I wiped her angry tears away with my tail.

"Five," she groaned, glaring at my prehensile tail.

"You have feet. They're so fluffy!" I cheered.

"Yeah and they can satisfy guys better than all five of your hands!" She puffed air out from her nose. "Okay. Gotta work with your strengths. Honestly you shouldn't be assigned one hero. Are you good with your feet?"

"Oh yeah. I'm an ace at footsies!"

"Show me!" Poppy sat down on the padded floor.

This whole place is so cozy.

I sat down and we pressed our feet together.

"Aww, our toes are hugging," I said.

"Would you stay focused?" asked the flustered Hapi girl.

I put all my energy into my feet, but she easily overpowered me.

Poppy grabbed my feet with her talons and flung me into the air.

"Summon your wings now!" she exclaimed.

I squinted but was unable to summon them and instead fell into her fluffy wings. "I nestled them. So soft."

"Yeah, but ugly. I tried painting them, but the color always fades. They're stuck…brown." She groans. "Forever."

"The color just makes your other colors pop more! That's why you're called Poppy right?" I ask.

"No. I'm called Poppy because when I'm around. It's always Spring!" she exclaimed, doing a cute twirl.

I hope Tumble is okay.

A ringing sound comes from outside.

"Lessons over! Time for the real thing!" exclaimed Poppy, pulling me out of her home.

"Huh? What's wrong?" I ask, almost falling over trying to keep up with her speed.

Poppy opened the door. Betrayer was just outside.

Oh no. Not him.

"You are needed," he said in a low voice.

Oh, it's not him.

"Nice to meet you, Sir. I'm Annie."

The RiftRipper's body twisted as it made circles around me. "You're new."

"Yeah, and you are?"

"Gloom. I hope you don't suffer the same fate as the last one," he said, before sinking into the shadows.

"What is he talking about?"

"There's no time to explain. We are needed in the morgue."

"The morgue. Hey, if there's no time, then just explain on the way."

"Maybe I don't want to explain. I'll tell you what you need to know. Got it?" asked Poppy.

"You don't have to blame yourself for her death," I said, grabbing her wing.

"What? She didn't die! She betrayed us! Ran off when things got tough. How dare you blame me!"

"Sorry."

The morgue was the darkest place of them all. There were skeletons hanged by the windows. The whole building was cloaked in fog too. I bet Racheal would get really hot in this place.

Maybe this is where we should practice kissing.

"Hey, you got a good wiggle going on. As for me. My power comes from my incredible throat!" Poppy breathed in and then the voice of angel came out from her lips.

"Darkness may come.

But there's no need to run.

You can fight

With my light!" hey voice coated her body in a bright white aura.

"Wow!!" I exclaimed, hugging her.

"Yeah. Bet you can't do that."

"I can't. That's amazing."

"Part of being a Hapi and a powerful one at that!"

"I bet your momma was a powerful and beautiful Hapi!"

"My mom is dead. Just…shut up and obey me." She pulled me into the morgue.

It smelled really bad and was really dark too.

Poppy ran across the room and sent her energy into the empty torches.

There were a bunch of dead heroes on the ground.

"Grab your pom poms!" exclaimed Poppy, pointing to the table behind me. "You're going to need them."

Poppy was led by a man in black to a dead hero.

I hurriedly went to her side.

Poppy tilted her head back and pumped her throat. She then released a globule of spit on the body. "Help me out, Lamby!"

"Yes, Sir!" I spit out as much as I could.

Poppy hummed while she rubbed the spit over the body's bare chest.

I copied her humming as best I could and followed along.

"For every hero that you see, ten don't even wake up after the trip. As angels its our job to resuscitate them the moment they arrive! I have about a 5% success rate. I know it's pathetic and I hate it." She punched his chest. "Wake up, damn you!"

I joined Poppy. "We punched his chest together."

Live! So Poppy doesn't cry!

My tattoos started glowing. Blue energy poured from my hands and entered the hero's body.

He coughed up water and then he opened his eyes.

"Nice work, Lamby. You make a pretty good assistant," she said, patting my head.

I nuzzled her wing and she smiled.

The hero sat up. "My legs. I can't feel my legs!"

I poked his feet. "Relax. They're right here!"

"I can't feel them!" yelled the scared boy.

Poppy combed his hair with her wing. "There's no need to worry. You're fine."

"Where am I? Monsters! There are monsters here!" yelled the man.

Poppy leaned up to my ear. "They usually act like this when they first arrive."

"What's wrong with his legs?" I asked in a whisper.

164

"Dimensional transfer is tricky stuff. He's lucky to be alive. Not sure how long he'll last."

He's just like Ruiz now and it's because I wasn't strong enough!

"Hey, no crying. Especially in front of the guys. Don't know what you think you know about tears, but they are a maiden's greatest weapon," said Poppy, whooshing away my sadness with her wings.

"I'll take him in!" I exclaim with a firm stance. "Is that okay?"

Poppy sighs. "Yeah, it's fine but he's not allowed to touch Virgin Lamb."

"Why are you always so mean to Rachie!" I yelled.

"I wasn't good enough, so how are you!" yelled Poppy.

Old Bat suddenly materialized in front of us.

"Do you need us?" asked Poppy, putting on a big smile.

"Just wanted to invite you to the festivities."

"Is today Gloom Shroom day?" asked Poppy.

"No. We're having an execution," said Old Bat with a warm smile.

Creepy. Wait. Creepy.

"Can you postpone it? I gotta find Racheal. I bet she'd love to see it!" I exclaimed.

She looks so cute when she gets all hot and bothered.

"She's already there! The star of the event."

"You mean she's the executioner?" I asked.

Old Bat slumped. She gave me an ugly glare. "Really? How dense can you be?" she asked, all the mystery of her voice gone.

Poppy held me with her wings. "Virgin Lamb is the one being executed."

No. No. No. No.

"You don't want to miss her big moment, do you?" asked Old Bat with a smile before leaving into a vortex.

Poppy pated my shoulders. "Let's just uh…keep training. Gotta get you strong if you're going to protect a boy who can't walk."

"We have to save her!" I exclaimed.

"Umm, how we gonna to do that?" asked Poppy.

Yeah. That's exactly the problem! I can't just beat that old lady. She's too strong!

"Face it, Lamby, your girlfriend is gone for. I'll be here to help out though. You can spend the night with me. I know, I'm sooo generous," said Poppy.

"Racheal is my friend," said a wispy voice.

Gloom!

"You have an idea of how to help?" I ask.

"Lalala! I'm not listening!" yelled Poppy, running off.

I turned to Gloom and looked at his blank face. "What's the plan?"

"Create a panic. A rogue RiftRipper going berserk and slaughtering people should do the trick." His faceless void shifted into a smile.

Chapter 10: Dark and Broody

Poppy ran back into the room. "You can't be serious! Those heroes and their essence belong to me! You can't just go around destroying my property! What makes Racheal more important than them anyways?" she asked, glaring at Gloom.

Gloom puts his hands over his chest and squeezes them.

"Boobs are overrated!" yelled Poppy.

"I don't think killing heroes is a good idea either," I said.

Gloom slumped. "Just a few?" he asked.

Poppy stomped her foot down. "No! Racheal is going to die and that's that."

Gloom wrapped around Poppy. "But you can stop it. This village is under your control. You could start an uprising, if you wanted to."

"Well I don't want to."

"Then your harem will shrink. One body a minute. Wonder how long you'll last," said Gloom, moving his bladed tentacle like a clock hand.

"You do that and you'll regret it!" yelled Poppy, her feathers flaring up.

While these two are bickering, Racheal is getting closer to execution!

I ran out of the training shack and saw a line of heroes, all dressed in black.

The air around them was heavy.

"Which way to the execution grounds?" I asked, tugging on one of the hero's cloaks.

167

"This is the line. I'm going to spend my food coin to see it. Better be worth missing a meal," he said, his shoulder's slumped.

"Racheal is a member of your village! Don't you care that she's going to die?" I asked with a look of bewilderment.

"Well yeah. I don't want to miss it. She's like the top hero. If I didn't care why would I pay."

"Huh?"

"Racheal would want us to watch. It's a sign of respect. This isn't the first execution we've had here. Won't be the last." He sighed.

Even if I have to do it alone, I'm going to save her.

I ran to the front of the line.

A row of CatBoy soldiers blocked the path.

"Please, there's been some sort of mistake. Racheal is a good girl. She wouldn't do anything bad," I said, bobbing around in a panic.

"If you want to know what she did, then keep your mouth shut and listen," said a CatBoy.

Old Bat was on the stage and so was a naked person with a bag over their head.

Oh no! That must be Racheal! She must be so scared.

Old Bat amplified her voice out with the motion of her wrinkles. "This hero is responsible for stealing property from our great leader, Flam!"

Flam! He's a bad guy. Is Old Bat the Wood Primordial traitor that Old Fool mentioned? If so, then Rachie is super in trouble.

Racheal stood up tall. "I did what all of us should have done a long time ago! Those animals were being bred for death! They didn't have any hope

168

and they didn't do anything wrong. I won't ask you to stop my execution, but what I ask from you, my fellow heroes, is to remember what I did! Remember that when we see someone in peril, it is our sworn duty to save them!"

"Racheal!" I cried out from the crowd.

She turned to face me, that dumb bag blocking her pretty face.

"Annie. It's okay. I'm not going to pretend I'm not terrified of dying. Peed myself a couple times just walking up the stage. And it sucks I'm dying a virgin, but hey I'm dying a hero, right? You inspired me to be who I really am! Don't let my death break you. Think of my bulged-out eyes, mouth with a bit of drool and oh geez! I'm getting excited now! Hey, when is the execution?"

This is how she deals with her fear. She's more of an angel than I am.

"When you are ready. There are still some heroes getting tickets," said Old Bat.

"Wow. So all the guys of the village are seeing me naked. This is crazy!" exclaimed Racheal.

"You're supposed to be my big sister forever!" I yelled.

"I can be! What I was going to say is when you think of my lifeless face, remember why I died not how I died. Wait up." Racheal turned her head. "How am I dying again?"

"Guillotine. Clean, quick, relatively painless. You served us for many years, it's our way of thanking you."

"I've been here for four years and yet that's the best you could come up with. I don't want some vanilla execution! I want to at least get crucified. Actually no. This is going to be my last death so it needs to be really flashy. Crucifixion, while hanging, while burned alive, and any chance I can get whipped while all that's going on?"

Old Bat turned and wretched.

She's trying to buy time, right? Right?

"I'm the top hero of the village. I won't allow a simple guillotine. And actually, before I go, can I finally get laid? I'm already naked. Just remove the bag and I'll pick my favorite guy. Consider it part of the event!" exclaimed Racheal, wobbling back and forth.

"The guillotine is already set. Now unless someone has an objection, then I suggest you lie down and die."

"Can I at least take this stupid bag off!"

"No."

"One of the heroes can shoot fire from his hands. Blaze, are you there?"

"Yeah. I'm here, Racheal," said a hero in the crowd.

"Can you please just set me on fire? That would at least be something new. I mean a guillotine is like a major downgrade from being skinned alive," said Racheal.

"No! Don't!" I yelled.

"Annic. It's going to be okay. I've lived a fun life. I'm not afraid to go," said Racheal, her voice soothing and calm.

Something flew onto the stage, grabbed the CatBoy executioner and tossed him into the crowd.

"I object to this execution!" yelled Poppy.

"What, wanna kill me yourself, Trappy?" asked Racheal with a laugh.

Poppy flared up but exhaled the rage and put on a big smile. "Racheal is one of us. If you want her, then you're going to have to take us all down!"

Vines crept up Poppy's legs.

"Be wary, boy. Your next action determines your lifespan," said Old Bat, her eyes vacant and merciless.

Poppy's smile dropped. Her body froze up and terror took over her eyes.

"Put our Mistress down, Old Bat," said a hero with a powerful dark aura around him.

Old Bat smiled. "No need to freak out, 5758762311. Poppy won't dare say a word. Our beloved angel is unable to even muster a grunt."

The hero masked the area in darkness.

This is my chance. Come on, Annie. You've got a great memory. You just gotta find her.

I used my sound powers to send Racheal a signal, a low tone Cuckatrice call.

She responded with her own call and, in this way, we came closer and closer, a few steps at a time.

"Poppy is more than just our Mistress," said the hero, his voice getting closer to the stage. "She is our salvation. If not for her my wrists would be red with crimson agony. I would have died alone and hopeless. Poppy is our sunshine. My darkness can't be contained when that sun is being threatened! Do it, Poppy! Burn away our doubts, burry our fears with your angelic hymns!"

"Well, I can't ignore the pleas of my adoring fans. ***Haremization!***" Poppy took a deep breath. "Save the lamb from slaughter. Save her life. Save her soul. Remember I brought you laughter. Follow my voice. Rejoice. And save the lamb. Your Mistresses commands it!"

Poppy's voice echoed beyond the stage, enchanting the crowd.

The dark fog was pulled into a rift created by Old Bat. "You've spat on our kindness. We've fed you, clothed you, and kept you safe. Yet you dare to stand against us! Do not bite the hand that permits your lives."

The heroes moved as a single entity, engaging in combat with the CatBoy soldiers.

Poppy licked her feathers and then sent them to her injured heroes after singing a short spell. The feathers healed the wounds of the injured heroes, giving them a second wind to stand against the CatBoy soldiers.

Racheal chirped one last time.

I grabbed her hand and tiny bells played in my head.

I've never been so happy.

I hugged her and sobbed.

Old Bat's head spun around three-hundred and sixty degrees.

"Whoa, that was sick," said Racheal, pulling the bag off her head.

"You've put everything I've suffered to protect at stake." Old Bat sobbed and then turned to face the crowd. "ENOUGH!"

The CatBoy hero battle came to a sudden halt.

"Racheal will not be executed."

Poppy raised her hands and the heroes cheered along with her.

"She is hereby exiled from Dark and Broody Village. Her achievements shall be torn down from the wall. Her possessions shall be burned and she will never be allowed in this village again." Old Bat sliced the air, creating a vortex that blasted everyone off their feet. "Is that clear?"

While she talked to the crowd Racheal and I ran off together.

"Thanks for not rescuing me," she said with a genuine smile.

"I'm sorry," I said in tears, getting choked up.

"I wanted to inspire my fellow heroes. Getting a bunch of guys to think of me every time they grip their steel. That's worth dying for. Though not to say I wouldn't have regrets. But it worked out great. Inspired a bunch of guys while being bare naked and got to live. I'm just going to get some clothes and then we're out of here!"

Something suddenly sped by.

Racheal fell to ground, four holes in her shoulder.

I fired a soundwave at the enemy but it flew out of the way.

"Four," said Poppy, with hollow eyes. "Four of my boys are dead. Your stupid heroism ended up getting them killed. It made me kill them! BatLover, DarkSunset, HollowMelody and Skullz,are all dead now! You're not getting out of here alive!" She swooped down.

Gotta protect Racheal.

I sprouted wings and slammed into Poppy. "Hurting Racheal just makes their deaths pointless. There's nothing you can do for them!"

"They didn't die for Racheal! They died for me!" yelled Poppy, sliding behind me and slicing my back with her talons.

My aura wings dissipated and I fell to the ground.

Racheal caught me and took a step back. "Stop! Don't hurt Annie! She brought someone back to life before. She can do it again! Go with Poppy. It was really great meeting you. I'll be fine on my own. You gotta work hard as angel here and get that boat so you can find your sister," she rubbed noses with me.

I grabbed onto her. "I have a big sister right here and I'm not letting her go."

Poppy landed and clenched her teeth. "Just get out of here! I don't need your help. This village was fine before you showed up." She ran off in tears.

"You might be able to save them, Annie. Even just one. If you really want to come with me, I'll wait at the clearing. The place where the Cuckatrices were." Racheal smiled at me.

I nodded and ran after Poppy.

Several heroes were screaming in pain at the execution grounds. Four heroes had a black towel over their faces.

"They died doing the right thing," I said to Poppy, spitting into my hands and healing the hero closest to me.

"They died because I told them to."

"What do you mean?"

"Mortals can't resist the power of angels. Surely you've realized that. It's why Racheal loves you. We have a powerful aura of seduction," said Poppy before turning to her patient and chanting a calming melody.

"Racheal and I get along for lots of reasons!" I exclaimed.

"Oh yeah, tell me what you two have in common," said Poppy with a grin.

"Well, we both want a boyfriend really badly. And we…like cute things."

"Is that all?" Poppy moves to the next patient.

I go to another hero but he's already gone. "Racheal is my hero and we're gonna be together foreva!" I yelled, tears coming up in my eyes.

"Heroes don't last long without an angel at their side. There's nothing else you can do here. Just go to your girlfriend." Poppy gestured for me to move with her wings.

"But you're supposed to teach me lots of things."

"What good does it do? My haremization technique has led to my heroes to their deaths. Just go away! I don't want to see you or Racheal ever again!" yelled Poppy, breaking out into tears.

I ran up and embraced her. "I'm super sowwy." My eyes built up sadness and then it all came rushing out like a waterfall.

Poppy hugged me for a while and then suddenly shoved me off. "Get going. And be sure to satisfy her," said the harpy angel with a lewd smirk, groping the air with her feathers. "Your teacher demands it."

I nodded and then flew off.

I arrived at the forest clearing to see my Rachie. My wings came out on their own and I flew into a hug. "I'm so happy you're okay!"

"Thanks, little sis. But we have to get moving or else we'll get hunted down."

"By who?"

"The time limit for an ex-hero is exactly one hour. We've got one hour before ISEKAI puts out a bounty on me."

I started wiggling with worry.

No. No. No.

Racheal started laughing. "Relax. Sorry. I was just joking," she said with an awkward smile.

I stared at her suspiciously.

"What?" she asked.

I summoned up her journal but she snatched it. "Come on. No need to check it. It was just a joke. I promise."

I sighed. "Okay."

"So, let's go steal us a boat," said Racheal, walking off.

"Huh? We can't do that."

"Your sisters are on a different island. It's exactly what we need to do. Oooh. Imagine if we run into a ghost ship while we're sailing! Wouldn't that be crazy?"

"You're so cute." I poked her leg. "Okay, I'll lead us to the shoreline so we can get a ship."

I closed my eyes and focused on my sisters. A pink string appeared.

Racheal held her hand up and turned it. "Whoa, uh, what does this mean?" Her freckled cheeks became flustered.

Why is it attached to her?

I tried again. Another string appeared.

"Oooh, are you sapping away my lifeforce?" she asked with wide-eyes, looking at the new string on her other finger.

I lowered my head. "I wanna find my sisters." I look up at her with a teary smile. "I guess you really are my sister."

"Yeah. So what's the plan?"

"Hate me."

"Huh?"

"Hate me. Break my heart so it can guide me to my sister."

Racheal crouched down. "Annie, I could never do that."

The pile of leaves next to us rustled.

A cute Tanewki angel popped out from it. "Looks like your journey has come to a sudden stop!"

No way. An angel and a Tanewki!? That's double rare!

"Whoa! Who are you and what do you want?" asked Racheal, stepping in front of me.

"I am Amorita!" she exclaimed, turning into a leaf, riding the wind, and then reforming behind us with a pop sound.

"And I'm super excited to meet a Tanewki!" I cheered, hugging the cuddly angel.

"And what do you want?" asked Racheal, crouching down to the extra short angel.

"Amorita appears only when needed. I haven't a clue why I'm here. Only you do. What do you need?"

"A boat!" I cheered.

Amorita shook her head. "No. No. That isn't it."

"Wait, you're telling us that we don't know what we need? You had better be some terrifying monster in disguise because otherwise you're kinda just a bother."

Amorita taps the string. "Oh my. Well, we have our answer." She claps her hands.

The leaves transform into a neon pink inn with a big heart on the door.

"Ummmm. What is that for?" asked Racheal with a raised eyebrow.

"Why it's for the two of you, of course. My hero no longer needs me so I've decided to only manifest when someone else needs me. You two need the right environment to express yourselves," said Amorita, putting my hands in Rachel's gentle grip.

"Hold up. What do you want as payment? I only have a bit of Cat Coin on me and I don't plan to waste it on whatever the hell that is," said Racheal, gesturing to the massive building.

"It's called Amorita's Sanctuary and only forbidden love is permitted in these walls! Once you enter, my interspecies love shack turns totally invisible, sooooo you can't be spotted by anyone! Total safe zone." She exclaims, creating a red carpet with another leaf in her pocket.

"This sounds a little too good to be true," said Racheal, scratching her head.

"Don't worry, I'll protect you," I said, puffing out my chest.

"No, you run if things get bad. I want all the terror and danger!" exclaimed Racheal, hugging herself as she rushed in. She pushed open the door.

A single small room was before us with one massive pink bed and scented candles.

"Yeah, I take it back. This is something I don't really know how to handle," said Racheal, picking up the pillow shaped like me.

I nuzzled up against the Racheal-shaped pillow. "Rachie." I grabbed my chest. "Amorita made all this for us. And I think she's right."

"Awww. You wanna snuggle?" asked Racheal, pinching pillow me's cheeks.

I have to do this. Otherwise I'll never be able to find my family.

I set down the pillow and stood on the bed.

"You look too cute in your sheepy jammies," said Racheal with a smile.

"Y-You're super cute too," I said with a mumble.

My heart is pounding. I gotta stop before it makes an earthquake in my chest.

"Rachie…" My tail came up in front of my hands. The heart-shaped arc of my hands framed the heart eye of my tail. I smiled through my embarrassment. "I wuv you!" I suddenly cried with relief.

Racheal's eyes went wide and her cheeks flared up.

We stared at each other before I jumped into her. I tickled her sides. "Say you love me too. Please. I need you too."

"Y-Ya know I love ya, Annie. But you're like a little sister and sisters don't…"

I made her moan by nibbling her neck. "Rawr. I'm a demon and you're my contractor. That means you gotta do what I say." I stuck out my tongue.

Rachie grabbed my tongue. "Nuh-uh. The demon has to do what the contractor says." She snickered. My hero then poked my belly. "And I want you to just calm down and think about your true feelings."

My tail wagged excitedly. It grabbed onto the Rachie pillow and gave it a super hug!

"I want you." I poked her tummy repeatedly.

She bent down from my sneak attack so I hopped up and aimed for her lips.

My kiss missed its target and hit one of her cheeks.

"See. It's totally platonic. We're platonic," said Rachie, patting my head.

"Then let's get unplatonic!" I stripped out of my jammies, leaving me in my pink bloomers.

"You are just too cute," said Racheal with stars in her eyes.

"Too cute to love unplatonically?" I asked with a frown.

"Nothing personal. I just like boys, that's all."

I grabbed her hand. "Me too! And I know it's not personal." I placed her hand on my bare chest so she could feel my heart beat. "But I really want it to be."

Racheal stopped for a moment.

My tail slid up her robe and pressed against her chest.

I can feel Racheal's thumps!

My eyes lit up. "You do love me!" My tail came out her collar and tickled her neck.

"Hey…uh no fair. That's cheating. You can't just target my weak point like that," said Racheal, her head in a daze.

We fell onto the bed side by side.

The ceiling above us lit up, creating constellations of various types.

"Soooo pretty," I said, looking up.

"Yeah, you're really pretty," said Racheal, fidgeting with her fingers.

I rolled on top of her and grinned. "I was talking about the stars."

My tail tickled her chin.

Gotta be careful. No force. I don't want to scare her like I did Yu-ki. I want her to relax.

I reached her shoulders with my arms and started rubbing them.

"Okay, so I gotta ask, why the lights on your nipples?" asked Racheal.

"It's an angel thing," I said with a shrug.

"Oh. Yeah…that makes sense," said Racheal, nervously looking away.

"Touch me," I said, grabbing her hand with my tail.

"Huh? Hold up there, Annie. Heroes and angels have a sacred bond that…okay, so every hero I know has sex with their angel but that's not the point at all!" yelled Racheal before covering her face. "I need to really just stop talking."

My tail pulled her hands away. "But you have such a pretty voice."

"I…do?" asked Racheal, peeking up at me.

I kissed her hands and nodded. "Now get out of that stuffy robe. I wanna count all your freckles," I said, poking each freckle on her chest.

"Okay. I guess we're really doing this!" Racheal hopped up and clapped her hands. The sound of demons screaming to a jarring melody came out as she enticingly took off her clothes. "I always wanted to strip in front of someone I love with heavy metal music playing. Who knows if I'll get another chance," she said, revealing her white bra with red swirls and black straps. She struck a pose alongside the sound of church bells.

"Strawberries!" I jumped into Racheal's thighs and nestled her crotch. "Do they smell like strawberries?"

"Oh, you mean my panties. Well, there's a very good explanation for that. See, I used to wear them in Middle School and well, I, uh. Nobody would ever see them so why change, right? Ugh, I'm so embarrassed," she said, covering her face.

"They are super duper cute! Can I have them?" I asked pulling them down.

Racheal grabbed them but not before I saw some cute ginger hair.

My hero is extra fluffy!

"So, there's something else I wanted to try with my uh partner." Racheal pointed at my bloomers. "Wanna swap?" she asked, covering her face.

I grabbed my chest. "It's gonna burst!" I exclaimed in terror.

Racheal poked my nose. "No it won't. You'll be fine. You uh, you don't have to trade if you really want to. I mean don't want to. Can we please trade?"

"I'd totally trade with my lover." I wiggled my hips. "Are you my lover?" I asked, pursing my lips.

Racheal crouched down and pulled me into a quick but loving kiss. "You felt that too, right?" she asked, her finger tracing her bottom lip.

"Yeah. It was like zap but soft like a cloud. A zap cloud!" I exclaimed, popping up into another kiss.

My tail slid off my undies and handed them to Racheal.

She covered her eyes from the blinding light.

"Can you turn down the brights there, Annie?"

"You wanna see me naked?" I asked, jumping up and down.

"I just want to see something," said Racheal, shielding her eyes.

My tail tripped her and took her strawberry undies.

"Sorry, Rachie. It has a mind of its own sometimes," I said with a cooky laugh.

Racheal put on my underwear.

I sat down and held out my legs and she put her underwear on me.

"I'm a strawberry angel!" I cheered, jumping to my feet and doing a little twirl.

"Hey, Annie. The strings they vanished after your little confession."

"It was a biiiiig confession. I'm just little," I said, tapping my cheeks.

"Maybe now you can find your sisters. Try summoning them again."

Good idea!

I nodded and focused my energy. Two strings appeared. They were wrapped around Racheal, coming together to make a bow.

"Wow, this is the cutest bondage ever!" exclaimed Racheal with a funny face.

"Why won't it work?" I asked with a sad face. "Maybe you really do need to break my heart."

"Nope. You still see me as your big sister. We just gotta change that. Okay, little angel, I'm gonna try to send you back to Heaven!" exclaimed Racheal, tickling me.

At first I giggled but then my breathing got heavy.

"You okay?" asked Racheal, slowly dragging her finger up my back.

My body wiggled in spastic ecstasy.

"Angels, when they're aroused, they're whole body feels good."

"Well doesn't everyone's."

"We become super sensitive everywhere," I said, my breath coming out as pink puffs.

Racheal leaned in and sniffed the puffs. Her eyes got hazy. "Whoa. Those are some crazy demonic pheromones you got there, Annie."

"I'm sorry. I didn't mean to! Please don't leave me!" I latched onto her leg.

"I'm not leaving you. I'm sending you to Heaven, remember?" Racheal pet my head. "That's my job as your girlfriend!"

I wiggled and grinded until I chirped.

I've never had so much happy tingles before.

"Cutest sound I ever heard," said Racheal with a smile.

"Oh, Tumble is way cuter than me," I said, holding my cheeks.

"Well then, let's go get her." Racheal flicked my string, which was now leading outside the building.

I bowed. "I'm sorry about all this trouble. I didn't do it just to find them. I really do love you."

"Yeah." Racheal's eyes watered up.

A third pink string connected from my heart to hers.

We hugged each other tightly and lied side by side.

"Let's get some rest. Tomorrow is a big adventure," said Racheal with a gentle smile.

I snuggled up to her. "I don't want to leave yet either."

We fell asleep in each other's warm embrace.

The next morning, we left the inn. We walked hand in hand, determined to find my sisters.

Part -4: The Power

of an Angel

Chapter 11: The Mortal Militia

Amorita pops into existence once we leave the love shack. She opens her palms, one with a purple mushroom, the other with a gray one.

"We're not interested in whatever you're selling. Got it, trash panda." Racheal signaled me to move along.

Amorita transformed into a leaf and then popped back into her fluffy form on Rachie's shoulders.

"Free of charge, like all good things. You've had an amazing night, so the question is…" she held up the purple shroom "is it so amazing that you want to remember it in extra vivid detail for the rest of your life? Or…" she raised the gray shroom "do you want to forget it ever happened?"

"I'm taking option three. Not eating suspicious fungi," said Racheal, setting down Amorita.

"What you experienced last night was just a sample of the freedom you can enjoy. If you're interested in more you can come to my hero's grand kingdom," said the racoon angel.

Racheal looked down at me and smiled. "I'm fine with just the sample." She turned back to Amorita. "Look, thanks for helping us out, but we need to be on our way."

Amorita turned the mushrooms into leaves and then stuck her hand in her leaf-filled pockets. "Before you go! A message for you." The leaf in her hand turned into a note.

The note read: "CatBoy General at occupied camp spotted. Need heroic assistance." The gold cane emblem signaled that it was an extra dangerous quest.

I tugged on my hero's cloak. "Rachie! If we do this quest, then we will have enough money to buy a ship!"

"Yeah, but it could be a trap. I'm a wanted traitor now."

"What? But you said that wasn't true."

"I didn't want you to freak out. Don't worry though. I've fought other traitors plenty of times. I'm good at fighting heroes. And this is our best bet. Thanks, racoon girl." Racheal gave her a thumbs up. "Actually. Here." Racheal offered her a handful of CatCoin. "Consider it a tip."

Amorita shook her head. "Your lovely sweat and virgin juices that you left on the bed are more than enough payment for me. I hope the love between you two blossoms even stronger!"

"Yeah…uh, we're just gonna go now," said Racheal, taking the note, picking me up and rushing off.

We ventured forward to our next destination!

I ride on Racheal's shoulders, allowing me a better view of the deadly swamp we entered.

"What did you say this place was called, Annie?" asked Racheal.

"The Swamp of Agonizing Regret. It's where our new friends said to meet us. We gotta get a crew together to sail the treacherous seas, after all," I said, making a slashy motion with my hands.

"More likely than not, this message came from some heroes at Dark and Broody. Those creeps aren't our friends, they're ex-coworkers. I saw them eying you," she says, carefully avoiding a puddle of acid. "And what if they're after us."

"My momma told me that not trusting is sadder than being let down. I will never throw away my trust in heroes. Besides, they were only eying me because I was stretching on the guild hall's dance poll."

"Well if you're okay with it, that's what matters. You sure do have a way with boys. Maybe you can give me some tips to find a nice boyfriend."

"Sure thing. You got the hips, so wave 'em, big sis!"

"Thanks! And look, just because you're a little Pollyanna doesn't mean you shouldn't be wary. Not all heroes are good."

My face froze up.

Racheal cradled me in her arms. "You're shaking. Are you okay?"

I nodded and wiped my tears. "Fine and dandy," I said before sobbing into her bosom.

I miss Mommy.

"Don't ever think crying makes you weak. Not crying is what cowards do. You're a strong girl and its perfectly okay to cry."

I looked up at her and smiled. "But it's so hard to cry when my girlfriend is with me." I playfully stuck out my tongue.

Racheal patted my head. "Stay sharp. Big frog thing. Is it hostile?" she asked, aiming her hands, ready to fire a sound shot.

The blue frog had an orange, red and blue fire brewing in his belly.

"Hiya froggy!" I waved at the BlasToad and he waved back. "Nope. He's super friendly."

"Wait, isn't that a BlasToad. I heard we lost a hero to one last week."

"Well yeah, but that was a different one. This one is friendly." I reached into my pack and tossed him some bread crumbs.

A trio of healthy heroes came out from the bushes after the toad left.

"Hey, heroes," I said, pushing up my boobies with my arms.

Gotta flirt with precision if I want a harem like Poppy's.

"Glad you could make it, cutie," said the most muscular of the heroes. He stepped back when Racheal glares at him.

"Where is the enemy camp, Steve? And are you sure we'll be enough to handle it?" asks Racheal.

"My name is Ebony Fate," said Steve.

"Well, we all were told to attack the same camp. Rather than fight over it, I think teaming up gives us all a better chance of victory," said the short hero with the blue glasses.

I don't recognize him. Is he from another village?

"I could take 'em all on my own! But I'd rather do it with it with my fellow bros." The third hero looked at Racheal and me. "And of course, my sistas!" The mohawk hero pointed to us with a grin.

"Do not call me sister, Acid Fantasy. You always ignored me back at the village. Now that I'm wanted, you want to get close. Sorry, that's too suspicious." Racheal stepped in-between the strapping young boys.

"We all needed Poppy since she was the only angel. But that's changed. Now we're free to mingle with all the pretty girls we want."

"Right now my priority is to finish this quest so I can help Annie. You want to flirt with me later, you're welcome to. But, right now, I don't trust any of you. How high is my bounty?"

"We're all deserters, so we all have bounties now. Come on, Silent Symphony, give me some lovin'," said Acid Fantasy, pursing his lips.

"I've had angel spittle. It's sweet, tangy and it stays in your mouth for hours. You can't tempt me with your normal saliva," said Racheal, crossing her arms.

Wow. Am I really that tasty?

Racheal blew into her hands, creating a foghorn sound. "You all rushed into this without thinking. Who even assigned this quest? Dark and Broody is under CatBoy protection, so it sure as hell wasn't a quest from our village."

"Some guy in a cloak. But it wasn't a RiftRipper," said the glasses hero.

"And who are you?" asked Racheal.

"I'm a hero helper from another village."

"And what village is that?"

"I'm here to help, don't worry."

"All three of you should just leave this to me. I already got some of you killed," said Racheal softly.

Acid Fantasy put a hand on her shoulder. "Hey now. No need for that. They died fighting the real enemy. Look, we got sick of hunting down rebels and working for those sadistic CatBoys. With you and your angel by our side, we have the confidence to really take a stand. You inspired us to do the right thing."

Racheal held her head and blushed. "Wow. So my speech really worked. I guess you don't need to die to be a martyr."

The glasses hero raised his hand and spoke. "I'm a scout from the group that created this special quest. We wouldn't have chosen you three if you had no chance at winning."

"What do you care? Heroes are a dime a dozen," said Racheal.

"Then let's increase our odds," said the glasses hero. "Angel, do you have any power vials with you?"

"My fluids are something I chose to give to people who are special to me," I said, snuggling up to Racheal.

The mohawk hero stepped up to me. "Well I may not have family back home, but I do value my own life. If we don't get powers, then we could all die."

"I only have one bottle. Maybe I'll give it to the sweetest boy." I licked my lips playfully.

Flirting is so much fun.

"I once saved a kitten from drowning," said Ebony Fate.

"That's nothing. I spent six hours at a convention helping a lost girl locate her mother," said the glasses hero.

"Forget about the power vial. There's another way to get an edge!" Acid Fantasy tore me from Racheal's arms.

Racheal pulled out her knife and the other two heroes drew their swords. "Put her down or I'll cut you down."

"I didn't ask to come here! My bandmates need me. The sooner I finish this quest, the sooner I can hang with my real bros back home."

"You're going to use the money for a return ticket?" asked Racheal.

"Yeah. I've been saving up. This quest will finally get me my out. Now step back. I'm getting powers now," said Acid Fantasy.

"Mark, calm down man. Just take the flask. We'll let you. Let's not create a conflict, okay?" Ebony Fate slowly approached.

"Aww, you boys aren't going to fight over my lips," I said in a teasing tone.

"You steal her kiss and I'll cut your legs off," said Racheal, pointing her dagger at the mohawk hero.

"Hey dad! I am special. I'm gonna do this and be just fine!" yelled Acid Fantasy toward the sky.

I hate being forced to kiss people so I might as well do the kissing.

I slurped the vial, then I grabbed his face and plunged my tongue into his mouth.

The other two boys stepped back.

I pulled away and turned to Racheal. "He was willing to risk it. Just calm down. He should be fine."

Huh? I'm falling.

The hero hit the ground and started shaking.

"Is he going to die?" asked the glasses hero, covering his eyes.

The bushes rustled and a CatBoy general steps out. "You all are," he said with a twisted smile.

The CatBoy had a slender body and a baby face. He was wearing a sailor-hat and jammies with sleepy faced kitties on them.

"Which one is he?" asked Acid Fantasy, holding out his sword.

"Must be new." Racheal stepped up to him. "We're from Dark and Broody Village. That makes us allies," she said, offering her hand to the general.

His gentle face suddenly twisted. He pointed at me with his clawed fingers. "You! Why didn't you stop me?"

Huh?

"At Sunny Village I killed my own parents. Why didn't you stop me!?" he pushed Racheal off and came rushing at me.

I stood my ground.

I'm not afraid. Nobody is going to stop me from reuniting with my family.

I held out my hands and fired a soundwave into him.

He was blasted off his feet.

"Nice one, angel girl!" cheered Ebony Fate. "Now hurry up and do something for Acid Fantasy. His whole body is in shock."

Racheal fired a shot near the CatBoy general. "If you hurt Annie. I will murder you." Her hands were trembling. "Don't tempt me because I really want to know what it feels like."

"My name is CatNap. You and everyone from your treacherous village are better off dead!" He dragged his hands down his wooly shirt and blew them at Racheal.

Wait wool. Oh no!

My hero fell to the ground.

"Can we not do this right now!? My friend is going to die!" yelled Ebony Fate.

"You'll be joining him soon enough. ***Fairy Dust!***" CatNap spread the SleepySheepy pollen but Ebony covered his mouth.

The hero rushed in and lashed with his sword.

CatNap slashed his legs, putting them to sleep.

I fired a sound shot directly at the CatNap's head.

Ebony Fate used this opportunity to pierce the general's chest.

CatNap then tossed dust into his face and the hero collapsed, still gripping his sword.

"No. I wasn't supposed to die. Not until I kill him. That detestable dictator!" yelled CatNap.

"Flam ordered you to kill your parents, didn't he?"

The General tore out the sword. "Sacrifice is power. The only way to grow strong enough to take what you desire is to kill what you love. That bastards savors this tragic contradiction." CatNap spat out blood.

"We are exiles from Dark and Broody. We came here to take down a CatBoy general at a nearby base. If you promise to help us, then I'll heal you. Deal?" I asked, holding a gobule of my spit just over his wound.

I was suddenly slammed to the ground by an unseen force. A clawed hand gripped my face and rubbed it into CatNap's bloody wound.

"We don't make deals with your kind," said the cruel voice of General CatScratch. "Spit on him or else I'll get the saliva from your severed head."

I cried and spit repeatedly until CatNap's wound was healed.

"Let's behead her!" yelled CatNap.

"And miss our chance to land a critical blow to Flam. I think not," said CatScratch. "We shall bring her to the fortress, along with these heroes. All except one." He yanked me off the ground by my hair. "And you get to choose."

I can't kill a hero. I'm supposed to save them.

"Let's just kill the girl. We don't want her attracting those dreadful machines," said CatNap.

"Hmmm. You do have a point."

My stomach churned. I raised a finger at the hero who was convulsing in agony. "I choose him…" I said softly.

"The obvious choice. All right. You can pick him. But you have to do it yourself." CatScratch pulled the dagger out of my pocket. "You have to kill him with this."

His family is waiting for him back home. He's so close to being reunited with them. Can I really end his story just to continue my own?

"She won't do it! Let me do it!" exclaimed CatNap.

"Give her a chance. It's her first time." CatScratch moved his sword up to Racheal's throat. "You know what happens if you don't do it."

I'm sorry, Mark. I'll never forget you.

My tears ran down my arms and became steam upon hitting the heated blade. I brought the dagger down. His screams tore up my insides and his blood splattered my face.

Warm.

I brought it up and down and up and down and up and down. The world became twisted and the sky darkened. I was no longer an angel. To save my family, I had become a demon.

He was going to die anyway.

I tried to comfort myself as I continued to stab. I don't even know why I kept doing it.

My whole world turned black.

I awoke in a steel cage with the sun shining in my eyes. There were many cages around me with heroes in them. I scanned the cages, searching for Racheal.

"Morning," said Racheal, leaning over me with a grin.

Does she know what I did? I can't tell her. She'll hate me.

"What are we going to do?" I sobbed but my eyes produced no tears.

"Look at all these heroes. There's like twenty of them. We have all the hero power we need to take over this outpost. Hey, Annie? Are you okay?"

Racheal shook me and smiled but everything still looked so sad.

"That general didn't touch you, did he?" she asked, clenching her fist.

I shook my head. I saw my hands and then hid them.

I can still see the blood.

Rain came pouring down suddenly.

Racheal nestled up to me, keeping me sheltered in her hug.

"I did something really bad," I said in a dead whisper.

"Well it doesn't matter."

"What do you mean?"

"If you do something bad, then you just have to move on and do more good things in the future. Don't worry about what you can't change, Annie." Racheal bent over and kissed my forehead.

Is it really that simple?

Screams were heard and then battle cries.

In seconds the CatBoy soldiers were engaged in combat with cloaked figures.

"See? All your good karma has given us an escape." Racheal held my fingers in hers. "You're a tough girl. Now come on, let's combine our powers so we can break out of this place!"

Racheal loves me despite what I did. And I love her. I really love her.

I feel energy around my body like zappy clouds. My jammies transform, sprouting a long frilly black skirt with musical notes, a pink blouse and golden sound amps on my wrists.

"Whoa! This is incredible! You're incredible, Annie!" exclaimed Racheal.

I turned and smiled at her. "It's cuz I love you super tons!"

"Awesome! Now let's break out of here and join the fight!" yelled Racheal, putting her hand on my shoulders and sending her energy into me. *"Reciprocal Bond!"*

I fired a powerful sound wave that blasted open our cage and then exploded into a watch tower.

The cloaked warriors and soldiers moved out of the way of the collapsing tower.

Good. I didn't kill anyone else.

Racheal fired a blast at a nearby cage. It wasn't as strong as mine, but still blasted the bars off.

Together we freed the captured hero's while blasting away enemy CatBoy soldiers.

The hooded warriors must be heroes too!

CatScratch held out his sword and pulled three cloaked heroes in, decapitating them. His bloody face then turned to us. "Destiny has given me yet another gift."

My body froze up but Racheal blasted him.

He stood his ground from the blast, and then raised the weapons of the fallen warriors all along the battlefield. *"Steel Dénouement!"*

The swords came down alongside the rain droplets.

I could see one headed straight for my Rachie.

I held out my hands and blue energy shot out. It encased my hero in a water bubble and stopped the swords on impact.

"Oh! I have a cool idea." Racheal turned the water bound swords around. She then put her hands to the hilts of the swords and then sent a soundwave out.

The swords shot out like bullets, taking down the incoming CatBoy soldiers.

"How did you even make this?" asked Racheal, poking the shield. "This is not my power."

Maybe it's my bond to Mommy!

CatScratch pulled the swords off the ground with his energy, directing them into the backs of incoming heroes. He then gripped the impaled swords and cleaved the heroes in two. "Heroes without powers are mere civilians," he said, spinning a sword in front of him to eviscerate an enemy.

"Stay away from the angel!" yelled a young hero, dressed up in a stretchy body suit and wearing a colorful mask.

"You had better have powers. My swords are getting thirsty for a challenge," said CatScratch, clanging his swords together.

The hero sliced the air with his fingers.

CatScratch deflected the onslaught of air slices.

"Prickly girl! I, uh, kinda need some back up!" yelled the oddly dressed hero.

The pitter patter of little feet on rain was followed by the most amazing sight.

Tumble!

I ran to her. I didn't see heroes or soldiers. I only saw my little sister.

Her eyes nearly popped when she noticed me. She ran to me and slipped on a wet puddle.

I was suddenly smashed against the ground by a sudden gravity wave.

"Two angels! What a delightful day this is turning out to be," said CatScratch, flinging his sword at Tumble.

A cloaked warrior stepped into the path of the sword and grabbed it. "It will be when your head lies at my feet," he said, rushing in. He whipped out a gun. "My friends are my greatest treasure," he said, before the gun shot out a line of bullets.

CatScratch deflected the bullets with a surge of gravity.

The cloaked warrior rushed in and kicked CatScratch. He then collected the water in the area, forming it into a river before sending it slamming into the general.

CatScratch coated his sword in his prana and sliced the river, dispersing it. The hero with the stretchy clothes rushed behind him and sliced the air, cutting the general's back.

The general lost focus and was blasted by the river into a house in the distance.

Tumble ran into my arms and healed my wounds with her spit.

I held her tightly.

It's her. It's really her.

I snuggled her as we both cried.

I watched the cloaked warrior approach Racheal as I snuggled my little sister.

"So, you have water powers too?" he asked.

Racheal looked up at him and her face went red. "Hot…I mean sound. I make funny noises and cool ones. I'm a girl!" she exclaimed, wobbling in a daze.

"Does this girl have a name?" The cloaked warrior held out his hand. "*Liquid Mist*." The water around the incoming CatBoy soldiers became a mist. "Friendship is the only ammunition the soul needs," he said, before spraying the enemy with his gunfire.

"Name! Yeah! Racheal! Like a sheep. Baaa," she said before covering her cheeks.

"Well, little sheep. I'm Braven."

Braven is alive!?

"That is a really hot name," she said with googily eyes.

"Wait?" He removed his hood. "Your power is sound? Are you the Silent Symphony?" he asked with wide eyes.

"Oh, so you've heard of me?" she asked with a giggle.

"I've lost a number of good friends to you and your detestable village. To think I'd get a chance to avenge them." He raised his gun.

"Stop!" yelled a tall and muscular hero. "The hero's here have all been exiled from their village. If you hurt any of them, you will be stripped of your ranks."

"Hey, I'm the one who brought you guys the angel!" he yelled.

"But it was our RiftRipper who saved your life." The hero removed his hood, revealing hazel eyes and a gentle smile. "I'm Ricardo, but my brothers in arms call me Dios Gigante. Welcome to the Mortal Militia," he offered Racheal a hand.

"Hey, angels. Don't just stand there. Heal the wounded!" yelled Braven, gesturing with his gun.

He doesn't seem to remember me?

I went to the closet hero and spit on him, but the wound didn't close.

Huh? Why isn't it working.

Tumble spit and the wound was sealed. She poked my cheek and tilted her head.

"I'm okay. Don't worry."

Did that transformation take up too much of my energy?

Racheal ran up and seized both of us in a hug. "It's her right? She's your little sister?"

"Yeah. It's really her," I said with a sniffle.

"I'm soooo happy for you! She's super adorable by the way," said Racheal, rubbing Tumble's head.

"Tumble, this is my girlfriend, Racheal," I exclaimed, grabbing Rachie's hands.

Tumble looked at Racheal with discerning eyes. She turned to me and nodded.

Yay! I have her approval!

"Stop stalling and heal the wounded!" yelled Braven.

I turned to Racheal, wiping my spit on a cut on arm.

"Hey, this is just a temporary thing. I'm sure you'll be back in action in no time!"

Tumble healed while I just did my best to calm down the injured. Once the enemy camp was cleaned up, Dios Gigante raised their flag. Two hands joining together with a blue sphere behind them.

Tumble was in my lap, fiddling with my hair. We were both watching things from the tower.

Racheal was scribbling on a paper some note to write to Braven.

I hope she doesn't love him more than me.

"Hey, Annie. I'm gonna go for a walk. You okay up here?" asked Racheal, tapping my head.

"Yeah. I'm okay," I said softly.

"I'm sure your healing powers will return. Oh, don't be late to the meeting. Meet me there, okay?" asked Racheal before skipping down the stairs of the tower.

Tumble snuggled my arm.

She hasn't let go of me since I got here. I'm not losing her ever again. But I don't want to lose Racheal either.

My thoughts about Racheal brought her book into form.

Tumble put her hand on my hand.

"You're right. It's not right to spy on her, but I have to find out what Braven's up to. He's dangerous."

Tumble rolled her eyes and released my hand, she then lied down on my lap and fell asleep.

Sorry, Rachie. I'm not the best girlfriend but I'm trying to be a good sister.

I bit my fingers and placed my hand on my girlfriend's journal.

I was skipping down the hall. "Hey, what's your name?" I asked the young luchador hero.

"You're Racheal, right? I'm Lopez. The most common Hispanic name, I know. My hero name is cooler. I'm the Luchador Espada!" he exclaimed with a dramatic pose.

"So, what brings you to the Rebellion?"

"I'm came from a village on another island."

"Was the trip difficult?"

"Nothing compared to my trip from Cuba to the Americas! We just hopped into a portal created by our personal RiftRipper."

"Does he have a name?"

"None I know of. Anyways, I joined because of my little sister, Kamila. She was held hostage so that me, Ricardo and our other brother Guillermo would fight for them."

"Then aren't you putting her in danger by creating this militia?"

"Oh no, we didn't create it. Ricardo is just in charge of the branch on our island. We came here to try and rescue some heroes for the new branch. Maybe you can lead them," he said with a smile.

"I was kinda an outcast in my village. Being the only girl there was rough. Do you have any girls in your militia?"

"Sorry, you're the only one. What brings you here?"

"Wait, so there aren't other girl heroes in your village? Like at all? That makes no sense. The RiftRipper who killed me specifically wanted me."

"And why do you fight now?"

"I need a trip to another island. It's for my…my girlfriend, Annie."

Yeah. She's my girlfriend. Nothing wrong with that.

"Ah, you're enchanted by the little angel. But there's more to this than just her."

"Well yeah. I want to go home and see my mom."

"And?"

"And I want to free the heroes who are being used by the villages!" I yelled.

Lopez patted my back. "There you go! There's that fighting spirit. But right now, you're looking for someone. Does your girlfriend know?"

"Probably. I'm not very good at hiding my emotions. I love her I really do, but I still really want a boyfriend! Tell me about Braven!"

"And spoil the fun of you learning about him yourself? Never."

"You're a nice guy. I'm sure your precious little sister will be freed in no time."

"Oh, my little sister is very precious to me, but she is fierce like a puma! Beats me and my brothers every time when we used to wrestle. She's stronger than me and Guillermo, and faster than Ricardo."

"Then she's probably lifting weights while she plans her own breakout. Things will turn out okay. You just have to hold onto hope." I smiled at him and gave his hand a good squeeze.

"We're going to raid my home village tomorrow and free all the prisoners. I will get to see my sister very soon." His smile, even hidden beneath the mask, exuded a powerful wave of positivity.

I smiled back at him and went down the hallway.

"Braven is behind the main lodge. He's always training!" hollered Lopez.

I skipped all the way to the lodge and then peeked out. My cheeks flared up.

He's sooooo hot!

"Come to take me down?" His eyes tossed daggers my way which I graciously accepted with open arms. Braven approached me while I just sputtered nervously. "That girl with you. Do you know what she is?"

"Adorable?" I asked with a shaky grin.

"She's a demon."

Yessss! I knew it!

"Demons are super cool, right?" I asked, leaning awkwardly against the wall.

"Demons take your affections and twist them. They turn bonds into bondage."

Bondage? Hot boy in bondage gear. Me in bondage gear. Both of us in bondage gear. Yes!

I swooned and he caught me.

"Are you listening to me? You can't trust those things. Not even her. She's just using you to find her family." His eyes turned dark.

That expression is too sexy. Oh no, I'm going to soak Annie's bloomers.

Braven grabbed my hand, which was still clenching the note.

He tore the note out and his eyes got wide. "You lust for me," he said softly.

I draw bunnies and rainbows and he thinks I'm being lusty.

"I uh...really like you." I covered my face.

I did it! I confessed.

"You know nothing about me." He turned away, his hair flipping in that sexy angsty way.

"I want to know more!" I screamed and then hid behind my hands.

He grabbed my hands. "Are these the hands that killed my fellow rebels?"

"Hold up. I've never killed anyone. Hour long daydream fantasies don't count!"

"Then they were captured? What do you think happened to them after that?"

"I...I don't know," I said softly, lowering my head.

He exhaled sharply and gripped my neck.

Is he going to choke me?

His grip tightened. He lifted me off the ground by my throat.

Should I fight back? I could kick him really hard. But wait, not yet, I gotta ride the high as long as I can.

Braven's eyes become gentle and he pulls me into a kiss while still crushing my throat.

Super hot and kinky as hell! Halleluiah!

He released his grip and I coughed. My hand casually lowers to my thighs and secretively massages my pleasure wound.

I'm sooo horny.

"Want to have sex?" I ask with a weird grin.

"You can be my pet. If you behave, I'll reward you."

"And if I'm a naughty pet?" I asked, wiggling my butt.

Braven's eyes widened. "Uh…then I'll abandon you. I order you to stay away from that girl." He lifted his shirt.

He's showing me his bare, muscular and scarred chest. Are those bite marks? Sooo kinky!

"Your little angel did this to me. She bit into my flesh with vacant eyes. She may act like an angel, but her true nature is that of a demon." His eyes darkened with passionate rage. "The road I travel is one of constant strife and loss." He outstretched his muscular arms. "Are you willing to follow me into the depths of Hell?"

Chapter 12: Dios Gigante

I feel something on my shoulder and I'm pulled back into my consciousness.

"What brings you here?" asked Gloom, looming over me.

I closed the book and stood in front of Tumble. "I won't go down without a fight."

I aimed my hands and focused my energy.

"I'm not here to kill you. I hate killing. I haven't killed since I was initiated. I'm not like the other RiftRippers. Flowers make me smile." Gloom's body contorted into a crescent shape.

"Then why are you here?"

"I asked first," said Gloom, pointing at me with several hands.

"I'm here because I was rescued. I'm going to find my sister while helping the heroes."

Gloom sunk into himself as he laughed. "These aren't heroes. They are rebels. They fled from their villages. They are deserters, like me."

"They want to help the other heroes. They're good guys."

"Things aren't so black and white. Even so, there's no need to give me those fearsome eyes. I'm the Mortal Militia's personal RiftRipper. Have been for years."

"But you were going to kill Poppy's heroes."

"Nope. I use threats to deal with my problems. RiftRippers are terrifying creatures. There's no need for us to kill unless we are transporting. My threats are so fearsome that my targets end up killing themselves." His body twisted and the stars in his eyes turned red. "I've said too much. You know my secret. I'll have to cut it out of your mind." Blades came out from under his cloak and gently poked my head.

I have to fight or I'm gonna die.

Gloom collapsed into a puddle. He reformed behind Tumble, encasing her inside himself in a cage of blades. "Choose how you want to end yourself."

How is everything falling apart? What should I do?

Tumble poked the knives playfully and silently giggled.

"That's enough games." Dios Gigante stepped up to Gloom.

"But look at her terror! It's adorable!" exclaimed Gloom before collapsing into a puddle.

"Your games have cost us the lives of several troops," said Dios, glaring at the puddle.

"Yes, but you need me soooooo you have to stomach it. I just hate seeing people fight. It would be so much better if they just turned their swords on themselves." Gloom impaled his body with multiple swords and let out a wretched scream that soon turned into laughter.

"Your flowers are getting thirsty. Best water them," said Dios.

Gloom nodded repeatedly and then slid off the rooftop.

"Are you alright?" asked Dios, patting my cheeks.

I was cuddling Tumble and crying. "You saved me." I gave him a warm smile.

"Gloom was just playing around. He wouldn't harm an angel. If a RiftRipper destroys an angel, their mind becomes even more twisted. He values his individuality. He can't harm you."

"Okay. Still…thanks," I said softly.

"Hey. I want you to stay here when we go on the next mission."

"Why?"

"It's dangerous and you're no soldier. We can bring the wounded back to you and your little sister."

"I'm a hero too. If I don't give it my all, then I'll regret it forever."

"We leave soon after the meeting. At least consider it."

"Your little sister is going to be just fine. You'll see," I said with a smile.

"Yep. I guarantee it! Hey, you know Braven, right?"

I nodded.

"He's so happy all the time. What's his secret?" asked Dios.

Braven is always acting happy so he can keep his friend's safe.

"He, uh, he trained himself to be happy."

"I'm heading off to the meeting. I hope you'll consider staying behind."

"Oh, I'll go with you," I said with a smile.

He shook his head. "Sorry. Heroes only. Some of the heroes have had bad experiences with the angels. They don't trust them. It would only cause problems."

"But what they don't realize is you can just read about it in your journal."

"Hey, I respect my hero's privacy," I said with a shaky smile.

Tumble rolled her eyes.

"Keep your little sister safe. She's run off before. Thankfully our RiftRipper found her and sent her back. She's extremely powerful but she doesn't take failure well."

So she was the angel before me that was at Dark and Broody. I've been following her little footsteps after all.

Racheal didn't come back to get me for the meeting. It's not like she said she would, but it put me in a sour mood.

I opened Racheal's diary but Tumble closed it. "Why should we be left out if we're going to be fighting with them?"

Tumble picked up an apple and tossed it. She then sliced it in half with an air sickle.

"Luchador Espada is your hero?" I asked.

Tumble nodded with a big smile.

I plopped her onto my lap and tickled her. "Have you two kissed?"

Tumble grabbed her cheeks and wiggled her body in joy. She then pats my head.

"Oh, so he gives you head pats."

Tumble nods and places my hand to her chest. It's racing.

Awww. My little sister's first hero crush.

Tumble and I practiced our powers while the heroes had their meeting. We came up with some cool combo moves that we could use in the next fight.

Tumble jumped into my arms and nuzzled my face.

I looked down to see stars in a black puddle.

"Hello," said Gloom, waving at us from below.

"What do you want?" I asked, pulling her close to me.

"It's time to get going. Are you suited up?"

I looked down. I was in the uniform I wore back when I was an angel at Sunny Village.

It feels so long ago.

Gloom tore open his chest, revealing a portal.

I looked down at Tumble.

She shrugged and then hopped in.

I followed her into the unknown.

Mist, smoke and the clashing of metal greeted us upon arrival.

I raised my hand to fire sound waves, but nothing came out.

Oh no. We practiced too much. I need energy.

Tumble sliced the hand off an incoming attacker by waving her hand.

Racheal blasted another enemy away. "They knew we were coming. Someone told them we were coming."

Someone betrayed the militia? But why?

Braven fired mist from his hand and then took down the confused enemy. "Avoid killing! They're heroes like we are!"

I went to Rachie and stood on my tippytoes. "Kiss me."

"Now really isn't the time," said Racheal, throwing invisible sound grenades at the incoming heroes. "What are Dark and Broody heroes doing here?"

"Please kiss me! It's so I can help!" I exclaimed.

"Okay." Racheal lifted me up by my booty and pulled me into a kiss.

I slurped up her saliva and my wings sprouted.

Racheal pulled away with flushed cheeks and heavy breaths. She then moved in for another kiss.

While we made out I could see Luchador Espada pick up my little sister.

He put her on his shoulders and the two of them fired wind sickles at the enemy soldiers.

"Where is Gloom? We need to evacuate now!" he yelled, setting Tumble down to heal his comrade.

Racheal's eyes were swirling with ecstasy. An arrow hit her from behind but she kept kissing me.

Oh no. I intoxicated her. Gotta keep her safe.

I tore out the spear and spit on her wound while I blasted incoming enemies.

"What did you do to her?" Braven tore me out from Racheal's arms. He smacked her cheeks. "Snap out of it!"

"Already getting into trouble?" Poppy was with five heroes, all armed with crossbows. "I taught you better. Split up. Take her down."

Poppy's main hero blanketed the area in darkness.

I used my sound powers to locate the heroes and then fired sound shots their way, but most of them missed.

Something suddenly slammed into me and pinned me to the ground.

"What are you even doing here?" asked Poppy, digging her talons into my arms.

"We're here to free the prisoners."

Poppy shook her head. "Idiot. It's impossible to win against them. All you've done is put your hero in danger again. You're really a terrible angel."

The four heroes made a circle around me.

"I'm sorry, my student. But more and more of my heroes, my boyfriends are leaving to join this pointless rebellion. The only way to save them is to destroy their hope. You and Lamby have gotta die," said Poppy, her face heavy with dread despite her smile. "Dark Passion, I order you to end her life."

Poppy's main hero lowered his hood. His pale as death face had piercings above his eyebrows. His eyes were a gentle blue as he raised his sword.

He was suddenly sliced by his fellow hero.

"Richard! What the hell are you doing?" yelled Poppy, rushing to Dark Passion's side and healing him.

Richard's eyes were blank. "Protect the angel," he said in a daze before striking another hero.

He's the one I brought back from the dead. The one who was killed by Betrayer. But he's not protecting me because he's thankful. He's been possessed. Is it my fault?

With the darkness seeping back into Dark Passion, I was able to get clear shots on the other heroes.

A group in the back raised their crossbows. Richard stood in the path and was pierced in my place. "Protect," he said in a daze.

"You're going to get yourself killed!" I flew into him and knocked him to the ground, having him dodge the next volley.

Blood wasn't the only thing coming out from his wounds. Water coated in blue energy was gushing out of him.

It's the energy. My aura must have messed with his mind.

I wasn't paying attention.

An arrow shot me from the back.

Poppy then landed on me. "Beg me to kill you, please. It will make it so much easier. All you've brought is misfortune to others. Give up your life and I'll make sure your little sister is safe."

Richard tore out the arrow in my back and pierced it into Poppy's chest. He attacked her repeatedly.

Poppy's claws dug into his chest. "You love me! Why are you helping her! Is it because I'm a boy? Am I too weak to keep you safe?" She cried as her claws dug in deeper.

Richard's eyes went hollow.

I spit on my wounds to heal them and fired precise sound bullets at the incoming enemies as I stood back on my feet.

Poppy kicked the corpse off her. "Stand back, boyfriends! I'm going to end her myself. I have to take responsibility." She glared daggers at me through her teary eyes. "I never should have saved your life."

Richard's body stood back up as if being pulled by an invisible puppeteer.

"Why won't you just die?" yelled Poppy, flinging a dagger at Richard's head.

It's not my energy…it's Momma's. Momma is protecting me.

I ran off.

Richard is already dead. But my Rachie is alive. I have to find her and escape from this place.

When I was running through the battle-field, I saw Tumble and Luchador Espada. Tumble fired a sickle that I imbued with sound. The ear-shattering noise took down a line of enemies.

I looked up at Luchador Espada.

"I'll keep her safe. I promise," he said, warmth emanating beneath his mask.

Tumble gave him a head pat, filtering her power through him.

"***Rebellion's Espada!***" he yelled, forming a wind sword and slicing through an enemy CatBoy.

Oh no. They're here too!

I ran off. My sister became smaller and smaller in my vision until I turned the corner.

Dios Gigante was four times his size and was smashing building. "Where are you?"

I looked up at him, took a deep breath and shouted. "We gotta go! They were waiting for us!"

"I know! That's not important right now."

"Have you seen Racheal?"

"You really should have stayed behind." Dios reached down and grabbed me. "Here! You want her? Is that want you want! Come on out, old fool!"

What is he doing?

The demolished building formed into a tower as an old wood primordial climbed up the rubble. The tower tilted to Dios Gigante.

"What do you want?" The old man was clenching a wooden staff. He had a green leafy beard and was most wrinkled of all the wood primordials.

"I want my sister!"

"What? You'll have to speak up. I don't have my glasses."

"You're blind!"

"Yes. And I don't want to go deaf either. Now calm down and speak clearly."

"I brought them all here. Now fulfill your part of the bargain. Hand me my sister!"

No. He was the one who sold us out. But he's the leader. And he was so nice.

My head was getting dizzy. I shook myself to my senses.

I have to find Rachie before it's too late.

I aimed at Dios' eye and fired a blast.

Dios' eye was unaffected.

"Sorry, boy. We're a poor village. We can't afford to feed the prisoners," said the old man.

"You let my little sister starve?"

"Never. Someone came to pick her up and we decided it was best to part ways. Women are a very dangerous commodity to hold onto."

"Where is she?"

"Who knows? Last I saw her, she was being taken away by a CatBoy. Maybe ask one of the generals."

"You lied to me! You said you'd let her go if I turned them in. I made the Militia to weed out the exiles. I brought them to you."

"How could you do that!?" I yelled, biting into his massive fingers.

"I had to do it for my sister!" yelled Dios.

I killed that hero for Rachie. But it was different. I had to make a choice. Dios didn't have to choose someone to die. He decided to betray his people all along.

The old man smiled with his wrinkles. "Family is such an incredible motivator. Tell you what, become our hero again and I will create a squad just for tracking your sister down."

"I'm never doing anything for you again!" Dios released me and barraged the tower with his massive fists.

I was caught by a shadow just before hitting the ground.

"Welcome to my village, little angel," said the RiftRipper known as Assailant.

The Old Man pushed aside the massive fists by releasing a spatial distortion with his hand. "We have no need for a hero who abandons his people

217

for selfish reasons. Chop him to pieces. Save the heart so we can pass on his powers."

"As you command." Assailant's tendril extended and set me on top of building. He then rushed into battle against the massive traitor.

He ran up Dios' arm, slicing it up in the process.

The giant slammed his arm into a building, but the assassin sunk into his shadow to dodge. He then hopped up the rubble and sent a tendril into the giant's throat.

"With a target this large, I think I can avoid unneeded casualties. *Misery Clad*." Assailant's entire body unfolded into spinning blades as he zoomed toward the giant's neck.

A white shadow rode up the giant's belly and to his throat.

It thrust a single blade into a portal. The blade came out of multiple portals around Assailant, parrying his attack.

The shadow took form.

Betrayer.

"Finally! I found you!" yelled Assailant, getting sliced while sending multiple bladed tendrils into the portals.

A single bladed tendril came out from the portal in front of Betrayer. He sliced it with ease, cutting off all of Assailant's tendrils in the process. "Did you come after me as a request or is this personal?"

"Die!" yelled Assailant, slamming into Betrayer after pulling a metal spear from the vortex in his chest.

"Ah, so it's personal. Your hatred is misdirected." Betrayer pulled Assailant into a gruesome hug with the tendrils coming out of his body. "I gave you everything."

"Then why do I have nothing?" Tears poured out from Assailant's entire body. His back elongated and shifted into a saw before it pierced Dios' throat.

"Dios has nothing to lose. For the first time he is fit to lead the rebellion. I won't let you kill him," said Betrayer, struggling to pull out his tendrils.

Assailant's cloak had hooked them in, keeping the tendrils locked in place.

Once the saw had sliced off the head, it went into a frenzy, chopping the giant to pieces.

He's dead. Just like that.

Betrayer sunk into his shadow and navigated through the fleshy chunks. His body expanded before devouring the heart of the hero. He then went into his own vortex and vanished.

The old man blasted a sever of Dios' falling flesh with a powerful barrier. He appeared before Assailant and spoke but I couldn't hear from where I was.

Chances are Tumble's hero is in danger! He probably didn't even know about the ambush. But what if he did? What if she's in danger too!

I climbed down the building.

The old man appeared in front of me. "Little angel, on behalf of the Village of the Doomed, I express my deepest apologies for what you witnessed."

Am I going to die?

"Your eyes should remain as pure as your spirit," said the old man with a smile.

His aura weighed down upon me. I couldn't move.

"If you spare the heroes, I'll stay with your village. I'll be your angel," I said in tears.

"Maintaining peace is no small feat. The sacrifices I've made to protect this village keep piling up." Tears gushed from the old man's vacant eyes like waterfalls. "We all have a role to play. And those who don't follow their roles…they don't last."

A rebel hero tossed a torch on the old man, setting him on fire.

Another rebel picked me up. "We're evacuating the area."

"But Racheal is still in there," I said in tears.

I tried to summon up my string or her book.

Nothing.

I was too weak and sad.

The heroes carried me out of the village and to the clearing.

"Gloom is going to meet us here as soon as he can," said a rebel.

Someone in the back screamed.

Assailant had found us.

I tried to shoot out energy at him but I was out of power. The old man must have sapped it from me.

I didn't run. I just watched as they died. Every…single one. The last body gushed blood on my face.

Warm.

Assailant, now red from those he killed, lifted me up. "No worries, little angel. I'll keep you safe. The wise elder has assigned me to watch over you." He wiped the blood off my cheek, accidentally cutting my cheek a little. "You can stay with me. Think of me like your papa."

I never had a papa.

I gripped onto him and cried.

To be continued in **Tragic Angel**
Coming Fall 2020

CLOSED BOOK

Tears drip from my eyes onto the pages of my journal. A hand rests itself on my shoulder. Tears drip on my back.

"I felt it all," says a voice that makes me shiver. "All your love, all your self-loathing, your desperation and your misery. Your life is truly a tragic tale and you've spun your words beautifully for those tragic twelve chapters. Why not stop there? Thirteen is an awful number. You've suffered more than any little girl should ever have to. You must despise being born as a cursed being."

I glare dark pointies at my captor. "Nymph Beasts aren't tragic. It's you whose made all the bad stuff in my life happen."

Flam. I swear, I will end you.

"All of it? You give me far too much credit, my dear. Do you think that if I'm killed, your people will be freed? I'm the one granting them their wildest dreams! I created a mystical wonderland for every one of your sisters."

His smile makes me tremble.

"Y-Y-You're just using them! Now go away! I have to finish my story." I pick up my pen and continue writing.

His scarf seizes it. *Dear Main, I love you so so much, like lots and lots, honey. And after my death I want you to kill the bad man who I blame for all my problems. Do it or my ghost will stalk you everywhere you go.* Flam tosses the pen aside. "There's your ending. Look, I'd love to stay and hear the rest but you have prior engagements." His scarf twists into a noose and pulls me out of my chair.

I grab the scarf and hoist myself up to keep my neck from snapping. "Please, I don't want to die."

"You already begged me to kill you. I can't go back on my promises and I won't be late. You'll be impressed. I made sure to round up quite the crowd for your execution." His scarf releases me and I fall to the ground.

I grab onto the journal and hold it to my chest. "When a hero dies, their diary goes away too. I wrote this down so that their memories won't be forgotten."

"Guardian Angel, such a sweet title for such a tragic book."

I hate this but I don't have a choice.

I push the journal into Flam's arms. "My last request is that you deliver this to Main. Please, that's all I want."

Flam looks at me with a wounded face. "I'll deliver it to him absolutely. Feel free to struggle and try to escape your demise. Don't think that any rebellion against me will make me break my promise to you." He bent down and kissed my hand.

Wait, does he want me to escape? What's his plan?

"Oh, before you go, you might want to check Main's journal. Your final hero could be dead for all you know."

I shook my head. "He's not dead...and he's coming to rescue me! I won't read his Diary because I have faith in him," I say as I try to keep my voice firm.

"Oh, the loss of that spark of light will truly make the world a darker place." His shoulders drop. His eyes then widen. "How about we play a little game. It isn't quite time for you to die yet. You have exactly seven minutes before you're due. In that time, I nor any of my soldiers, will interfere with whatever you do. Think of these seven minutes as your last moments of freedom. You're free to do whatever you want. But all good games have a penalty. If you're late, the execution will be just as fast but soooo much more painful. Better hurry." He opened the door.

I ran out the door.

He's still playing mind games, but I don't have time to figure out what he's plotting. I'm going to take a gamble. I won't go down easy.

I rush down the hallway but it starts moving beneath me.

Of course, the carpet is alive.

"You're not supposed to interfere!" I yell as I stomp on the bad carpet.

"I'm not a soldier. The master of the castle said we can do whatever we want before your execution. So I'm having fun!"

The carpet grew spikes that pierced into my feet.

I focus my energy into the blood, intoxicating the carpet with rage. It thrashes around in a mad state, allowing me to slip by safely.

My blood can bring this whole castle down, but that's not what I'm after.

I sprout wings and fly down the hallway, dodging various pots, pictures and other items that try and attack me.

The steps bend and try to create a small tunnel to crush me.

I create a water trail and it speeds me through the tunnel and out of harm's way.

Probably have only five minutes left, but that's all I need.

I land in the main hall, which was where the hero statues were.

Flam said they aren't really heroes, but I remember now. He turned Ruiz to stone. There's no CatBoy general with that power. That leaves only one option.

I fire a concentrated jet of water from my hand. It slices the head off one of the statues like a blade.

I climb up the statue and look at the sever where the head once was.

No sculptor details the insides. I was right. These aren't statues. Damn it.

I bit my lip.

My gamble was correct. But that only leaves a larger gamble.

I fire another shot, slicing off another statue's head.

Please, let that be the one.

I lap up my tears, turning my sadness into determination.

"What are you doing?" yelled a CatBoy.

It wasn't just any CatBoy. It was YarnBall, the creepiest of all the CatBoy generals.

"You can't interfere! Flam's orders!" I yell, shooting and killing another trapped hero.

"Rules are made to be broken. But I won't fight you. I want to help? Is this the one?"

My eyes widen.

Yu-ki...no.

"Stop! Don't touch that one!" I yell, turning my sights on Yarny.

"I'm just helping you win the game! I'm not allowed to interfere but I'm certainly allowed to help." He broke off one of Yu-ki's fingers.

I fire a water bullet right at him.

It hits his chest.

Yeah. Kill Flam's Generals. Not a bad way to spend my last moments!

YarnBall grip his chest and begins to walk toward me.

I fire another bullet into his head. Blood gushes from the hole.

"Stop." Tears came from his closed eyes. "I'll strike a deal with you. Just pick three more. Choose three heroes to sacrifice and I'll tell you which one is the right one. If I'm lying, you can kill me. I won't lie." He was shivering but it looked like it was more from excitement than fear.

He's wasting my time. If I get it right on the next shot, then I won't have to wait for his answer. Wait, I'm the one with the upper hand here.

"Every hero that dies means one less power for Flam! One less bond for him to exploit!" I yell.

"So, you're just going to kill them all?" Yarny was wiping his eyes.

"Tell me who it is now. Not for me, but for your boss."

The curtain on the wall moves and Flam emerges. "I accept each loss with glee." His smile and eyes lit up with sparkles.

He's trying to psyche me out. My next move is critical. I can end this even if I don't know who has the stone power.

I aim my hand at the statue near Flam. It's the statue of my third hero, Ruiz.

Flam's smile drops. "You wouldn't dare," he said with a dark tone.

My body shivers but I keep a steady aim. "Ruiz' powers allowed you to map out Sunny Village. They let you take down the Wood Primordial. You need his powers."

Flam smiles with a nervous twitch. "You love him. You won't kill him. Not when just one more sacrifice could set him free."

He's stalling me. What do I do?

Flam stood right in front of the statue. "Do you remember when he sold you out to save his own life? Doesn't that bother you?"

Why is this man so cruel? Wait. He's perfectly lined up. I have to take the shot. Sorry, Ruiz. I wanted to save you but I have to do this for Main. For the guy who doesn't care about me. No! He's coming and I'll show him just how awesomeriffic I am by killing Flam right now!

I fire an extra strong shot.

Flam's scarf is unable to react fast enough.

The Dictator's head…along with Ruiz' fall to the ground.

I turn to YarnBall, ready to fire again. "Which one is it?"

He points behind me. "T-T-Ten seconds left."

Damn it all!

I fire at two more heroes with faces I don't recognize.

"A deal is a deal." YarnBall moves his hand off his chest, the bullet wound is petrified.

As my eyes go wide in horror, his smile spreads with joy.

It wasn't any of the statues. It was him. I…killed them for nothing. YarnBall has to die now!

Something wraps around my legs. I fall to the ground and am reeled into Flam's sickening embrace. He caresses my hair while keeping my body bound. "Time's up. You far exceeded my expectations. I thought you would go after your fellow angels and try to free them. But no. Instead you try to wound me by killing my lovers. Oh, you are a dark creature indeed," he says with clenched teeth.

"I hate you!" I yell as I try to wrestle out of his grip.

"Don't worry. All the important heroes, the ones with powers, are in my chambers." He shows me the decapitated head of Ruiz, but I did relocate the powerless ones here, of which you killed four of. Powerless or not, I loved them dearly. I'm going to make your death four times as painful."

Pointless. It was all pointless. He can't be beat. He twists everything.

Flam grips my cheeks. "Those broken shall feel once more when this body is clad in pain." He slices my arm with his fingernail.

"Free my Yu-ki. Please. I won't fight anymore." Sadness overwhelms me and I break out into sobs.

I can't fight. What's the point? I just have to do one last good dead before I die.

"Will you accept the most painful death I've orchestrated for you."

I nod in tears, unable to talk.

"Very well then. Yarny, free Yu-ki. Have him join us at the execution grounds."

I'm powerless. I've always been powerless. My vision blurs. The world is black. The book of my life has closed.

Exclusive Chapter: Yuki's Secret journey

I never thought I'd be in a situation like this. Here I am, in a bed of leaves with a young angel that wants to make love with me. I placated her by snuggling and now she and her little sister are asleep. I have a decision to make.

Annie is strong. I nearly did something regrettable. I escaped her powers of seduction this time, but who knows what will happen next time? I have to bring her to the next village and then…I have to leave her.

Something rustles in the bushes.

I draw out my legendary dagger, Catalyst, and infuse it with coldness.

"You don't want to fight me," I say, pointing the blade.

A girl comes out from the bushes. It's the little Gobli girl I had rescued from Street Trash's slave auction. She looks at me and the two girls by the bed. Her eyes flare up with rage.

"Hold on there! Nothing happened. No need to get jealous."

Gobliy, the name I decided to give her, doesn't heed my words at all. She raises her spiked club, ready to attack either me or the angels.

The best way to fight a battle is to surrender.

I drop my sword and grip my shirt. I then seductively remove it.

Gobliy's cheeks turn pink and steam comes out from her head. She wobbles back and forth, allowing me to gently lower her battle club. She grabs my hand. "Mine," she says in an impish voice.

I twirl a bit of her hair with my finger. "I was smitten by you the moment I saw you. Let's get out of this place. I'd love to see your home."

She swoons.

That's it. If I can just get her to faint, then victory is mine.

Gobli slams her foot down to secure her balance. She is breathing heavily.

Here I was told they had weak resistances to charm. Then again, judging by her pink school girl uniform, she's a rather high class Gobli. The more accessories they have, the more respected they are.

Gobliy picks up her club, points at the sleeping angels and makes a slamming motion.

"Do that and the flower in my heart will wither and die. Come on, let's leave them be and go find your place."

Gobliy's eyes shimmer. She pulls me along while skipping with joy.

"Gobliy, is it true that your people network with other races?" I ask with a smile.

"Yes. Goblis great at trade! Super fantastical!" she exclaims.

Maybe I can locate Annie's mother with their help. If she's still alive, that is.

"You are super fantastical," I say with a wink.

Gobliy stops. She grips her heart and has shallow breaths. The flustered girl faints but I catch her.

"Are you okay?" I ask with a look of concern.

Gobliy nods. "Thanks for saving me…again. Gobliy has best boyfriend!" She grabs my hand, gets flustered and then lets it go. She took a moment to catch her breath before continuing to lead the way.

"Was it bandits that captured you?"

"No! Gobliy greatest bandit. Never lose to others. It was hero. He hurt Gobliy."

What kind of hero attacks little girls? Was it a quest or some kind of vendetta? Goblis are known for using violence if met with resistance when they steal. I have to find out who this hero is and make sure he doesn't hurt this poor girl.

"What did he look like?"

"Scary." Gobliy hid her face under her hands.

I hold her in my arms. "I know you don't want to think about it, but I want to help. Did you see his face?"

Gobliy shook her head. "Hood."

"Well that doesn't narrow it down at all. Are we close to your cave?"

Gobli nods. She then pushes herself out of my arms and picks up her club. "Bandit time!" she exclaims with a big grin, pointing to a carriage coming down the path.

I could tell her that as a hero I don't steal unless it is necessary, but she'd probably just ignore me.

"Gobliy, you're used to attacking carriages as a group. It's not safe to go in alone."

Gobliy nods. "Yuki back up!" She then charges toward the carriage. "Raaaawr!"

I follow after her.

She busts the wooden carriage open with a single swing.

I unfasten the binds on the horses. "You're free now."

Gobliy signals me to look inside.

There's nobody here.

Her eyes widen when she notices a treasure chest. "Treasure!" She nibbles on the lock, trying to get it open.

Nobody is here and there's a treasure chest inside. A rather large one. This is too suspicious.

Gobliy abandons her mace and picks up the treasure box.

We arrived at the cave entrance.

"Is it true that trespassers are torn limb from limb when they enter a cave inhabited by Goblis?" I ask her, standing my ground as she tries to drag me in.

"Oh. Good point." Gobli slams her club into my belly, sets the chest on top of me and then drags me into the cave.

Within seconds we were swarmed by a dozen energetic Goblis, all wearing skirts only.

Must be her tribe.

"Big sista!" "Onee-san!" "Sissy!" they cheer.

"Treasure!" yells one.

The others immediately leave their big sister and start wrestling over the treasure chest.

Gobliy picks me up and brings me to a spot with some fancy sheets and a broken mattress. She fiddles with a chain on a pole and then attaches it to my hand. "Boyfriend!"

I'm really popular with the girls lately.

"You saved Gobliy's life." She grabs my head and lowers it. "That means you owe her life debt! You will be Gobli tribe's big brother forever and you must be Gobliy's boyfriend. This is great honor; you must accept!"

These Goblis are just too cute.

"What happens if I happen to slip up?" I ask with a nervous smile.

"Dinner!" Gobliy opens the curtain, showing off human skeletons next to eating utensils.

Better make myself useful if I don't want to be dinner. I probably should just seize an opportunity to escape, but if there really is a hero going around and capturing Goblis, then I need to track them down. It's possible that doing so will even give me some insight on where Annie's mother is. She wanted me to be her hero and I will not let her down.

All the Goblis slam their clubs into the chest together.

The chest opens up and a bunch of CatCoin spills out as they ravage it.

I pick up the coin and unwrap it. "One-hundred percent coco. They must have followed us to the den. Gobliy! You have to let me go! We're all in danger."

Gobliy doesn't hear me or rather it seems she can't hear me.

A hooded figure enters the den.

"Worry not, handsome damsel, the Silent Symphony has come to your rescue!" exclaimed the figure, pantomiming putting on boxing gloves.

I've heard of her. Incredibly powerful and crafty. Time to get some answers.

I imbue the chain with heat until it melts and then rush at her.

She punches but I dodge.

The sound of a train erupts from her fist, disorienting me.

She leaps up, kneeing me in the face before wrapping her legs around me and throwing me to the ground.

Gobliy slams a mace into the girl, knocking her out in a single hit.

I check her pulse. "She's still alive."

"She's the one! Bad girl kidnapped Gobliy!" yells the Gobli girl, raising her club for the finishing blow.

"Hold on. We need to find out why she did it. Leave her with me, okay?"

The other Goblis look to their big sister. "Hungry."

Gobliy pats my head. "Stay, Boyfriend." She then hoists up her club. "Looting time!"

They cheer and rush out of the cave, leaving me alone with the girl.

I pull her onto the mattress and hold up one of my empty canisters "***Imbue***." My power activates and angel saliva fills the container. I pour it out on the girl's head injury. "Come on, don't be dead."

The girl opens her eyes. Her cheeks flare up.

"Hey, don't worry. I didn't do anything. I'm not interested in romance."

"So then, you just want sex?" she asks with wide eyes.

"No. I just want to help people. Honestly I'm gay so you're not exactly my type anyway."

"But I'm also adorable, right? I could pull off a boy! We could pretend!"

"Hey, calm down. I have some important questions to ask you. Why are you going after Goblis?"

"I rescued you! The damsel is supposed to give the hero a kiss not an interrogation." She crosses her arms.

I roll my eyes, grab her and pull her into a kiss.

She wiggles around as my tongue enters her mouth.

I've lost track of how many strangers I've kissed. Still, this is the first girl I've kissed. Hopefully she'll be more compliant now.

I broke the kiss.

She points at her throat, fires an invisible bullet into it and then screams out in absolute silence. She skips around with glee and then pats her throat. "Wow! That was amazing! Let's go again!"

"Yeah. I can give you another kiss." I hold her back with one arm. "But after you answer my questions."

"Okay, so I'm Canadian, I loooove horror and gore! I'm also an independent comic creator! My name is Racheal Summers." She shakes my hand repeatedly.

"Were you the one who kidnapped that Gobli girl and handed her over to be sold at a slave auction?"

"They kill people. You do realize that, right?"

I grab her hand. "Was it you?"

"Maintaining the village isn't easy. The elder needed some extra money so we turned her over to Isekai. Someone there must have put her in the slave trade. It wasn't me. I just captured her after she murdered a traveling family from my village."

"I'm sorry."

"Don't be fooled by their innocent looks. Those creatures will tear you apart." The girl bit her lip. "Imagine your arms being torn from their sockets. Your screams only serve to excite them."

Okay. She's certainly an odd one but she doesn't seem to be mean-spirited.

"Hey, uh, Racheal?"

"Yes, handsome guy?" she asks with shimmering eyes.

"Who exactly did you turn over the Gobliy girl to?"

"All clients are confidential. Sorry, bud," she slugs my shoulder.

I lean into another kiss. "Are you sure?"

"It was a RiftRipper. They handle all negotiations."

"From what village?"

"I can't recall."

I kiss her again.

"Doomed Village! Wow! Funny how I suddenly remember, isn't it?" she asks, bobbing back and forth.

"What about a mermaid angel? Did you ever capture one of those?"

"I didn't even know there were mermaid angels. Hey, damsel boy. How about you and your hero leave this Gobli den together? We can come to my village. You can even come into my room." All her bravado suddenly drops and she grips my hand. "Please come into my room!"

"I probably should go with you. But I'm going to stay and protect them?"

"But they're murderers. They can protect themselves. Please, come with me. I really like you." She looks at me with a sad face. "What's your name again?"

"I'm Yuki, the Pacifister." I offer her my hand.

Racheal twists it behind my back and kicks me to the floor. "You've caused a lot of problems for my friends."

What is she talking about?

She pins me down with her foot. "You're coming with me to answer to your crimes, traitor."

How did I forget about my bounty? She seems harmless, but really she's quite fearsome.

"I have to stay here because I'm in love."

"What?"

"With Gobliy. She's my type."

Okay, kinda making this up as I go along, but I just need to buy time till I figure out how to get out of this mess.

"I thought you were gay. Was that a lie? It's me, right? You just didn't want to date me so you said you were gay? Wow, low blow."

"Are you really going to tear me away from my soulmate?" I beam at her with my charming good looks.

"Hey, stop looking at me like that?" She hides her face under her hood.

I throw a smoke bomb to the ground and then imbue my dagger with electricity.

Good thing I got the legendary weapon duped. Thank you, Merchant.

Her body convulses before she collapses.

Great, back to square one.

I set the girl down far away from the cave by a tree around some bushes. When I returned to the cave, the Goblis were having a big feast. Gobliy snuck away while the others were eating and pulled me to the back of the cave. She lifted up a rock. Beneath it was a crown.

"Gobli King!" she exclaims, jumping up to try and put it on me.

I crouch down and hug her. "Don't worry. I'm not going to ever leave you."

The other Goblis stop eating and bow once they notice me, though they continue chewing. Gobliy pulls my head down to make me bow. "Still big brother and Gobliy's boyfriend."

"As you command, my liege," I say with a sweet smile.

Gobli grips her heart and collapses.

Before I can go to her side, her fellow Gobli's beat her chest.

She comes back to her senses.

These poor girls have been abandoned by society. No wonder they are going on raids. These aren't the only Gobli tribe around. I should find the others. I'll keep them all safe and repurpose their bandit skills for the good of all.

The next couple months Gobliy and I would go out and locate the other Goblis. She shared the story of my bravery but they weren't impressed. It wasn't until I took off my shirt that they all bowed to me. Cave by cave we took over. I created new rules for their banditry, which also weren't agreed upon until I sang to them with my shirt off. The new rules were: no killing unless provoked; only go after horse-drawn carriages - only the privileged class have those, after all; free, instead of eat, the horses; all items obtained will be equally distributed among the tribe of Goblis. The last rule stopped infighting. Gobli tribes, with my help, started trading amongst themselves. Within seven months, we had a network all around the island of Sun Bleached. I helped them establish trade with a troll who went by the name Merchant and by the end of the year we had enough funds to create our own village within the mountains. This village was a place where the Gobli big sisters could meet up to discuss future plans. There were times they fought over me and I was nearly torn apart on several occasions. Thankfully a few head pats and romantic poetry were all it took to pacify them.

Gobliy and I were on a play date. We never did anything sexual thankfully. Being her boyfriend just meant giving her head pats, holding her hand and occasionally kissing her cheek, which was of course followed by resuscitating her from the shock. We were picking some BloodMelons off the Crimson Palms that had sprouted from a warzone. She didn't care about who was fighting who or why. They were dead now and their blood had been collected by the Crimson Palms to make melons. I certainly cared about them. Most of the bodies were heroes and many of them looked like they had been killed by water bullets.

After all this time, I finally have a lead. Maybe she is being used as a weapon. But why are two different factions of hero's fighting each other?

Gobliy threw a rock at me to get my attention.

There was a figure approaching. A RiftRipper.

"War is just another word for misunderstanding," he said, sulking along the battlefield.

"What the hell is going on here?" I ask with an intense voice.

"A survivor? Why haven't you killed yourself? Aren't you sad about all the death?"

"Did you do this? What's your name and village?"

"We are nameless beings and I have no village. You should never assume."

"What happened here?"

The RiftRipper looks around. "Death, war, bloodshed. Can't you tell?" His body twisted around me.

"Oh wow." I blush and twirl my hair. "You can twist like that."

Gobliy understood that I wasn't really into him but still couldn't watch so she put her hands over her eyes.

"Yes. I can bend into any angle I want."

I grab his thick body and stroke it. "That's so sexy!"

The RiftRipper pulls back. "Affection is a no no no no no no!" he wailed as his body bobbed in multiple directions.

I pick up Gobli and run.

The RiftRipper notices, shifts into a shadow and follows along. "Why are we running?"

"Just stay away or I will cut you." I draw my dagger and infuse it with acid.

"I'm here for the pick up. Battle's over. Gotta get those stragglers. You're supposed to be miserable and broken, but that's okay. You can join us anyway."

"Join who?"

"I can't say unless you agree to join."

"Do you know of a Mermaid Angel that was sold at an auction?"

"I know of one that was killed at an auction by my…uh…some guy I know."

She really is dead. That poor little angel lost her mother.

"And what does he call you?"

"Gloom. Wait! You tricked me!" His tendrils hoist me from the ground and spin me around. "Excellent job! You're hired!"

This is the most insane RiftRipper I've ever seen. Makes the rest of them seem mentally sound.

"I can't join someone I don't trust. Tell me what happened here," I say with authority.

"Misinformation. Each side was told the other side was wrong and then they fought. Typical, but still oh so fun."

"And why are you here?"

"To recruit the broken for a good cause. We want to free those trapped by the system."

"What system?"

"I can't say."

"Gloom!" A hero in Luchador attire comes out from behind a tree. "You found a survivor. I was beginning to lose hope."

Clenching his leg was a familiar little angel.

"Tumble, remember me?" I ask.

Tumble hops up to me and smiles.

"How did you come into possession of this angel?"

"Me!" cheers Gloom.

"You can't trust this guy," I say, pointing at the RiftRipper.

The Luchador lifts up his sleeves, showing he is missing bits of flesh. "Yeah. I know. But we need him. Thanks to him we were able to save some heroes from this mess."

"Why are the heroes fighting each other?"

"They are from two captive villages. It's around festival time, so it was either they fight each other to the death or both their villages would be destroyed. The winning village gets supplies too and the losing village…wiped off the map. The Love Dictator is the cruelest man imaginable."

"Who lost? We have to go save their village."

Gobliy grabbed my arm and shook her head. "Boyfriend stay," she commanded.

I crouch down to Tumble. "I don't know how you two got separated but your little sister is no doubt looking for you. Your mother is…"

"Alive," says Tumble with a firm look.

Oh, she can talk.

"Don't spoil the surprise! The twist is so important and you just ruined it!" Gloom's body turned in on itself, coming out as a monster of black spikes. "I have to kill you all now and I hate killing!"

"Get out of here! Tumble and I can calm him down!" exclaims the hero, sending air sickles at the rampaging RiftRipper.

"Hey. I'm kinda a veteran." I throw three containers filled with water and then rush up with my dagger. The ice-coated dagger freezes the RiftRipper inside the ice, completely immobilizing him.

"Wow! You're amazing! Are you the Pacifister? I'm a huge fan!" exclaims the luchador, shaking my hand. "I'm Luchador Espada."

My grip slips and I lose consciousness.

I awake in a bed of leaves, my body feels weak.

Gobliy leans over me. "Stay alive, big brother or Gobliy no longer love you! We break up if you die and then Gobliy's tears are your responsibility."

"Why didn't the angel save me?"

"Prickly girl try to touch boyfriend so Gobliy scare her and her boyfriend off with big club. You may praise Gobliy now."

Shit. That RiftRipper must have cut me without me realizing it. And now I'm going to die because Gobliy is too clingy. Okay, gotta make the best of my remaining time.

"Thanks for protecting me. Look I…you're going…you need to lead the Goblis now."

It took so much effort just to speak.

"Well, well, what do we 'ave 'ere?" asks a troll merchant.

Gobli raises her club. "Uncle?" she asks.

"Yeah, that's right it's me," he says with a rocky smile.

"Big Brother hurt. Uncle must save him or no longer allowed to spoil Gobliy with birthday presents."

"Don't think I'd be able to live without that privilege. Look, I know how to save him but it's not easy."

"Gobliy is super easy!" she exclaims, proudly standing.

"You need a Fairly. Small, hard to hit, and fairly vengeful. You need its blood. Kill a few and you can cure just about any poison."

"No. I'm not living…if someone has to die."

I already got Richie killed. I won't let anyone give their life for me.

"Shut up while Gobliy is rescuing you! Where is Fairly?"

"They are incredibly rare. I do happen to have one on me though. You'll have to kill her to save him." He holds up a bottle with a Fairly inside.

The poor creature is shaking with terror.

"There's gotta be another way. She's just a girl, like you," I say weakly.

Gobliy smashes the jar with a single swing. "Nope. Fairly is just paste. Thanks, Uncle!"

"Yuki is one of my best customers. I can't let him die, but I also can't directly kill, part of the merchant's code. I'll be off now."

Gobliy put the blood from her mace to my mouth.

The fairy's legs and organs were on my lips.

This is terrible.

"Gobliy deserves praise! Praise me!"

"You killed an innocent girl."

"Yeah! Gobliy loves you lots and lots."

A buzzing sound was heard, suddenly there was a swarm of twenty Fairlys.

"Get us out of here!"

"Gobliy great at this game!" She slammed her mace into the Fairlys, knocking them out of the sky. She stepped on them, grinning when she heard the pop.

Racheal was right. I tried my best but I can't change their nature. They revel in violence. How can I change a world that doesn't want to change?

I pass out.

I awake, starring at a blood and guts drenched Gobliy.

All this happened because I upset that RiftRipper. More are dead and it's all my fault.

"I can't keep doing this. Gobliy. Kill me. I feel terrible."

"Nope. You saved Gobliy so you owe Gobliy life debt."

"But now you saved me. Doesn't that mean that...?"

Gobli put her hand over my mouth. "It just means Gobliy is a good little sister." She smiles with bits of Fairly in her teeth.

With my energy restored, we journey to the gobli village to inform them about the hero war.

The two guards at the front were sleeping.

That's odd. They're usually very diligent.

I shake one and realize she has a spike coming out her back.

She's dead.

"Stay outside," I say, drawing my dagger.

"No! Gobliy protect little sisters!" She ran in with tears in her eyes.

I follow after.

There are a few dead Goblis on the ground but most are trapped behind a wall of spikes. Sitting atop the cozy hut of the queen, Gobliy and my home, is a CatBoy General.

Why is NeedleStack here?

"What do you want?" I ask, pointing my dagger at him while I grab a container.

The cat-faced general snaps his fingers, having unseen needles grow and pierce my legs. He hops down and lands in front of me.

I'm so terrified.

"Has anyone ever told you how adorable your nose is?" I ask, poking it.

He blushes. "No…they haven't. They keep saying I'm more cat than boy. I flirt but they say, sorry, I only love cats platonically. Only Momma Cat cares about my feelings but eww, she's a girl."

Is he still going on?

"Doesn't bother me one bit. The extra fur just means I get tickled when I kiss you." I lean in and press my lips to his.

Gobliy sneaks up behind him but suddenly screams.

A needle grows in her head.

"Stop! Don't kill her! What do you want?"

"I'm here for you. There's a certain group causing trouble for my boss. You're going to help me destroy them."

"I love helping! Let her go! I'm your guy."

"No! You no leave. Gobliy die without you."

"Big Brother just has some business to take care of. I'll be back," I say.

"No leaving Gobliy!" she cries.

The needles in my legs shrink and I fall to the ground. A barrier of needles blocks Gobliy's path.

"We're going to need to get that healed." NeedleStack picks me up and heads toward the cave's exit.

"Gobliy will find you and then bonk you really hard for abandoning her! Bad big brother!" she yells.

NeedleStack takes me outside and drops me to the ground.

A white RiftRipper appears alongside a familiar girl.

Shade. Why is she working with a CatBoy General? Annie is going to be so happy when I bring her Luna back to her.

"Good kitty," says Shade, petting NeedleStack with his own shadow.

"We thought you were dead," I say, sucking up my pain.

247

"And I thought you were going to be by my sister's side. She was nearly killed at Sunny Village. I had to step in to save her."

"Do you know where she is now?"

"No. She left my range just yesterday."

"I want to help you find her."

"You left her to keep her safe, didn't you? You're a wanted man. But enough about her. Let me heal you." Shade's saliva came out from her fingertips and sealed up my wounds.

"That's new."

"Yeah, I've learned a lot of new tricks."

"Why are you with him?"

"Hey, don't be rude!" yells NeedleStack.

"Shush, kitty or no pets," says Shade.

NeedleStack put his hands over his mouth.

"There's a militia of exiled heroes. They are growing rapidly."

"And you want me to kill them?" I ask.

"Of course not. We want them on our side."

"And what exactly is your side?"

"We want Flam dead and we aren't going to rely on Isekai to get it done. There's a whole village of Gobli's who will be torn apart if you decide not to help us. We're not asking."

"What do you need me to do?"

"Go in the portal." She gestures to the white hooded RiftRipper.

"Did you kill Annie's mother?" I turn to Shade. "Why work with the man who killed your mother?"

She clenches her teeth. "Without a RiftRipper we can't enact our plan. We need him."

"I'll go with you." I clench my fist and walk into the portal.

I will bring your sister back to you, Annie. I'll be your hero. I won't fail you!

The Main Character!: The Hero's Epic Journey Continues!: Chapter Zero

I tread through Throbbing Forest, using my unique hair powers to keep the vines from hugging me to death. "I don't want your affection, damn it!" I yell, punching a vine repeatedly in the face with my sexy hair.

Why did she have to get captured here? There are plenty of places that are easy to break into. Glam's Castle ain't one of 'em.

I tear a particularly cuddly Weech off me. It stares at me with kawaii eyes, but I'm immune to its psychological attack of cuteness.

I slice open a path with my hair while I pat my chest. "Stay calm. We're almost there."

The last bladed leaves blocking the view to Glam Castle are cut down.

I see the rainbow framed colorful castle shimmering below the night sky before me.

My stomach churns. I turn over and wretch.

I hate this place. It's so tacky.

The castle's drawbridge expands and transforms as I slide down the hillside.

"Hey, get off me, wench!" I yell, shooing away a bloated Blood Bat. "You already got a sip, so just be happy and move on!"

By the time I reach the bottom of the hill, the drawbridge had fully transformed into a stage.

"We're out of range of the BladEagles. Time to hit the skies!" I turn around and climb on my predator drone.

"Nice to see you again," said the drone in a monotone voice that warms my wounded heart.

"Nice to see ya too, my acquaintance." I give the drone a slight smile.

Acquaintanceship and I are close. Perhaps too close. But it's just a robot, right? So does it really matter?

I shake myself back to my senses as we lift off the ground and soar high above Glam Castle.

The stadium lights up with artificial light, most likely from GMO Lamperns.

I notice what looks like the entire CatBoy army in the crowd.

"Bring us down steady. We don't want to get noticed."

"Okay, I guess I will."

Always so calm and focused. You're the only one I trust to have my back.

We land in some trees near the stadium.

"Maybe I'll see you again," I say with a slight nod.

"That would be nice," said Acquaintanceship.

I adjust my cat ears and make sure my CatBoy soldier suit is up to date.

Back in my hero days, I'd go for a flashier entrance.

I press my finger into my fangs until it draws blood.

Alright, definitely sharp enough.

I sneak through the crowd. Unable to control myself, I graze shoulders with many of the CatBoys, yearning for a slight acknowledgement of my presence.

Damn it, get your shit together! You're supposed to be undercover.

Hey, I can't help who I am.

What kind of lame excuse is that?

I argue with my asshole of a conscience as I sneak ever closer to the stage.

"Stop right there."

Oh, shit, I see a sailor hat. Had to bump into a general. Rival you're such a pathetic failure!

"I'm not a failure, shut up!" I yell while punching my head.

"What did you say?" asks the general, who was clad in a military uniform.

I thought all the Generals wore fetish gear. What makes this prick think he's hot shit?

"Yes, sir? How can I help you?" I ask, batting my eyelashes to seem meek and impressionable.

"You're just a soldier. You have to stay behind the line. You can watch the execution from there."

"Yeah. Learn your place," said the glowing yellow line under me.

I don't even know what the hell that creature is.

"You're General PurrGrim, the hero of the Dark and Broody Village massacre," I exclaimed, channeling my inner fanboy.

The general blushed a purple color. "I am merely an instrument for our fabulous leader. Besides they all killed each other, I just played music."

"But you played it from the heart," I said with a childish smile.

A heart I want to fuckin' tear out and shove down your entitled throat!

The general gave a gentle smile. "You know. Most of the soldiers are thin little toothpicks. Only worth one good strum before they break." His creepy, long nailed fingertips crawl up my body and caress my epic muscles. "But you're a strong one. How would you like to come to my bedchambers later? Music that induces mass slaughter isn't the only melody I know. I could soothe your precious body." His hands slid down and grabbed my package. "Oooh. You're a big one. I'd love to tame you." His eyes got wide.

This fuckin' creep needs to learn the difference between idolization and me wanting to be his sex pony! If I say no, though, I can't save the girl. Is angel loli sweet enough to brace the full wrath of barbed CatBoy cock?

I hear sobs coming from the stage.

She's crying. My precious little damsel is crying. I gotta buck the fuck up and rescue her before they murder her!

I point to the yellow line, which glares at me and growls. "I'm only a soldier. I'm not worthy of being with a legend."

"Then perhaps, I'll get you promoted to Captain. If you don't die before I'm satisfied, you'll be more than worthy," he said, licking my neck with his weird fingernails.

Shit! He's actually really good at this. I'm teetering off the edge here.

I slap myself.

Get it together! You don't like fuzzy sausage! Just save the loli and lets skedaddle!

"You're right."

Inner me may be a total prick, but sometimes I need a good nudge to sort my thoughts out.

"Of course, I'm right," says PurrGrim, pulling me past the grumpy yellow line on the ground.

"I'm super excited to see that little girl scream as she dies. Is it okay if I meet up with you after her eyes pop out her sockets?"

Ugh. I'm making myself sick with this fake sadism. Real sadism is great, but faking it makes me nauseous.

"It may be your last night, so enjoy," said PurrGrim with a warmth that made me shiver.

My hand started pulsing. Shit. Not now.

"I want him dead too, but right now we have a loli to rescue," I said, glaring at my hand.

It glares back at me and then gives me a peace sign.

Sheesh, living with myself is driving me insane!

I scoot by the other commanders until I make it to the very front of the area. Thankfully, nobody notices that I'm not decorated with the commander's emblem.

I look up at the stage and my eyes widen.

The angel is naked.

Those canonical censor bars are ruining my life!

I slap myself and look again.

The innocent angel is tied to a spiked metal pole. Her hands are pierced along with her legs. If that wasn't bad enough, the pole was superheated.

A cooking crucifixion. The brochure said it was going to be a quick, flashy death. Something is off. Flam isn't one to lie. He doesn't need to. The truth bends to his fancy.

The curtain opens and Flam appears.

He's right there. I want to kill him so badly.

And blow your cover? You're such a moron! I raised you better!

I grip my aching head. "Shut up." I steady my breath.

Flam is right there, wearing a painfully glittery dress tuxedo hybrid. He raised his voice to bury the bound little angel's wretched screams.

I fall to my knees in tears.

Mommy. I'm scared. The noise it won't stop. I hear her. I hear her suffering.

"You all must be dying to know what sort of fantastical method of execution our little angel is going to get. Now, as you all know, I don't normally kill angels. And I bear no ill will to this girl. Her constant struggling against me has only served as friction for the fires of tragedy. She begged me, with stars in her pretty pink eyes, to end her life. Now those eyes are gushing with terror and agony. She now covets the life she once handed to me. But I won't let that bring me to break my promise to her. Bonds are sacred and a promise is a powerful bond indeed." He dances around the stage as he spouts venom with his sickly sweet words.

If I only I had killed him when I had the chance.

You're such a stupid child! Regrets will only bring you down. Has all your miseries taught you nothing?

"Yeah, yeah, shut up," I say to myself.

Flam continues his nonsensical speech while I brainstorm on a way to get her out.

She's terrified. She peed herself. By god, she peed herself and it's glistening! Do I see a freakin' rainbow!?

My hand smacks my face.

Stop thinking with your dick and figure out a way to save her, you degenerate.

My shoulder's slump.

I hate it when he calls me that.

Flam grabs the curtains in back. "I promised this girl a swift death, but here I am cooking her alive as she bleeds out. What kind of cruel man does this, you ask?" His scarf becomes a whip and hits her back.

She squeaks.

So fuckin' cute! But damn it! Belly pokes should make her squeak, not psychotic torture!

Flam grabs the little angel's cheeks. "I got this wonderful idea from your story. Just as the RiftRipper who killed your girlfriend got the idea of skinning her alive from her comics, the method of your execution spawned from her beautifully twisted mind."

The girl's mouth shivers. She stifles her screams and glares at him. "This is nothing compared to the loss I've faced."

I grip my chest.

She's so daring and willful! I can't let a treasure like her be destroyed!

"I'm well aware. I just thought it would be a bitter sweet gift. You gave your heart to her and she abandoned you. I wanted you to have one last gift from her before you left this world. I am more than merciful, I'm benevolent." He pats her head.

My sexy purple hair became jagged.

Kill. Kill. Kill.

Hey, hair! Keep your shit together. We can't take him, and you know that!

"I'm going to be rescued! You'll see!" she yells before the whip made her body spasm.

Is she talking about me? She must be? I think she looked my way. Eeeeee! I'm so excited. She believes in me!

Yeah, too bad she'll be disappointed. You're a total failure and a creep! She'd never like someone like you.

I broke down in tears.

"You're right but it's not about that. I have to save her. Must protec!"

"Dude, do you realize you're muttering to yourself?" asks a CatBoy commander.

"Sorry." I make my cheeks flare up on command. "I'm just thinking of how to confess to a really cute boy I saw."

The CatBoy blushes and turns away. "Oh."

Flam amplifies his voice through the stage. "She wants a hero! Well, we most certainly must oblige!" He opens the curtain.

The Main Character!: The Hero's Epic Journey Continues!

That's the Pacifister, Yuki. I thought he was dead!

Yuki's eyes and mouth are bound by living leather straps that chuckle at his plight.

The angel's eyes lit up when she saw him. "Yuki…it's really you."

"Yes! It's really him. The hero who abandoned you. Well I have some wonderful news for you. Your darling, Yu-ki, was kidnapped. It took a long time for me to finally track him down. But now he's here and I'm going to free him just like you requested."

"No! Please don't kill him!" The little angel's tears splashed out from her eyes.

"I won't. But he is going to play a very special part in your execution!" Flam's scarf wrapped around Yuki's arms. It went up his hands too, completely coating them. The scarf made Yuki draw his dagger.

"After all this time, you've been reunited with your first hero! And with your spilt blood, splashing onto his nubile body, he shall be cleansed of all transgressions against me. Your death will free him absolutely! A single well-placed stab is all it will take."

This is really bad! He's trying to break one of the greatest heroes. Well, ex-heroes. Forget about finding an opening. I have to try or I have no right to have ever been a hero!

"Killing me will destroy Yu-ki. It won't free him. Please, leave him out of this."

"You can't decide your fate, my dear. You can only scream and struggle as you die."

True terror seized the angel's eyes before she fainted.

Smart girl.

Flam whips her back, but she doesn't awake.

"No. How dare you!" He throws the whip aside.

The Princess' Beauty Sleep. Using a damsel in distress technique is risky as hell. I didn't even know that dangerous art was still passed on these days. To think she used it to her advantage like this. That's one hell of a little lady. Flam won't lay a finger on her as long as she's catatonic.

"Yuki!" Flam pulled the hero up to him and tore off the leather strap over his mouth.

Yuki suddenly grabbed Flam and dipped him. The legendary hero's lips were just inches from the cruel warlord's. "Let her go. I'll be yours forever if you do." His eyes sparkle with charm.

I grabbed my heart. Shit! I'm not gay! I like girls!

Oh really, then what's with your ol' Trap squeeze?

Hey, Traps are sexy noble warriors! Shut up, me!

Yeah, you're right. Sorry. Traps are fuckin' awesome.

Flam presses Yu-ki's lips into the sleeping angel's.

If this doesn't work, then I've already won.

Flam pulls Yuki off and throws him to the ground, strangling him with his scarf. "How dare you not love her after all she's done for you?"

"Not used to your plans failing, are you? She's a dear friend to me. But only her true love can awaken her now. You'll have to cancel the execution!" he exclaims while glaring at Flam with his gorgeous eyes.

"Damn it. I guess I am gay for him. But he's too damn hot. Guys shouldn't be that hot unless they are traps!"

The CatBoys around me stare at me with weird looks.

The Main Character!: The Hero's Epic Journey Continues!

Aww man. Did I just announce that to the world? Whatever, at least I got the spotlight now. I can feel my energy growing. All these people are about to become acquaintances.

"I'm a lolicon. I'm exactly what you need." I walk onto the stage.

The crowd looks up at me with confusion.

"It's a pleasure to meet you all. I am that which opposes all that you are. As long as someone strives for power, I will be there, competing alongside them. Names, Rival. Fancy meeting your acquaintance." I wave at them and they wave back.

Oh yeah. Jackpot!

"You weren't invited here," says Flam as he steps up to me.

"Doesn't matter. I just captivated your whole audience. Now you gotta listen to me. Release her from her shackles. Give her some damn clothes and only then will I give her true love's kiss."

"You fear attachment. You wouldn't dare risk it."

"Dude. She's sleeping. She'll never even know," I say, slugging his shoulder.

Flam, your sadism has given me the open window of opportunity!

He glares at me with distrust but knows he has no other options.

"Release her," he says softly.

The heated pole cools and the nails in her body wiggle out before falling to the ground.

I catch her and wrap her in my robe.

She looks so peaceful and vulnerable. Must protec.

"Go on, then. Kiss her. Wake up our little angel and I'll allow you to choose how she dies," says Flam.

Yeah and if she wakes up mid kiss and miraculously falls in love with me, then I'm freakin' screwed. I gotta keep interactions to an absolute minimum. No way am I risking it.

A container lands next to me. A pillar of smoke pours out from it, enveloping me.

Who needs friends when you have acquaintances! Hell yes!

My hair stretches to the pink section of the smoke pillar and grips onto Acquaintanceship. It then snaps me right up to my on and off kinda sorta co-worker.

Flam's soldiers aim at me, but he signals them to stop.

He knows when he's beat.

His scarf presses to the ground and expands. He rises all the way up to me and then casually sits on his scarf like a throne. "You've only postponed it. I will execute her. You know how unbreakable my bonds are." He touches my lips.

Eeew. I don't want cooties.

"I'm gonna find a way to wake her up. You have to let Yuki be free. It's only fair."

"I only promised that if she cooperated. In the end she sabotaged the execution, escaping the role of a damsel by using a Damsel In Distress technique. I admire her clever nature, but will not abide to my part of the bargain after she denied her part."

"Do you still love me?" I ask, looking away with rosy cheeks.

"Now and always," he says, grabbing my cheek.

"Then make the deal with me."

"And what do you offer me?"

"Dude, seriously? I came all this way to rescue her and I didn't kill a single one of your troops. And I'm going to personally deliver her to the Hero of Destiny before I beat his pathetic ass. What more do you want?"

Flam's eyes widen. "Tee-hee. You're as strong as ever, I see. Very well, I shall free him as you requested. No tricks. He can go where ever he wants."

"Good. Glad ya get it."

Flam looks at the angel in my arms. "Do you have any idea who she really is?"

"Not a clue. The brochure didn't say and frankly, I don't want to know. She can casually tell me her name when she wakes up."

"Very well, I leave you to it! Onward, my love! Let the hero's epic journey continue!"

To be continued in *The Main Character: The Hero's Epic Journey Continues!*

Coming Fall 2019

Annolette, Rival, Old Dude, Flamboyant Villain, Assailant, Poppy and others will be returning for *The Main Character!: The Hero's Epic Journey Continues!*

The Main Character!: The Hero's Epic Journey Continues!

Annie here with a request for my fans!

If you want to help shape my destiny and support my newest hero Main, then please make a loving subscription to his Patreon. There are great perks there that get me mega excited!

https://Patreon.com/sphere_of_compassion

Also, if you enjoyed my story then you'll love the *Of The Exps* serieis (3 sci-fi/fantasy books are currently available in eBook and print form).

https://amzn.to/2IN29eR

And subscribe to the website too!

https://sphereofcompassion.com

https://www.patreon.com/Sphere_of_compassion

REBELLION OF THE EXPS

BOOK 1

Alexander J. McCarty

Art by: Gabriel McCarty

TRAILER!

Awakening

Exp 8 Trailer

"Freedom is a shackle."

Exp 8 could only faintly hear these words. Nonetheless, they repeated fervently in its mind.

There was no world for Exp 8. It had no identity. All it knew, all it was, were those words: "freedom is a shackle." Despite this, it didn't have a clue what they meant. They were merely noise.

A mechanical sound broke through the mantra as an automatic door opened. Voices could be heard but only as whispers.

Exp 8's nervous system slowly activated, allowing it to feel the gelatinous fluid that encompassed him. Its eyes opened, frightening the people who were gathered around.

"It's waking up! It's finally waking up! Hurry, go inform Devlin," exclaimed a scientist, his hands trembling as he looked up at the creature in the incubator.

Exp 8 was an imposing height of six feet five inches, towering over the other life-forms in the room. The creature's body was clad in blue-tinted, platinum-colored quicksilver armor an inch thick. The sleek armor shielded all but the being's piercing black eyes. Those eyes had a depth as overwhelming as space itself.

Around Exp 8's head was a cybernetic helmet that protected the soft flesh within. Horizontal slits were carved into the center of the two slabs melded along the jawline, forming a mouthpiece. The slabs curved upward above its head, creating long, functionless ears. Protruding from the back of its helmet were metallic tendrils, wispily floating in the gelatinous fluid. Embedded in the crown of the helmet was an empty clear orb.

A motherly light started to bloom inside the orb as the system booted up. Exp 8's metal-plated chest was concave, funneling in like an ant-lion trap. A dimly lit, sky-blue sphere filled the cavity. A five-foot metallic tail was limply swaying in the liquid.

The creature had strong, thick legs. Sharpened metal plates formed three bladed talons on each foot and one blade in the back for support. Energy gathered in the orbs embedded into the being's large hands. The being's trembling fingers tensed up into fists.

Exp 8's head turned slowly, examining the immediate surroundings. The new life-form deduced that it was floating inside a large shell.

A mere moment ago, Exp 8 would have been unable to understand the concept of *shell*. But for some unfathomable reason, its meaning was clear. Now the creature understood what a shell was and simultaneously felt the desire to escape from it. The reason for wanting to escape had yet to be formulated.

Exp 8 reached out, bumping its hand against the glass.

The creature was imprisoned in a clear incubator filled to the top with a light green liquid.

Exp 8 felt a strange sense of fellowship with this liquid. Both of them were seemingly trapped by nothing.

A large number "8" was painted across the incubator's surface.

Exp 8 dragged its fingers across the number, following its curves. It soon became entranced in the act. The creature felt something both real and fanciful as its fingers made loops around the image. This symbol was somehow a part of the curious life form.

Exp 8's arm moved instinctively, breaking free of the trance. Struggling to move the rest of its body, the creature realized multiple tubes and wires had penetrated through its armor and were embedded deep into its flesh.

Now that Exp 8 was aware of their existence, the creature felt pain. It didn't fully grasp the concept, but it was certainly not fond of this new sensation.

Curling up, Exp 8 loosened the pull on its body. Pain still lingering in its eyes, it looked beyond the encasing and into the world outside its little eggshell.

Everything was gray, structured, and lifeless.

It looked beyond the immediate surroundings, peering through the wall and into a hidden room.

Exp 8 was not alone.

Inside the metal room were multiple incubation chambers. Inside each was a life-form, curled up like a fetus. Some of them were missing limbs and others had holes in their bodies. One was belly up, its eyes glazed over.

Exp 8 watched their lifeless bodies attentively and waved its hand, willing them to awaken.

They remained motionless.

Fear of death struck Exp 8 even before the being could fathom its meaning.

Exp 8 saw the shell in a new light. The desire to escape was now wrapped in a layer of fear. The being pushed its trembling hands against the encasing. This world was no longer a shell; it was a cage. The word *cage* brought up the all-too-familiar word *shackle*.

Exp 8 feared that it would die shackled inside its prison. It tried to thrash around but was only able to flail its arms. The creature's head moved the slightest bit forward, but it was unable to reach the encasing. In Exp 8's peripheral vision, something caught its attention.

Beyond the encasing was a group of strange creatures. These life-forms had no prison and were gawking at it with wide eyes.

Exp 8 did not feel threatened by these creatures. The being knew intuitively that, if it escaped, they would be unable to stop it.

The foreign creatures continued to stare, none of them uttering a word.

Exp 8 was befuddled by their astonishment. How could its imprisonment be more astounding to them than their own freedom?

Freedom! The word trapped Exp 8 in a torrent of desire. It did not matter what preceded it. Freedom was now its goal. And escaping from this prison was its only means of attaining it.

The scientists approached closer, their eyes filled with admiration.

Exp 8 peered down at them. They appeared to have skin outside rather than within. Their external material appeared to be more malleable than its own armor and looked completely functionless for self-defense. One creature looked at a metal device on its arm and smiled. Suddenly the lab's twin iron doors flew open, releasing a puff of steam.

"Devlin!" they exclaimed, shaking with excitement and apprehension.

The steam dispersed, revealing a proud grin. Devlin was a loose-bodied youth with a piercing golden right eye. A clump of jet-black hair covered his left eye. He wore a black, unbuttoned lab coat with a cloak that draped over his arms like wings. Beneath the glossy coat was a spiffy blood-red undershirt. From the neck down, he was shielded by a black skintight bodysuit.

Devlin stepped out of the foot-high layer of steam. His feet were comfortably situated in custom-designed metallic boots that gleamed black with a bright red trim. Wrapped around his throat was a necklace with a metal double helix pendant.

Exp 8 could not fathom the idea of arrogance, but Devlin's smile perturbed the creature. It did not seem genuine.

"My creation has finally awoken!" exclaimed Devlin in a dramatic, youthful voice.

The men in the room bashed their hands together gratuitously and smiled as if they relished it.

The notion of these creatures enjoying pain disturbed Exp 8. The creation feared not knowing what these life-forms were capable of.

Devlin looked down at his kin. A cruel smile spread across his face as he opened his lips to speak. "Enough! Enough applause. We can celebrate my success later. Leave us! I wish to speak with Exp 8 alone," he whispered in a harsh, commanding tone.

"Congratulations!" they exclaimed, striking Devlin's shoulder as they left.

The doors shut automatically.

Exp 8 was all alone with Devlin.

TO BE CONTINUED IN EXP 8: REBELLION OF THE EXPS

NOW AVAILABLE IN EBOOK AND PRINT FORMATS.

SEARCH EXP 8 book @ amazon.com

Link: https://amzn.to/2WQAHC9

REBELLION OF THE EXPS BOOK 1 Exp 8. Copyright © 2015 by Alexander J. McCarty

ISBN 978-1-9437-3302-6

Published by Sphere of Compassion, Inc.

Cover design by Gabriel McCarty

RESURRECTION OF THE EXPS

BOOK 2

THE HERO OF SEL

Alexander J. McCarty

Art by: Gabriel McCarty

TRAILER!

The Crimson Coliseum

The Hero of Sel Trailer

Previously: Exp 8 was knocked out by the Prince of Pleasure's poison. He awoke on the ashy floor of a dark room. "Where the hell am I?" He rattled the searing hot iron bars.

"Calm down. Wait your turn," said a demon.

Exp 8 recognized him.

It was the same crispy demon captain that had led him up the mountain.

"Where is this place?" asked Exp 8, pulling his hands off the bars.

"The center of entertainment, the Crimson Coliseum!" The crispy demon pulled a lever that rose the iron bars up.

"Don't die, alright? You did a good thing in Respite, saving those kids. Beg if you have to. Strike a deal. Don't piss him off," said the charred demon commander.

Exp 8 stepped out of the prison cell and entered the Crimson Coliseum. The structure itself was made from bones, making it more durable than the fleshy buildings he had previously encountered. Tens of thousands of demons were stationed at the pews. Nearly all of them cheered when Exp 8 rose up his fist. There were only a few thousand that raised their fist in solemn silence.

Exp 8 got into a fighting stance as the bars of a nearby cell opened up.

The Baroness of Blades emerged, leaping onto the blood-soaked fleshy arena stage.

"What are you doing…?"

"As Etah's proudest warrior, I will strike you down, hero." She gripped the hilt of one of her rear swords and rushed up to her competitor.

"We can take him on together," said Exp 8, skipping back while using his jets.

"My pride will not allow it. *Ignition!*" The Baroness unsheathed a sword, super heating it in the process. The blade missed Exp 8's head but sliced off one of his tendrils. She swerved out of the way of an orb directed at her face and slammed her bladed foot into her rival.

Exp 8 slid back, directing the momentum to get behind her.

The Baroness grabbed the hilt of a blade at her front and gouged it in.

Exp 8 ducked under her reverse jab and used the opening to stab his talons into her legs.

She ripped the dagger out of her head and jabbed it at his throat, blocked by his arm at each thrust.

Exp 8 gripped the arm holding the dagger and slammed his head into her face. "If this is some kind of ploy, best to end it soon. I don't want to kill you by accident." His turrets rose out from his shoulders.

The Baroness stopped all movement. "I may be incognito, but this fight is real. The winner gets to face Etah. This may be my one chance at taking him down. *Ignition!*" She pulled out a dagger from her knee, set aflame by her boiling blood.

The blade slid up Exp 8's torso and sliced open his shoulder.

Exp 8 gripped onto the blade and twisted the talons he had imbedded in her leg.

The Baroness collapsed to the ground alongside her rival.

Most of the protruding blades slid off Exp 8's armor, but two or three found the gaps and pierced his flesh.

"I don't believe you. You've had plenty of chances to fight Etah." Exp 8 twisted her arm, making her drop the dagger.

"Calling me a coward!" she yelled, biting into his neck.

Exp 8 slammed her against the bloody floor. "You want an audience! You need someone to see your victory. It's not tactics; it's your inflated ego!" He created an orb, gripped it with his gravity field and slammed it into her head repeatedly.

"That's right! Everyone is watching! I won't fail now!" She twisted one of her blades as she tore it out, blinding her rival with a gush of steamy blood.

Only able to see red, Exp 8 felt something slam into his chest. He was rolled onto his back. His vision adjusted through the blood to see a long slab of steel between his fingers. "Make it look good."

The blade slid through his fingers and into his chest.

The Baroness plunged the blade all the way through. "It's over." She stood up, yanked the sword out from his chest and raised it. "I won! I am the greatest warrior."

A few members of the audience cheered. Most were either silent or weeping.

Etah leaped off from his decorated podium.

The impact from his landing splintered the ground.

The God of Hate backhanded the defiant demon lord. "What have you done?"

The Baroness slid back and jabbed a sword into the ground, slowing herself to a halt. "They're all watching. All of them! My pride is at stake!" She rushed at the Deva, wielding two swords in each hand.

"He was supposed to win! To triumph against an unstoppable force! How dare you deny these people their hero!" Etah's aura was sucked into his bulky body. "Death would be mercy. You shall be disgraced!"

The Baroness ducked under his fist and sliced his belly.

Etah's legs slammed into her body like battering rams.

The Baroness jabbed two blades into the Deva's knee and kicked off the ground. She rode the momentum, slicing the god's shoulders and positioning herself behind him.

Etah spun around. "All of it ruined! You want to be a hero so badly! Hmmhmmhmmmhuhuh! The job is yours!" He parried each strike with an equally powerful punch. His foot slammed down on hers, flattening it along with her pride. "Everyone behold! This is the embodiment of your hopes! She alone can save you from your judgment!" The god gripped her swords between two fingers each.

Nearly the whole stadium cheered for their new hero.

"You've taken up their dreams. You've stolen Exp 8's mission by striking him down. Can you live up to their expectations?"

"You will fall with all of Sel watching!" The Baroness dropped the swords and stabbed a dagger into Etah's throat. She twisted it as she ripped out the scorching blade. Lava gushed out of the deity's wound. "Never underestimate me!" she yelled in a frenzy, stabbing his throat with various daggers.

Etah knocked her off.

The Baroness rushed up to the Deva, her hands ready to unsheathe two more swords.

Etah's aura burst out and gripped her hands. His tattoos lit up once she was within range. His hands went around hers. "And so, the rebellion dies!"

"*Ignition!*" The Baroness pulled her blades out halfway before they were pushed completely through her.

Etah twisted the blades and cleaved her body in two.

The Baroness joined the blood-soaked floor.

Moans, screams, and anguish from the pews blotted out all noise.

"This despair, it's superficial. Not nearly enough," said Etah with a clenched fist.

Exp 8 spat out blood.

Etah turned his attention to the fallen hero. His grimace shifted into a wide grin. "Still alive! Heal him!"

Four demons with white wolves and tigers on a leash came out from the sidelines. They went to Exp 8's side and placed their paws on him.

"I'm sorry, I couldn't free you," said Exp 8, tugging at their collar.

White energy poured out from the paws and entered Exp 8.

Within seconds his wounds had closed. Within half a minute, he was glowing with energy.

Etah pulled the leader of the Freedom Forcers off the ground. "Residents of Sel! Your hero has returned from the dead! The battle you came for will now commence!"

The stadium shook, each cheer contributing to the quake of support.

"Come, hero! Fight me here and now in the Crimson Coliseum! End my reign, if you can," said Etah with a beckoning hand.

"No."

Etah took a step forward. "What?"

"I won't move a muscle until you heal her. I know you can do it," said Exp 8, patting his helpers on the head.

"You think a warrior like her would die so easily?" asked Etah, lifting up the demon lord's upper half.

The Baroness ripped out an arrow and jabbed into the tyrant. "Die! Die! I'm not done yet! I won't lose to you!" she yelled, unable to pierce his hardened muscles.

Etah flung her aside.

"Heal her or I'm out."

The God of Hate glared at the defiant hero. "You don't get to command me."

"Have it your way." Exp 8 flew off the ground. He slammed into a thin red aura.

"As if I'd risk letting you leave. Come down here and face me!" yelled Etah.

"Look everyone! See your ruler! Look how he struggles when things don't go as he plans. Marvel at his frustration," said Exp 8, flying circles around Etah.

The deity bit his lip. "Heal her." He turned his head to the demons. "I said heal her!"

277

The demons dropped their leashes and picked up the Baroness' halves.

"Wait. Stop." Etah looked at the hero and smiled. "I have a better plan. Either fight me…." His red aura shot out like a bullet. It exploded into the crowd like a grenade, killing seven demons immediately and injuring eleven more. "Or I'll dispose of the audience. It's your choice." The merciless tyrant gathered energy in his hand, aiming it at a group of child demons near the front.

Exp 8 sent a volley of orbs at the detestable deity while making circles in the air.

Etah redirected the blast at the Exp, followed by a volley of smaller bursts.

The Ultimate Exp enlarged an orb as he swerved around the attacks, all the while firing at the god's face to disrupt his aiming.

"Your hero will do anything to protect you! Come down, hero, or face the consequences," said Etah, aiming his aura at the audience.

Exp 8 swooped down and slammed into the deity. "I will take you down! BIG BALL SHOT!" He fired off the orb, sending his enemy back a few feet. After reengaging his thrusters, he pummeled Etah's chest, keeping steady fire on the god's face.

"Stop! I'm not done! He's mine!" yelled the Baroness, using her dagger to scale up the arena.

Etah's aura gripped the orb and rammed it into Exp 8. He then grabbed onto the hero's leg.

Exp 8 slammed his talons into the arm holding his leg. He twisted out of the iron grip after firing a pebble-sized orb point blank at the god's face.

"Better hurry," said Etah.

The massive orb from earlier was now heading to a crowd that wasn't dispersing fast enough.

Exp 8 supercharged his jets and slammed his body into the orb, redirecting it to the ground. His jets flipped and backed him out, but he was still caught in the periphery of the blast.

Etah leaped off the ground. His massive hands grabbed onto Exp 8's torso. "You should pay attention."

The hero's jets flipped around again and blasted the god's face.

Exp 8 zoomed by, slicing Etah's back with his elbow talons. "Stop dragging this out. The longer it goes on, the more casualties there will be."

"Hmmhmmhmmmhuhuh. I'm well aware." Etah fired out heated blasts at the hero.

Knowing that a misfire would result in a casualty, Exp 8 slammed into each blast. The freedom fighter then crashed to the ground.

"Even when his life is on the line, the hero defends you! He protects people he has never met! Such valor!" Etah pinned down the mortal with his foot.

"These people aren't strangers. They're enslaved...like I was. We are made kin by our oppression!" Exp 8 struggled beneath the Deva's foot.

"Such powerful words! Though you could have picked a better time for them," said Etah, stepping on the hero's legs with his other foot.

Exp 8 punched the god's foot with great strength but it wouldn't budge. His tail smacked against the God of Hate's leg.

"What was that? Are you mocking me?" asked Etah, glaring down at the nuisance.

"Haven't quite gotten the hang of fighting with my tail, that's all," said Exp 8, struggling to push the god's foot off him.

"Behold: the Hero of Sel is unable to move! I could crush him at any moment! And if he dies! All of you die!" yelled Etah.

Exp 8 supercharged his jets yet again, sliding out from beneath the powerful legs and then quickly turning around to punch the god's face.

A stray arrow pierced into the gap in Exp 8's arm.

"I told you. I will kill Etah!" yelled the Baroness, ripping out another arrow from her body.

"How are you still alive?" asked Exp 8, rapidly dodging the tyrant's punches with properly timed jet-boosting.

"You know so little." Etah opened his fist and grabbed the hero's head. "Demons don't die, only suffer. Those children you failed to rescue. The ones you saw beheaded before your eyes, they are alive. I don't kill rebels, merely repurpose them! That's what happened with the Baroness! I break wills, not destroy lives. You are fighting to save them from nothing. What will you do now, hero?" asked the Deva, smearing Exp 8 with the blood of the wounded.

The Hero of Sel wrapped his legs around Etah's left arm. "Everyone dies. That's not what I'm against. Everyone suffers. Trying to stop that is pointless. What I fight for…what I died for is freedom! Slavery takes the meaning out of life and the purpose out of suffering! As long as living beings, whether sinners or saints, are trapped in a system of exploitation…as long as willful beings are treated as property, not people, I will keep on fighting! Until the system falls, I will stand and fight!" His jets went into overdrive.

Etah's arm twisted up and then back. The sound of it snapping ringed across the Crimson Coliseum.

Exp 8 careened into the ground and slammed into the wall of the arena.

Etah's left arm shook but he could not raise it.

The people cheered. They climbed out of their seats and charged into the arena, raising their blades, fists, and tendrils as weapons.

"Enough!" Etah's aura burst out from his body, melting anyone who entered it. He stepped up to the defiant hero who was still getting back on his feet.

"The people have stood up to you. You lost. The rebellion won," said Exp 8, gripping one massive orb in between his palms.

"Not another word!" Etah's aura burst out and slammed into Exp 8 from below.

Before the hero could reorient himself, the god gripped his arm.

Exp 8's eyes went blank as his left arm was torn from its socket.

Etah slammed the hero back and forth against the ground by flailing him around by the dismembered arm.

Exp 8's working hand disengaged his grip on the orb. He fell flat on the ground, his palm facing up.

Etah's aura crept out from his feet and held the hero's legs in place.

Exp 8 stood up in a daze, his eyes fixated on the god. His still-attached arm was too weak to form a fist.

Etah's aura shot into the mob. It pulled them in and contorted them into a chair.

The God of Hate created a barrier between him and the mob with his aura. "Listen to your hero now. You'll find his words deficient in valor now that his life is in my hands," said Etah, his aura climbing up the broken mortal's body.

"I can't move," said Exp 8, tears dripping from his helmet.

"Hero. You may live yet." Etah sat down in his living chair and assumed a lax position. "I'm going to give you one chance. Abandon your ideals. Let go of your morals. Stand by my side as a new god of this world. All you have to do to rule alongside me, almost as equals, is lower your head. Bow down to me or perish," he said, staring at Exp 8 with his eyes aflame.

"In that simple gesture lies the injustice of surrender. I will not bow to anyone, neither mortal nor god."

Etah's fiery aura came out from his hand and pressed down on the hero's back.

The Ultimate Exp fought against the weight. He pressed off the ground and looked up at the tyrant, crouched on one knee.

"Ah, much better."

Exp 8 raised his head, his body still held in place by the god's aura. "I will not bow down to you. Even if you break my neck, my willful spirit will wholeheartedly oppose you," said the leader of the Freedom Forcers, his resolve firm and tall like a mountain.

"A fool in the realm of the living and beyond. Such a shame. Your false hope has brought you so much determination, yet in the end, you had to surrender your life to be free."

"I chose to die. I did not surrender. I died for freedom! I am liberated now!" exclaimed Exp 8, raising a defiant trembling fist at the tyrant god.

"Utter nonsense! If you were truly free, you could have chosen to enter the portal of light like you desired. You were brought here by my willpower. Your freedom is an illusion. I own you, body and soul! You do not choose what path you take; I do," said Etah, clenching his fist.

"You may have sent me here, but I choose my path. I also decide what actions I take," said Exp 8, creating an orb in his fist.

Etah snapped his fingers. A figure in a clear cloak came out of the audience and rushed to his side.

"Such a blessed shame! You would have been perfect. You believe in this freedom so fervently you have deceived yourself into thinking you have attained it. Logic and reality have no power over your delusion. It matters not. By opposing me you have become a hero. All sinners, behold: the Hero of Sel stands against me even now! He values your freedom above his own life!"

Sinners throughout the arena raised their fists in solemn silence.

"By refusing me you have created a burning hope. A hope that is inextinguishable no matter what truths ram against it. You are a threat, a true threat. A psychopath who can deny the facts of life can only be tamed with insanity. Soon, you shall become like all the rest here, a brick supporting my foundation. All sinners, behold: I banish this hero to the realm of Absence! When your hero returns, he will be my new footstool!" Etah punched the Hero of Sel, his massive fist a blur.

The legendary leader of the Freedom Forcers was sent flying back. He was gobbled up by an unseen portal and vanished from the Crimson Coliseum.

<u>TO BE CONTINUED IN THE HERO OF SEL RESURRECTION OF THE EXPS BOOK2</u>

<u>NOW AVAILABLE IN EBOOK AND PRINT FORMATS.</u>

SEARCH *HERO OF SEL* @ amazon.com

https://amzn.to/2IN29eR

RESURRECTION OF THE EXPS BOOK 2 The Hero of Sel. Copyright © 2016 by Alexander J. McCarty

ISBN 978-1-943733-033

If you enjoyed this story then you'll love the ***Of The Exps*** series (3 books currently available in eBook and print form in the link!).

https://amzn.to/2IN29eR

And subscribe to my website too!

https://sphereofcompassion.com

About the Author

Alexander McCarty is an animal born on Earth who actively seeks freedom for his fellow animals. He enjoys watching anime, playing video games, reading books by other independent authors, being an activist, writing anime-style stories, and living a vegan life. Having graduated from college with a focus on Asian and Religious Studies, he now spends his time as a writer and as an abolitionist vegan advocate. He listens to any and all comments, suggestions, reflections and criticism.

Please contact me with a link to where you placed a review for any of my books (Of The Exps/ The Main Character) and I will answer any single question as one of my characters for **FREE**. If you do a review (and point out where) in addition to submitting fan art, I will write a **FREE** short 2–4 page story (with my characters) in a scenario of your choosing. =(:3)*

Bloggers who wish to review *Exp 8: Rebellion of the Exps* or *The Main Character: The Hero's Epic Journey Begins Part 1* or *Guardian Angel* may request "Review Copies" at the links below.

authoralexandermccarty@gmail.com

facebook.com/authoralexandermccarty

Annie's Special Message

Animals have families just like we do! You wouldn't want to hurt an animal if you didn't have to, right? Great news! You don't have to. You absolutely have the power to live Vegan! Vegan living means no buying animal products whether they are food, clothing or cosmetic related. It also means not supporting places that exploit animals for entertainment like zoos and aquariums. Be my hero by living Vegan and inspiring others to do the same!

If you need resources, the ones below are the absolute best.

http://www.adaptt.org/

http://www.abolitionistapproach.com/

veganeducationgroup.com